DATE DUE

APR 02 2022			
R 02			
JUN 2 9 2022			

Struggle

Struggle

Sara Zyskind

Lerner Publications Company • Minneapolis

Dedication

Thanks to Ester and Morris Biederman
for their help to the author.

Originally published in Hebrew by Beit Lohamei Hageta'ot
Edited in English by Sandra K. Davis.

Library of Congress Cataloging-in-Publication Data

Zyskind, Sara.
    Struggle / by Sara Zyskind
        p. cm.
    ISBN 0-8225-0772-2
    1. Zyskind, Eliezer. 2. Holocaust, Jewish (1939-1945)—Poland—
Brzeziny (Łódź)—Personal narratives. 3. Holocaust, Jewish
(1939-1945)—Poland—Łódź—Personal narratives. 4. Auschwitz
(Poland : Concentration camp). 5. Jews—Poland—Brzeziny (Łódź)—
Biography. 6. Brzeziny (Łódź, Poland)—Biography. I. Title.
D804.3.Z97 1988
940.53'15'039240—dc19
[92]   88-6092
                                                              CIP

Manufactured in the United States of America

2 3 4 5 6 7 8 9 10 97 96 95 94 93 92 91 90 89

Contents

Prologue

Eliezer, my husband,

I am writing your memoirs, but I take the license to write them in the first person, as if they were my own. Often they remind me of my own past. Similar things happened to me in those horrible days, and sometimes even in the same places, although we did not yet know one another.

I write these things because your story left a very strong impression upon me, so strong that despite all the years since then, years filled with contentment and many events, I have forgotten nothing. More than anything else, your courage and sensitivity to justice were engraved upon my heart. Of that I wish to tell.

We met at the end of the Second World War, after the horrible Holocaust that struck our people. We met on the way to Israel, two lonely creatures, lone survivors of large extended families.

We were young, 17 or 18 years old. We met like every other adolescent boy and girl, and like them we felt mutual attraction and the desire to be close to one another. We were filled with a sense of warmth and mutual understanding, as though we had known each other for years. But, despite our young age, we were very different from other adolescent boys and girls in love.

We met in the wonderful spring season, yet we said nothing about the glorious nature surrounding us—not of the blossoming trees nor of the intoxicating fragrance of the lilacs, which were then in full bloom. Never did we speak of the moonlit nights during which we strolled in marvelous parks, nor of the birds' clear songs.

We needed to speak only of the past, to tell about ourselves. Perhaps we wanted to prove that we too had once had a home, a father, a mother, a little sister. We needed to tell one another of our parents, whom we had prematurely lost, of the house out of which we were jolted, and of our lost childhood. My stories became so familiar to you that they could have been yours, and your stories became so familiar to me that they were like my very own. Thus the passing of so many years since I first heard them is of no importance. They remain etched in my memory as if I were hearing them today.

As I remember, your first story was about Gereck.

Chapter One

Gereck

Although I hated Gereck, I could not deny that he was a handsome fellow. He had a typical Slavic beauty: blonde, flaxen, straight hair, blue eyes, and an upturned nose. He was taller than other boys his age. He was always surrounded by a group of Polish kids—we called them *shkotzim* (peasant boys). Gereck was their leader.

I despised these shkotzim, but I particularly hated Gereck, and not without reason. Ever since my early childhood, his fair, arrogant appearance had disturbed me. Every time he saw me, he barely noticed me or he would make a face at me, sticking out his tongue and hissing: "Dark, filthy Jewboy!" I could feel the blood rush to my head. I would have attacked him, but I was smaller than he, in both years and size, a Jewish boy with black curls, dark eyes, and swarthy skin. All I could do was make a fist and curse him silently.

As we grew up, Gereck's confidence and haughtiness increased, particularly when he was surrounded by his gang of friends. Their common interest was hating Jews and they constantly searched for ways to persecute them.

9

By the last hour of each school day I was worrying that I might run into these shkotzim on my way home. I never walked home alone, but always surrounded myself with a group of my classmates, Jews like me. Even so, I worried. We were always afraid that around some street corner or from behind some thick bush, we would be assailed by rocks and curses: "Filthy Jews, go to Palestine!"

When we were attacked like that we would all break out in a mad dash, scattering in every direction. I would arrive home puffing and sweaty. With the exception of my little sister, Talka, who knew all of my secrets, I told no one of these encounters. My mother would then admonish me to walk properly, and not run like a madman.

Luckily, these attacks on the way home from school occurred infrequently since the shkotzim were older than we and finished school after we did.

Every Sunday, school let out earlier than usual. We had both Jewish and Polish teachers, and the Polish teachers were absent from the school on their Sabbath. We, of course, took advantage of the free time to play. Like a wild gang we tore out of the school gates, racing through the streets of our town and across the bridge over the Mrozitzka River. At the meadow on the other side, we arrived breathless to the green grass, dense trees, thickets, stalks, and bullrushes of the river bank. The meadow became our dreamland for all kinds of games— soccer, hide and seek, track competitions. I was champion in the running races. No one in school could keep up with me. Here we amused ourselves and ran freely without disturbance—until Gereck and his gang discovered us.

The Christian church stood at some distance from the bridge and every Sunday it was full of churchgoers, including Gereck and his friends. At the end of the prayers they would cross the bridge to look for us, and if they spotted us, they wasted no time chasing us.

We knew Gereck's schemes and ran far from the bridge to hide. Someone would stand guard to warn us when the shkotzim were approaching. But they almost always discovered us and surprised us. While we were in the middle of a game, rocks would fly in our direction from all parts of the bullrush, accompanied by insulting and abusive language. We scattered in every direction, searching for cover to protect ourselves from the barrage. Several of us might be injured in such a surprise attack, returning home dripping with blood from a rock that had reached its target. Back home, I was scolded about my dirty clothes, torn shirt, and scratched body.

The attacks occurred nearly every week, intruding upon our happiness. The disturbance of our games, the hurling of rocks, and the insults, all scorched my heart and made me indignant. Lying in bed awake at night, I would spin plots of revenge. Even though I knew very well that we had no chance of carrying out my plans, I kept on plotting. We were smaller and weaker than they, and to top it all off—we were Jews. Gereck and his friends felt that in this land they were the masters.

Despite all this a plan was finally hatched. We could not silently accept these insults and injuries. This would only lead to disaster. We had to strike back! Perhaps they were not really such big heroes. After all, didn't they always attack us by surprise, from a safe hiding place?

After an incident between Vitzek and me this thought would not give me peace. Here is what happened. Vitzek was the son of the gatekeeper in the adjacent house. He was one of Gereck's gang, and like them he was a virulent anti-Semite. Whenever Vitzek spotted a Jewish boy playing alone, he would quietly sneak up on him and violently kick him. The boy would flee and Vitzek, pleased with his courage, would chase him, shouting: "Coward, miserable Jew!"

I was infuriated by each boy's injury, and by the fact that

Vitzek was never punished for his actions. The decision was made. I would teach him a lesson! I waited for the first opportunity, which soon arrived.

One day, while looking out the window, I saw Vitzek sitting calmly on an empty barrel in the courtyard. I descended to the courtyard, pretending I hadn't noticed him. I bent down, and began to draw numbers on the courtyard floor, following Vitzek out of the corner of my eye. Indeed, I was not mistaken. He jumped like a cat from the barrel, and was very soon behind me. His leg was already poised for the kick when I sprang and deftly caught him by the throat. The boy was so shocked that for a moment he did not even fight back. He had not imagined such a response. But he quickly recovered and struck my face. It really stung, so my grip loosened a bit. I immediately received a second blow. I knocked him down with a kick. We struggled, sprawled out on the floor, with me on top of him. I then hit him in the face with all of my strength. Vitzek barely freed himself from me and fled. From that day on he avoided me whenever he saw me, pretending that he had not noticed me.

But this did not completely settle my account with Vitzek. Though he left me alone, he continued to persecute the other children. One day I saw Vitzek knock Srulik off his bicycle, give him a violent kick, and take the bicycle. This infuriated me. Srulik was not only my friend, he was also a relative who lived two floors above us.

Most of our family lived in the same building at 10 Shventa Anna Street. My grandfather ensured that his relatives, and particularly his children, lived nearby. Thus, grandmother and grandfather also lived in our building, and above them Srulik and his parents.

Srulik and I sometimes played together, but we were very different from each other. Srulik was a serious boy, devoting most of his time to holy studies. He wore the black garments of a Chasidic child, which added to his grave image. He had playful blue eyes, but from beneath his black, thin-brimmed hat they looked very serious. Srulik's parents wanted him to do something other than study all day, so they bought him a sparkling new bicycle. I helped him learn to ride it. Although I was two years younger than he, and could barely reach the pedals, I already knew how to ride well standing up, with one leg under the middle bar.

So when I saw Vitzek persecuting Srulik I was especially angered. To surprise Vitzek, I quietly slid down the banister in the hallway and crept up behind him. With one hard push I knocked him off the bicycle and before he could get up I sat on him, pummeling him with my fists. I hit him in his face and all over his body, shouting in his ears: "You will never again lay your hands on a Jewish child! Do you hear? You will never again lay your hands on a Jewish child!!"

I eased off on Vitzek only when I saw that his nose was bleeding. I told Srulik to grab his bicycle and the two of us fled. I walked into the house as if nothing had happened. But after a short time we heard shouting and the blows of fists on the other side of our door. My mother, pale as a ghost, with my sister Talka behind her, went to the door while I hurried into the kitchen to hide.

In the hallway by the door stood the gatekeeper Voitzechovsky, his wife, and their son, Vitzek, who held a blood-drenched handkerchief to his nose. Before my mother could even ask what had happened, the Voitzechovskys had already shouted: "Where is your little bastard? Where is he hiding? We'll break his head open!"

My mother, shaken, looked at them as she anxiously whispered: "What? What happened? What has my son done, Mr. Voitzechovsky?"

The gatekeeper did not answer. His face became redder and redder as his curses got louder. "You filthy Jews, how dare you attack our children! I'll show you! I'll kill your little bastard son!" And he tried to force his way into our apartment, right between my mother and my sister.

"Who do you want to kill, Mr. Voitzechovsky? And who here is a little bastard?" we suddenly heard from above. "And what is all this shouting? Can't you speak more quietly? Mr. Voitzechovsky!" The noise suddenly abated. Everyone turned their heads upward. On the stairs stood my uncle Avram, my mother's younger brother, tall, strong, and self-confident as always. On his hip I saw the pistol that he always wore. Avram's pistol was both a puzzle and a wonder to me; he was one of the few Jews in town with a license to carry one.

When I heard my uncle's voice I breathed freely and emerged from my hiding place.

"There, there he is!" called the gatekeeper pointing at me. But now his voice was several octaves lower. "Your Luzer almost killed my son!"

The gatekeeper's wife whined: "Look, Mr. Avram, at our poor child. Look how his nose is bleeding."

"I don't think that Eliezer attacked your son for no reason, but we'll find out what happened immediately. If Luzer did start it, we will punish him appropriately," my uncle answered.

Avram's restrained voice and his confidence gave me courage. "Vitzek knocked Srulik off his bicycle, and kicked him, and took his bicycle away! Vitzek beats up and kicks every Jewish child in our courtyard," I shouted, standing close to my uncle.

"Did you hear?" Avram turned to Voitzechovsky. "Well, Vitzek, what do you have to say: Is this true or false?" Vitzek did not respond. He hid behind his mother's back. "And now get out of here and don't you dare lay your hand on my nephew!" my uncle roared as he pulled me into the apartment. Even after the door was closed, we continued to hear the gatekeeper and his wife, cursing the Jews who dared lift up their heads too high. We also heard them scolding Vitzek, admonishing him never again to start up with this Luzer. These words must have been accompanied by blows, since we heard Vitzek crying.

From that day on, I never saw Vitzek in our courtyard, and Srulik rode his bicycle freely.

This incident and my uncle's firm stand gave me confidence and led me to think about the whole affair. I saw clearly the importance of the pistol. From then on my uncle's pistol was a source of pride to me. I secretly dreamed that I would also own a pistol when I grew up. Then I would walk as close as I could to Gereck, the pistol in its holster at my hip, and look him straight in the eye. We'll see if he'll dare to bother me.....Wait a minute—what am I thinking? Why, by then, when I grow up, we will have long ago moved to the Land of Israel!

Religion and Zionism were well integrated in our home, all of us dreaming of immigration to the land of our fathers. My father, a religious man and a strict observer of the Torah's commandments, was also an enthusiastic Zionist. For as long as I can remember, he was active in the "Mizrachi" movement. Meetings, decisions and discussions took place in our home, and important people visited us from Warsaw and Lodz. My father also took care of distributing the immigration certificates. He was very kind, always taking care of others—sometimes even more than he took care of himself and his family. My two aunts, my mother's sisters, Lea and Bracha, had already moved to Palestine with their husbands. I heard a rumor that when our turn arrived, my father gave it to another family—thus saving them from forced separation —and as he handed them our certificates, he said: "It's okay, we'll go a different time."

Now I knew that my father was trying to get certificates for us. My father told me that he had written to Palestine, to the director of the agricultural school, "Mikvah Israel," and had requested that he save me a place for the next school year. We had even prepared photographs.

Meanwhile another Sunday passed, a day of games in the meadow, accompanied by the usual fear of the shkotzim who were likely to discover us. This time it was my turn to be the lookout. Before they could find us, I spotted them hiding in the bushes. I could make out Gereck's blonde forelock and blue eyes. I could also see the other members of the gang, including Vitzek. I was sure that Vitzek had not told them of the confrontation that I won. He would never admit that he had lost a fight to a Jew. As soon as I saw them, I whistled sharply. My friends stopped their game, and without delay, before the shkotzim had a chance to throw any rocks, we all ran away.

That night, I remembered the change that had taken place in Voitzechovsky and his wife, and I knew that we needed some kind of weapon for protection. I thought of using slingshots. Did not little David defeat mighty Goliath with the help of a single slingshot? Then, too, the Philistines mocked the Jews—and how bitter was their end.

On the way from school I told my friends my plan. Each of us would make himself a slingshot from a branch shaped like the letter Y, tied at the ends with rubber straps attached to a piece of leather where a stone could be placed. We would carry small stones in our pockets and practice shooting at a target. I had to work hard to convince them to accept my idea. In Poland, Jewish children never fought back against non-Jews. I explained to my friends that we had nothing to lose. If we did nothing the shkotzim would continue to persecute us anyway, and maybe they would leave us alone only when they saw that we would fight back and protect ourselves. I told them about Vitzek, who had stopped coming to our courtyard and pestering the Jewish children after I beat him up. I also told them how Vitzek's parents reacted when my uncle Avram appeared with the pistol at his hip. Finally they agreed.

From that day on we practiced shooting at any target: felling chestnuts from treetops, chasing away pigeons from rooftops, and even breaking the window in the forest guard cabin. I set a record when I hit a rat in full flight.

Now we felt a newfound strength; it was as though our fear of the shkotzim had melted away. We were ready for the battle. We counted the days until the next Sunday.

On the Sabbath before that Sunday, my father wondered what had happened to his son. Instead of getting up and running away immediately after the Torah lesson, which my father taught me every Sabbath, I asked him if we could once again learn the story of David and Goliath.

The special Sunday arrived. This time my friends and I did not look for a far off, hidden place; instead we began a game of soccer not far from the church. But we did not all play the game. Five of us hid among the rushes and watched the bridge. Indeed, immediately after the service, before Gereck and his gang reached the bridge, they spotted us. With a flash of victory on their faces they ran over the bridge, Gereck leading. He passed by me. Our glances met, but only for a moment. My slingshot was aimed directly at him. He did not have a chance to bat an eyelash before the stone left my weapon and hit him on his forehead. His scream of pain split the air, as blood streamed from his head. Gereck collapsed and fell. I just managed to see his friends running toward him as he was sprawled out on the ground. But that was all I saw. Like an arrow I shot off in a run. My friends also fled.

Huffing and scared from what I had done, I covered great distances to reach my home indirectly. As I ran I saw Gereck's blood-drenched face in front of me. Almost breathless I broke into the house. There must have been some special look on my face, because despite my wild entrance my mother did not say a word.

With failing legs I passed through the corridor and entered the fabric room, filled to the ceiling with large rolls of fabric. This was the room in which I would hide and be by myself when I had done something wrong. I sat down heavily on the floor between the fabric and the wall. The thought that Gereck might die, that I killed him, would not leave me alone. I saw police coming to arrest me and take me to prison.

"Zezka! What happened to you? Calm down." A small pair of arms curled around my neck. My whole body trembled. I hadn't heard this name for years, ever since my sister was a baby, when she did not know yet how to pronounce my name. Talka did not wait for my answer. She understood that something terrible had happened to me, so terrible that I didn't even have the strength to answer her. She sat down beside me and we held each other until my mother called us to dinner.

The War

The events of the next few months made me forget Gereck and his defeat, and many other things as well. The school year ended, summer vacation arrived, and our family traveled as we did every year to Glovno, a vacation village. Every year when the time came for our trip I felt almost choked with happiness. Here in the village we were surrounded by fields and forests. The house that we rented stood on the edge of a large forest bordered by expansive fields. We were far from Gereck and his gang. Our relatives lived in nearby bungalows and I felt as though everything around me was created only for me.

That was the case for every year except this one, this 1939.

A heavy tension filled the air. Everyone spoke of the upcoming war, of Hitler's declarations about parts of Poland, which he claimed belonged to Germany. We had already heard of Germany's annexation of Austria and of the German invasion of Czechoslovakia. We were told the armies of those countries had not fired a single shot against Hitler's conquering armies. Poles let the world know that they would fight to defend their homeland. Men were drafted into the army, vehicles appropriated and work begun on trenches.

Jews were particularly afraid. We'd heard rumors of the persecution of the Jews in Germany long ago. Everyone knew of the horrors of *Kristalnacht*, when German Jewish businesses were systematically destroyed by Nazi mobs so that everything was covered with glass, or crystal. Such news was particularly frightening when it was corroborated by those few Polish Jews who had been expelled from Germany, reached the border town Zbonshin, and some of them then came to our town. At first we were only worried about the well-being of our brothers over the border. But now fear struck us as well. We were so uneasy that we hadn't the patience to stay in our vacation village and enjoy the delights of nature. We returned home early, before the vacation was officially over.

On September 1, 1939, before dawn, the German army crossed the border. From that day on our town, Bzezin, never looked the same. Located on the main road between two large cities, the industrial city Lodz and Poland's capital, Warsaw, Bzezin bustled with activity. Endless convoys of the Polish army streamed through town to Warsaw. We saw tanks, artillery, cavalry and infantry flowing by day and night, past our windows.

Not only did soldiers flood into Warsaw, but the panicked civilian population, seeing Warsaw as a safe haven, migrated towards the capital. Among the migrants were people loaded down with bundles, people pushing hand-carts, bicycle riders and pedestrians.

Most of them were Jewish men. Because of rumors of the poisonous hatred Hitler planted in his soldiers toward the Jews, especially toward young Jewish men, many of them decided to flee to Warsaw, which they saw as Poland's fortress. Separating from their families was very difficult, but they believed that they would soon be reunited, for Hitler had announced that this would be a blitzkrieg, and the war would be over within a few days.

Many of the men who marched from Lodz and passed through our town stayed in the homes of other Jews for a night's rest. Since the beginning of the war, I had not slept in my bed. Talka and I slept with our parents, giving our beds to strangers who stopped off at our house. Several times, when there were many guests, my mother arranged linens on the floor.

My mother now took upon herself additional work. In large pots she cooked food for those who sought refuge in our home. Strangers sat around our table. My mother also prepared sandwiches and bottles of tea for their journeys.

The migrants discarded many objects in the streets to lighten their burden: coats, blankets, even various pots.

One morning my uncle Avram showed up at our door. He had come to say goodbye to us. My grandmother cried bitterly, but she did not detain him.

My father stayed home. He believed that it was impossible to escape fate. He trusted in God. On the radio we now heard Polish marching tunes, interrupted occasionally by declarations of Polish heroism. Other times the songs were interrupted with announcements that a German fighter-plane had been seen in Polish skies, but the plane had been turned away.

In accordance with the instructions of the Polish police

and giant posters which had been glued to the walls of houses, we covered our windows with dark blankets or black paper. Inside the houses kerosene lamps or candles that gave off a faint light were used instead of electric bulbs. The streets were silent and dark. Every once in a while one could hear a few random shots. We slept in our best clothes, with our money and valuable possessions close to our bodies.

On the sixth or seventh night after the outbreak of the war, a strange thing happened. We had just heard an announcement that planes had crossed the Polish-German border and suddenly, as if guided by some mysterious hand, all the lights of the city went on. Bzezin was illuminated in a way we'd never seen before. Panic struck everywhere. The refugees scattered in every direction in search of shelter within houses and corridors. Chaos, shouts, curses rose up—but the lights were not extinguished, and they kept shining for hours to come. Rumors spread that it was the work of spies, since our town was populated by many Germans.

The next day our town was bombed. We were just getting ready to sit down to breakfast when we heard on the radio that a squadron of planes had crossed the border. Before the announcement ended we could hear the heavy grinding of airplane motors. Frightened, we ran out of our apartment, calling to Grandmother and our other relatives. We met them in the stairway. They were as frightened as we. We did not know where to run. There were no shelters. But one thing was clear—it was stupid to stay in the house, especially in the upper floors. We needed to find shelter below ground.

Suddenly there was a tremendous, deafening explosion. Within seconds strangling smoke covered the street, and the smell of fire hovered in the air. In the midst of confused shouting we ran out the gate. The street was full of fleeing people. We were still being knocked about in the thick smoke when a second and third explosion hit. In all of the smoke and confusion I lost everyone; I could barely see the person next to me. I was pulled along with the crowd towards the fields, as planes hovered directly over our heads. With the next explosion I fell to the ground. I buried my head in the earth and shut my ears so that I would not be deafened by the explosions.

Little by little the shelling subsided. The planes left. I raised my head to look around. I just had time to see my father's head lifted as well. Then another squadron of planes arrived, and another shelling brought fire and smoke everywhere. I thought the world was coming to an end.

The shelling lasted hours that seemed like years. After the second squadron, a third came, then a fourth, and only when day was changing to night did the last planes turn back leaving behind them pillars of fire and smoke.

I crawled to my father and helped him up. He was in shock. He barely managed to mutter, "Lord of the Universe, what will we do now? Where will we find Mother, where is Talka, Grandmother, what has happened to them?"

We could hear a man croaking beside us. It was a Polish soldier who had been hit by a bullet.

We turned towards town. I will never forget that sight. The town stood in flames. Tongues of fire laced with smoke could be seen on all sides. Dazed, we approached our house. It was seized by flames—the house in which I was born and raised, the house in which nearly all of our family lived. We stood like statues, unable to move. Many people stood around us. Suddenly we saw someone run toward the burning house, ignoring everyone's warnings and pleas. He was quickly swallowed up inside. We did not see his face. The several seconds that passed until we saw him come out running from within the flames seemed much longer. In his hands were his tallith and tefillin. Now we recognized him. It was my Uncle Chamota, the husband of Chandzia, my mother's sister.

After a few moments the house collapsed. First the upper floor, where Grandmother and Grandfather lived, gave way, then the floor where Srulik and his parents lived, crumbled. The upper parts of the house caved in on the lower stories. Our legs weak, we slowly moved away from the place.

On the other side of the street some houses remained undamaged from the shelling. Someone said that the wounded had been taken to these houses. As if seized by a *dybbuk* (evil spirit) we burst in. We were met by groans and the smell of blood. On the floor, on beds, and on tables lay the wounded. Suddenly, my father screamed. My mother lay on a long bench, her face drenched with blood. One eye had come out of its socket, hanging by only a fiber on her cheek. I was terror-stricken. Father bent over her. For the first time in my life I saw him cry. But he recovered quickly, tore his shirt and ran outside to wet it with water.

"Zezka," a weak voice reached me. I bent down to where the voice had come from. On the floor beside the bench lay my sister, Talka. Her legs were covered with blood.

"Talka! Talkale! What's happened to you? What happened to your legs, what happened to them?" My little sister just smiled. "It's so good that you're here. We were so worried about you."

Father returned with a pan full of water. He cleaned my mother's face, placed her head on his coat, cleaned Talka's legs and with his fingernails removed the fragments that were sticking out. Talka yelled and cried from the pain. Afterwards, Father went out to search for a doctor. But no doctor could be found. Dr. Warhaft, our doctor, had been drafted into the army at the beginning of the war.

Outside, it sounded as though heavy vehicles were coming closer, causing the walls of the house to tremble.

Father returned, pale as a ghost. "The German army has entered the city," he said. "Bzezin has been conquered by the Germans."

Homeless

That night we stayed in the house where we found my
mother and sister. All night people milled about. Some of
them entered hoping to find their relatives and left in despair after not having found them; some rejoiced when they
found their loved ones; and others, seeing their dear ones
wounded, burst into tears.

One woman brought towels, sheets and cups for first aid.
My father went from one wounded person to another— cleaning wounds, wetting parched lips, giving water to those who
were desperately thirsty—and I helped at his side, refilling
the pan with water each time it was empty.

Despite the trauma, I fell asleep. When dawn broke I found
myself curled up, dozing beside my sister Talka. I raised my
head. All around me I smelled blood and heard sighs and
moans. Talka slept, but she groaned in her sleep. My mother
did not sleep. Her eye had nearly returned to its socket.

I was still thinking of the previous day's events when
suddenly a horrible thought rocked my head: Lord of the
Universe, we are homeless! What will we do now? Where will
we go? We were left only with the clothes on our backs. And
not only us—there were many others like us.

I then experienced mercy for the first time, a trait which,
according to my father, had always been characteristic of the
Jews. Early in the morning, even before sunrise, residents of
our town arrived with food, sheets, and clothes. They offered
living space to the homeless, even though many of them
lived in very close quarters. They also told us that many
people were killed and missing, and they suspected that
others were trapped under the ruins of houses. We learned
that Grandmother and our other relatives had managed to
flee and were safe and sound at the house of a friend, but
Pola, Uncle Avram's young wife, had been killed in the
shelling.

My Uncle Avram had married a short time before the war. When he could not find a home near our house he had rented an apartment in an area far away from us which had not been hit at all in the shelling. Since Uncle Avram had gone off with those who fled to Warsaw, Pola was left alone in the apartment. Hearing the echoes of explosions and seeing the town in flames, she hurried toward our house to find out what had happened to us. We had managed to get away, but she was killed by a bomb that landed beside her.

My mother fainted when she heard this news, Talka broke out in screams and could not be calmed, while I was seized with chills at the thought of how my Uncle Avram would react to the tragedy!

Finally a doctor arrived. He dressed the wound on my mother's head. There was not much he could do to help, but he gave us hope that the eye would return with time to its socket, and indeed that is what happened. But she lost her vision in that eye forever. With forceps and a knife which he had sterilized in a fire the doctor removed more shell fragments from Talka's leg. My sister's screams were heart-breaking. Afterwards, the doctor moved among the wounded and did whatever he could to help.

Towards afternoon one of our relatives arrived and proposed that we come live with him. In his courtyard was an empty storage room and he promised to set it up as a dwelling place. My father accepted his offer with thanks, as we had no other place to go.

We lived in that room for a number of weeks. We slept on blankets spread out on the damp floor. Mother and Talka were still not able to get up from where they lay. We ate the bread people gave us.

The rest of our family was also scattered among relatives and acquaintances. Finally my father decided that we could no longer continue living like this and that we must move to

Uncle Avram's apartment. My sister Talka had contracted a high fever which made her wounds drip with pus. The nights were getting colder and we suffered from chills. One night I woke up abruptly, screaming and terrified. A rat was standing on my face, biting at my lips. Mother, who at the time of her own terrible injury had not cried, was now hysterical. Father bent over me. He cleaned and washed my face and on his face was etched the decision: we would get out of there.

"Tomorrow I will break down the door of Uncle Avram's apartment. Why didn't I think of that before?" he said to himself.

And on the next day, together with his brother-in-law Chaim-Mordecai, whom everyone called 'Chamota', he broke the lock and the door opened. We all moved to the apartment— Mother, Father, Talka and I, Chandzia, my mother's sister, with her husband, Chamota, and their two year old baby Abonik, as well as Grandmother.

When I lay down to sleep at night, for the first time in weeks on a bed, on a clean white sheet, I could not fall asleep. I thought of all the horrors that had befallen us in the few weeks since the outbreak of the war.

German Rule

The Germans entered the town and began to appropriate public buildings which had not been hit in the shelling, including the municipal building, the court-house, and the schools. These buildings now served as headquarters and living places for the German soldiers and their officers.

The schools did not open at the beginning of the school year and children were everywhere. They stood in lines to receive foodstuffs, sold homemade sweets, matches, and cigarettes to the soldiers, and wandered in the streets with nothing to do.

German soldiers seemed to be everywhere. They walked

about in groups, their loud laughs grating on everyone's nerves. They looked at the astonished population as inferior slaves, and they were particularly amused at the sight of bearded Jews who wore the traditional black garments.

Our town changed its appearance. In addition to the ruined houses, the piles of rock, the masses of German soldiers, one could now also see long lines stretching out in front of the grocery stores and particularly in front of the bakeries.

Only nature remained undaunted, continuing its cycle as it always had. The beautiful Polish autumn arrived. The ruins and the lines of homeless people did not interfere with the unfolding drama of nature. It remained as beautiful as it had always been. But to us Jews, the air was congested and suffocating. People passed by hurriedly in the streets, afraid to look right or left, especially the Jews sneaking by as close as they could to the walls of the houses. It was as though they wished to cling to the walls for shelter.

And indeed there was good reason to be afraid, especially for Jewish men. Every day, without warning, a truck would stop in one of the streets. German soldiers armed with rifles would jump out and choose from among the passersby any man that looked Jewish. For this purpose they were aided by the Polish residents of the town. To identify Jews whose dress was traditional, or who wore beards, the Nazis did not need the help of the cooperative Poles. Amidst blows and abuses they would push the Jews into trucks and take them somewhere to perform various tasks. Mostly they were taken to the public buildings in which the German soldiers now lived. There the Jews were commanded to wash the floors, clean the hallways and bathrooms, shine the commanders' boots, wash pots, peel potatoes, and perform other menial tasks for the Germans.

While the Jews, many of them old and unaccustomed to such work, tried to do their work as they were commanded, the bored German soldiers stood by with whips, occasionally striking one of the workers. They would burst into laughter when the stricken man stumbled, the bucket of water slipping out of his hands, pouring out and causing others to stumble as well. The soldiers immediately hurried to those who had fallen, forcing them up with blows. The man whose bucket had slipped from his hands would have to bend down on his knees and gather the water from the floor with his coat. Only in the evening would the men—beaten, exhausted, and hungry—return to their homes. Sometimes the men who were returned from work were caught again on the street and did not reach their homes at all. They disappeared. They were never seen again and their fate was unknown.

The bored soldiers looked everywhere for amusement. They would latch onto a bearded Jewish passerby or pull a man out of the foodstuffs line, shear his beard or pull out his hairs until blood oozed. Sometimes they would also force him to dance, accompanying his dance with blows and kicks, while the Polish crowd which had gathered looked upon the spectacle with laughter and applause. Not all the Poles acted like that, though. Some secretly wiped away a tear.

The Jews were seized with fear. Many exchanged their traditional garb for more normal clothes. Many shaved their beards, and others tied handkerchiefs around their chin and cheeks, as if they suffered from a toothache. But even in disguise they were rapidly discovered with the help of the Poles. So Jewish men rarely left their homes. All outside tasks were performed by women and children. But the Germans needed workers, so they searched and found a solution to this as well: they broke into homes and routed out the men who had hidden under the beds, behind the closets, or inside them. The soldiers also broke into Jewish stores, taking whatever they wanted.

With pain and clenched fists I watched the new world as it

unfolded around me. Father, meanwhile, trusted in God and believed that these difficult days would quickly pass. "England and France proclaimed war on Hitler, and clearly they will defeat the Nazi enemy," he said. "And perhaps we Jews sinned too much and needed such a reminder?" my father asked himself. "All this suffering will pass like a storm, but like a storm it will leave behind destruction, mourning and death..."

Because of the danger out on the street, my father and his brother-in-law, Chamota, stayed in the house. I was also forbidden to go into the street; I could easily be identified as a Jew, with my dark eyes and black hair.

During this time the stock of food in Pola's kitchen — things like flour, sugar, and potatoes — was giving out. The lines for foodstuffs were long, and my mother, who had still not recovered from her wounds, was too weak to stand for hours in line. Talka was also weak and confined to her bed. The entire burden therefore fell upon Chandzia, my mother's sister.

Chandzia would leave early in the morning and return, after many hours of waiting, with a loaf of bread or a little flour. Sometimes she would return only towards evening and other times she returned empty handed. Sometimes, as her turn nearly arrived, they suddenly announced that the item had run out, and that she would have to wait until the next day for a new distribution.

I was indignant at having to sit idly in the house. I was a young boy and I believed in my abilities. I was sure that I could succeed in getting food, and I was ready to take the risk of being caught for work. But my parents and family were opposed.

My patience quickly gave out, and, one day, when I saw that Chandzia was long overdue, I stole out into the street and stood in line in her place. As a disguise I wore my Uncle Avram's wide-brimmed hat that had been hanging in the hall. It was larger than my head and hid my dark hair, while the brim hid my eyes. With this hat and my checkered, wide shorts I looked so much like a Polish youngster that my family did not recognize me when they saw me in this disguise for the first time.

After I succeeded a few times to sneak outside and return with the longed-for food, my attempts became more frequent. Until the moment my family saw me come in they were, of course, terribly worried. My mother was particularly anxious. My father would calm her and say that I could be counted on. He believed that with God's help I would somehow manage.

Thus days passed into weeks, and there seemed no end to this situation.

My father and Chamota worriedly counted the few coins which remained. The money, according to their calculation, would last for another two or three days and no more. And what then? What would we eat? How would we buy flour and bread? We did not even dream of luxuries like milk, butter, and meat. We had forgotten such things long ago. But where would we find bread?

Each day seemed longer than the previous one. The idle sitting and the smaller portions of food began to affect us. We became pale and depressed. Seven-year-old Talka seemed to have suddenly matured. And two-year-old Abonik was no longer the cheerful imp he had been.

One day, as we all sat around worrying about money for bread, my mother suddenly cried: "I have it, I've found it!"

"What, what happened, what have you found?" we asked.

"An idea popped into my head," said my mother, "We'll earn money from the sale of butter!"

We looked at her, frightened. Had her thoughts, God forbid, become confused? Where would we get enough butter to sell, at a time when we were starving for a mere piece of dry bread which we had no way to purchase?

"Don't be frightened. I haven't gone mad yet," my mother replied to us, "Only listen to me. Surely you remember Yanina, the young Polish girl who used to work for us as a washerwoman?! I remembered that her parents had a farm with cows and that they made a living from the sale of milk. It's not so far from here. If you leave the city and walk in the fields to the path leading to the village, it should be about five kilometers away. It's good that we have a few more coins left, to pay for the milk that we'll buy. From this milk we will make butter. Only yesterday Chandzia told us that German soldiers asked the people standing in line where they could find butter. We'll sell the butter to the soldiers and we'll live on that. But," my mother's stream of speech faltered, and she continued in a more moderate voice, as though thinking aloud: "The question is whether these farmers still have cows and even if they still have them, who could carry milk-filled buckets such a long distance, particularly when the men do not even dare leave the house?"

"Mother!" I broke in, "that's an excellent idea! I will go to buy milk!"

"No, my son," my mother replied, "You must not take the risk; German patrols are everywhere. They will arrest you, the color of your hair and eyes will give you away. Do you have any idea, Lazerke, what I go through from the moment you leave to stand in line until I see you return safely?"

"No, Lazerke will not go even if we have to die of hunger," Grandmother chimed in.

"I'll go anyway! You don't need to be afraid—nothing will happen to me, I know how to take care of myself. And anyway, we have no choice. What will we do in another three or four days when the money runs out altogether?" I raised my voice to almost a scream, but when I saw the frightened eyes of Mother and Grandmother I spoke more softly and convincingly. "You have nothing to worry about. The Germans will not identify me. Even you did not recognize me when I put on Uncle Avram's hat for the first time. Look, I've found another important thing in the closet—suspenders to keep up the pants. This will really make me look like a village boy."

I went out to the hall and over my wide, torn shirt I put the suspenders, connecting them to the checkered knee-length pants with the clips which were made especially for that purpose. I put on my uncle's hat with its brim drawn down over my eyes. Then I went back into the room. Despite the tension, everyone broke out in laughter at my appearance. In this outfit I truly looked like a Polish peasant boy. No one could possibly imagine I was a Jew. I promised my mother, who was still full of apprehension, to be careful. In the end they agreed, though with a heavy heart, that I could go out on my mission, but not alone—Chandzia, my aunt, would accompany me.

My aunt also changed her appearance. She wore an embroidered blouse which she had found in Pola's closet, and a wide flowery skirt. On her head she tied a red kerchief. She looked like she had been born a peasant.

Equipped with two pails and the last of our money, we were on our way before dawn. Darkness still reigned and the air was cool. We each carried a prayer in our hearts—that the farmer would still have cows, that he would be willing to sell us milk, and that the German patrols would not stop us.

By the time we reached the village day had broken. We found the farm owner in the barn, sitting on a low stool, milking. After morning greetings my aunt asked him if the milk was for sale. The man told us the price of a liter of milk. When we heard his words we finally breathed freely. The money that we had with us would be enough for fifteen liters.

Chandzia brought the man our buckets and he filled them from a big jug without measuring. He wordlessly took the money. We parted from him with a blessing and turned homeward. Now we walked carefully, so as not to spill the precious liquid. I felt my heart expand from so much happiness. A new energy surged through me: I was helping to support my family! I was so delighted that I hardly felt the weight of the bucket. My fear of the Germans also melted away. Chandzia was exuberant too. She whispered: "Did you see, the farmer did not even measure the milk. I think we have more than twenty liters. Talka and Abonik will also be able to drink milk..."

At home we were met with open joy. Within minutes my mother had turned our apartment into a churn. I don't know where she learned how to sour the milk in special pots, to separate the cream from the sour milk, to churn and churn the cream until the butter could be seen. Everyone helped with the work.

My mother put one pot with milk on the fire to boil, and not only Abonik and Talka, but all of us were fortunate enough to drink a small portion of boiled milk.

After a day or two when the butter had hardened, my mother tore a clean sheet into pieces with which to wrap the portions of butter. She even made use of what remained after the wringing of the butter, adding to it a little bit of flour and making a delicious soup for us.

As soon as we had the butter, Chandzia and I tackled the most difficult task—selling it. Most of the population had not worked since the Germans' entry, and commerce had come to a complete standstill. People guarded their last coins to buy bread, flour, and potatoes. The little commerce which still took place in the city was only with the German soldiers. Thus we had to walk right into the lion's den to sell our butter to the soldiers.

Everyone was apprehensive. Grandmother clasped her hands, and my father took out his prayer book, and prayed for the success of the mission. Only my uncle Chamota calmed everyone down when he said with a smile, "There's nothing to worry about. In those clothes they look just like Poles. You'll see how those pigs will jump for the bargain. They won't even ask where the butter came from. Only don't forget that you don't understand German. The Germans know that the Yiddish language is similar to theirs and that the Jews understand them. The Germans must not discover that you know Yiddish."

I was excited at the prospect of the upcoming adventure. I was doing something for my family, which desperately needed help. But when we arrived at the schoolyard where Hitler's soldiers lived, I felt butterflies in my stomach. We found a place in front of the building, both of us carrying packages of butter. Other children were already making the rounds, loudly proclaiming their goods, homemade cigarettes and sweets. Chamota was right when he said that the soldiers would pounce on the butter without making further inquiries. Not much time had passed when two soldiers left the schoolbuilding-turned-barracks.

"Butter!" one of them let out a yell.

"How much does it cost?"

We pretended not to understand his words. The soldier came right up to us and began smelling the butter. Chandzia took out a knife, cut a piece of butter, and brought it to the soldier's mouth.

"Good," said the soldier, turning to his friend.

"Very good, real butter. Give us two packs."

We stood motionless, as though we did not understand him. The soldier took two packs from the basket and Chandzia signaled to him with four fingers. She pointed to one pack and showed him two fingers. The soldier understood her signals and gave Chandzia four marks. The second soldier also bought two packs. The soldiers did not even have time to enter the building before three more soldiers came out running. "Butter, butter!" their yells rang throughout the yard, "Where is butter?"

When we were left with only five packs, I pointed to my mouth and said "Brout" (bread), in the tonguetied way that the Poles pronounced this word. One of the soldiers said: "Wait a moment!" Again we acted as though we did not understand, but remained standing. After a brief time the soldier reappeared with a second soldier carrying two loaves of bread. He gave me the loaves and took my last packs of butter.

Delighted, we hurried home. We did it! We were successful beyond our wildest expectations. We brought with us both money and bread. My mother's brilliant idea had saved us from hunger.

From that day on Chandzia and I got up early every morning to go to the farmer's house for milk, from which we continued to make butter, and sell it at the school-building. The soldiers were waiting for us when we got there and in exchange for the butter gave us sugar or flour, and sometimes even a sack of potatoes.

We no longer suffered from hunger. We ate to our heart's content, and we believed that we would make it through the war.

One morning, before we had a chance to leave the house to go to the village for the milk, we heard loud knocks on the door. We held our breath, sure that these were soldiers searching for men for work. Father and Chamota hurried to hide behind the closet and we all helped move the closet back in place. My mother opened the door.

On the threshold stood my Uncle Avram. He had returned from Warsaw. He was dirty and covered with dust, and he stared at us wildly, as though he didn't recognize us. His hair was a mess, his shirt torn—and we understood that he had already been notified of Pola's death.

My mother gathered up her brother in her arms and
Grandmother embraced him. But he disengaged himself and
ran from room to room, tearing out his hair and yelling, "I
am responsible for her death! Why did I run away to Warsaw,
leaving her alone? Why did I think that only I was in danger?! Nothing happened to me while my Pola has been
killed."

"No Avram, you are not the guilty one," my father tried to
comfort him by reminding him that the Germans were the
guilty ones. He rationalized by saying that there is no escap-
ing the hand of fate.

Uncle Avram refused to be comforted. He did not flinch
from the danger lurking in the streets of the city. He would
return only towards evening, tired and broken.

One day, shortly after Chandzia and I returned from the
village with the buckets of milk, Avram burst into the apartment. He was pale and his coat was torn. "Our synagogue is
burning" he said, trembling. "Those bastards set it on fire.
The entire synagogue is in flames. The bastards even
prevented the people who wanted to save the Torah scrolls
from entering the burning building."

We all stood in shock. The synagogue was the pride of all
the Jews in Bzezin. The building was old and magnificent,
with colorful stained-glass windows that sparkled in the sun.
Father stood with his hands stretched upward. "God," he
whispered, "Avenge us, Lord, and don't allow them to run
free in sin without punishment!"

Avram continued telling the story in a shaking voice. The
officers had Rav Boornstein, our revered rabbi, wrapped in
a *tallith* (prayer shawl) and commanded him to write that he,
Rav Boornstein, had set fire to the synagogue himself. The
old rabbi broke down in sobs and collapsed. But the Germans caught him with their whips and quickly stood him up
on his legs.

"Enough, enough!!" my father screamed. "I don't have strength to hear any more!" Father put on his tallith and covered his head, and only his moans could be heard.

That day we did not sell butter. That day we fasted—not a crumb of food touched our mouths. We were all stunned and depressed.

Towards evening word reached us that in Lodz and Warsaw the Germans had burned all the Jewish synagogues.

Before falling asleep, I thought of my grandfather, may he rest in peace, and how proud I was of him when I was little. He was well-respected in our town, even by the Polish residents, and was very involved in the life of the city. He served as the Jewish representative in the municipality and was the only Jewish representative in the regional council. In his youth he was active in the fire department. He kept his fire hat and uniform in our house. Sometimes I would put on the hat and pretend I was a gallant soldier. My grandfather had even earned many medals for excellence from the Polish government, medals whose value I don't know now, but I remember that he kept them.

Since I was his first grandson, Grandfather loved me especially deeply, and I returned his affection. In the synagogue I always wanted to sit beside him. Even though I was a mischievous child I often sensed that he was still proud of me, particularly when I was accepted in the choir of the Great Synagogue. I had a beautiful voice and sometimes I sang solos. When my voice echoed throughout the synagogue, I would glance at my grandfather to let him know that I was thinking of him. And when our gazes met I could see that his eyes were full of love and excitement.

When Grandfather contracted a fatal illness, a delegation of the city's Polish honorables came to visit him at his sickbed. He talked with them for several hours. We were later told that his words were a sort of will and testament, and he asked that they behave kindly to the Jewish people in Bzezin. Grandfather's funeral was widely attended. Stores closed, and many of the town's residents came to pay their respects.

Suddenly I was overwhelmed by a feeling of joy. How fortunate that Grandfather had died then, before the war broke out. How fortunate that he did not see this degradation, that all of these sorrows were kept from him.

The next afternoon we went once again to sell butter. On our way to the school we passed the charred remains of the synagogue, where I used to sing solos accompanied by the choir. My heart was pained at the sight and my eyes flowed with tears. Where the beautiful building had once stood I now saw sooty walls, burnt doors and windows, piles of junk, and fragments of glass.

Rage and contempt filled my heart: Weren't all the tortures and humiliations which they perpetrated against us enough? Why did they also have to destroy the holy places? This question persecuted me relentlessly. But no one could answer me.

When we arrived at the school building, the soldiers were standing in front waiting for us. They asked why we had not brought butter on the previous day. As usual, we stood beside them without answering, as though we did not understand their language or their question. But in my heart I replied: If I could I would bring you poison rather than butter...

We heard rumors that it was now forbidden for a Jew to travel on the trolley in Lodz and Warsaw. Jews were also forbidden entrance to the main roads, and they had to wear a yellow ribbon on their left arms—a decree which made our blood freeze. Now the Germans could easily identify Jews, even without the Poles' help.

There were more rumors: in Lodz they were building a ghetto in which to concentrate all the Jews of the city. They were building the ghetto outside the city in the Baluty quarter, where most of the houses were small, and the city's poor lived along with many people from the underworld.

"How will all of the Jews of Lodz, whose numbers are estimated at several hundred thousand, find housing in this quarter?" asked Father.

Meanwhile, autumn had passed. The cold, short winter days arrived. Now we would go to buy the milk at night while it was still dark. Strong winds and rain, and sometimes even snow, pelted us on our way.

Weeks turned into months and the war was still not over. We were told that all of the Jews of Lodz had moved into the ghetto. They were allowed out for only a few hours each day, and after five o'clock, when that gate was closed, they were forbidden to be in the city. If someone was caught, it meant only one thing: death. People who did not manage to return in time were shot to death. Jews from Lodz wrote to us about hunger and shortages in the city. Food coupons had been distributed in the ghetto, but so little food was available that it was not enough to meet the population's needs. Jews were not permitted to buy goods outside of the ghetto, and searches were made at the gate. We could see that our situation in Bzezin was inestimably better than theirs.

The Jews of Bzezin pooled together to help the Jews of Lodz. There was hardly a household without relatives or friends in Lodz. We sent packages of flour, sugar, and coffee.

One day, when my aunt and I were walking with our baskets of butter, we stopped dead in our tracks. On the walls of the houses were plastered posters, in both German and Polish: "Every Jew in the city of Bzezin must wear a yellow ribbon on his left arm. Anyone violating this law will be shot."

We stood still, looking at one another fearfully. We were both thinking the same thing without exchanging a word. We knew that our business was at an end, that we had lost our family's livelihood. Obviously we could no longer walk around without the sign pointing out our Jewishness. Some people had already identified us, including our Polish neighbors in the building. They were all liable to hand us over, which would mean sure death. At home, no one would hear of our going back to our business.

"Thank God we have enough to live on. You must not risk your lives," said Father. "In any case you wouldn't have been able to continue buying the milk. The frost is increasing, the winds are fierce, and the blizzards are already starting. Thanks to your hard, daily work, after all these months we now have enough money to sustain us for a long time to come. What will be after that—we have a God in heaven and we must put our faith in him. The war will ultimately end, it can't go on forever. . ." Father tried to encourage us.

Indeed, the next day, while we were still allowed to walk around without the yellow ribbon, we were forced to return home without the milk, for a snowstorm raging outside kept us from walking. Poland suffered a difficult winter in 1940. In addition to food we now had to worry about materials for heating the house.

After a number of weeks with the ribbon on our sleeve, there was a new order; to replace the ribbon with a new sign that could be seen more easily. A piece of yellow cloth in the form of a Mogen David—a six-pointed star—with the word "Jude" was to be on every Jew. A mark of shame which we called "the yellow badge" was sewn to our garments on the chest and on the back. My mother sewed the yellow badge on everyone's clothes.

I felt horrible in those first days wearing this new yellow badge. This sign was different from the previous one. I could hide the ribbon by hanging the shopping basket on my arm. I could always move the basket and reveal it, so I couldn't be blamed for hiding it. Now things had changed. The two stars could be seen from afar, so that everyone could know the identity of the person wearing it. Running, I would sneak through the streets. I was covered with sweat at the thought that I would run into Gereck or Vitzek.

Slowly I got used to this situation as well. We had long ago stopped selling butter, but I did not lack for work. Every day I walked to stand in line to buy bread, potatoes, heating materials, and other goods. I sometimes walked to the post office to send a package to our relatives in Lodz.

One day when I came to the post office I met my friend Dutzik Coopermintz, who was two or three years older than I, and had succeeded in getting a job there. He stopped me and told me to take my package back home. At first I thought he was joking, but he said seriously: "From now on it is impossible to send packages to the Lodz ghetto. It has been sealed off. No one goes in or out. We have no contact with anyone there."

Not much time passed before a rumor spread like wildfire through the city. That which we had feared and not dared to discuss was verified: they were setting up a ghetto in Bzezin as well. The very next day we saw plastered to the walls of the houses posters with the new edict:

"The Jews of Bzezin will be permitted to live only inside a defined area, which will stretch from Koshtzyushko street to the Mrozitzka River. All of the streets within this area, including the street on which the synagogue had stood, belonged to the ghetto." The posters also declared the date when the edict would take effect, after which time Jews would be forbidden to live outside the ghetto.

The very next day the Germans began to fence in the area. They could not afford to give up Koshtzyushko street, the street on the border, which merged with the main road leading to Lodz, and include it completely in the ghetto, so they divided it into two parts. One side of the street would belong to the ghetto, while the other, which included the road, sidewalk and houses, would belong to the "Aryan" side. The road was divided by barbed wire in front of the houses that bordered the ghetto sidewalk. Uncle Avram's house stood outside the ghetto, so we had to leave it. Once again our wandering began.

Father did not lose hope. He continued to believe that things would be better someday. Soon after the establishment of the ghetto he went there to search for a place to live. Soon he found an apartment for us. An acquaintance had given him the keys to the apartment of a relative who had left when the war started. The apartment was located on Koshtzyushko Street, and from its windows it was possible to look out beyond the ghetto. The apartment had only one room, though, so our family had to split up. Chamota's parents, who already lived within the ghetto area, now took in their son and his family as well as Grandmother. Other ghetto residents also opened their apartments to their relatives or acquaintances.

My Uncle Avram moved in with a friend who gave him one room of his large apartment. Once again the town took on a new appearance: a winter day, a rampant snowstorm, and a convoy of Jews exiled from their homes, dragging themselves and their belongings toward the ghetto, some of them bent under the heavy burden, some pushing various kinds of carts heaped with tables and chairs, bedding, kitchenware, and other belongings.

We too joined this caravan with heavy burdens on our backs. Two or three times a day we made a round trip in order to move a few more things. "I believe that with the help of God this will be our last stop before the end of the war," said my father. Then, looking very grave, trying to justify our new fate, he added: "Maybe it will be better for us in the ghetto, since here we will be separate from the non-Jews and will not have to wander among them with the yellow badge, inviting persecution and humiliation."

In the Ghetto

The Germans appointed a man named Fishka Ika head of the ghetto and ordered him to choose a *Judenrat* (Jewish Council). Jews said that the Germans did not just happen to choose him, but that this Fishka had cooperated with the Germans and had given them the names of rich Jews, making it easier for the Nazis to confiscate their wealth. Soon the Judenrat drafted men as "police" to keep order in the ghetto. My Uncle Eli, the husband of my mother's younger sister, Sara'le, was one of those drafted into police duty. The policemen were promised better living conditions in return for service.

We were told that from then on we would have to work to earn our bread. We had to sew uniforms for the German army and all the tailors were ordered to sign up.

It was not by chance that the Germans had chosen our town as a center for sewing uniforms. The primary industry of Bzezin's Jews was clothing. There were hundreds of tailors of various kinds and clothing contractors who supplied them with cut fabric. In return they received finished garments, which they exported to the other Polish cities and even to foreign countries. I was told that before the First World War, Bzezin's products reached all the way to the edges of Siberia.

We were also clothing contractors, and as a child I witnessed negotiations with tailors who came to our house to get the materials and return with the finished products: coats, jackets, and pants. Big trucks from Lodz or Bialystock brought us rolls of cloth. The wings of our house served as storage rooms and workshops for cutting the fabrics into various sizes. My father was the storage man, while my uncles, Avram and Yankel, were the cutters. After it was purchased the merchandise was sent to its destination within Poland or to England, Spain, and other countries.

Rumors spread that we had received work sewing uniforms for the German army, not only because the city, Bzezin, was a town of tailors but also because a number of men from the Judenrat had proposed the idea to the Germans. In addition they had also slipped the German officers a lot of money. Among the members of the Judenrat there were precious people who were prepared to do much to save the Jews of Bzezin. They saw sewing uniforms for the German soldiers as a guarantee that the town's Jews would survive. Among those who did much for the local Jews, Yasha Zagon, who more than once risked his life to save another's, deserves particular mention.

Jews who had never been tailors also signed up for the tailoring jobs. Everyone saw this work as our salvation, for we believed that nothing bad would happen as long as the Germans needed us. My father, Chamota, Yankel, and Avram all signed up.

A large workshop was set up in the ghetto. Wagons loaded with rolls of mostly olive-green fabric, sewing machines, and other accessories came to the workshop.

The Judenrat set up groceries and bakeries in the ghetto. Food coupons were distributed to every Jew, in exchange for the money we earned at work. Foodstuffs, called rations, were provided us once a month. Potatoes, flour, oil, sugar, various groats, and a coffee substitute were distributed. Once a month or so we were given a little meat. We also received distributions of small amounts of coal and bread. In fact, we received everything in small quantities. We never saw milk or fruit. We made do with what we had. All we wanted was to hold on and survive the war.

A hospital was also set up in the ghetto. Dr. Warhaft, the only Jewish doctor, who had served as an officer in the defeated Polish army, returned and set up a hospital in which he served as doctor and director. He obtained a house on Hoifgass (Stashitza) Street, and brought in 25 beds. He was assisted by a medic, Kleinert, two nurses: Tushinska and

Rosenberg, the midwife, Buki, and Mrs. Oister, our teacher before the war.

Mrs. Oister, the nurses, and the doctor's wife worked very hard. They went from apartment to apartment collecting sheets, blankets, towels, and other accessories required for the hospital. Anyone who needed medical treatment received it in this hospital. A number of women gave birth there. In fact, that was where my aunt gave birth to her daughter.

We obtained medicine from the only remaining pharmacy in the area of the ghetto.

Life within the ghetto became more organized and even the most pessimistic began to believe that we could get through the war. The name of Bzezin was changed to Levenstaad and it was joined to the Reich.

During the confusion of these events the winter passed and spring arrived. Snow was replaced with rain, and sometimes, between the clouds, the sun peeked through, each day a little more, until it was powerful enough to melt the ice from the rooftops, adding much dampness.

The swamps slowly dried up and the fragrance of flowers perfumed the air. Spring planted in us a hope that things would be better soon—but then the Germans closed the ghetto and we were cut off from the world.

During this time I was very inactive. I sat in the house with nothing to do, especially when it rained, and I joined Talka who spent most of her time standing by the window. We would move the blanket which covered the window a little to the side and watch what went on outside of the ghetto on Koshtzyushko Street.

And indeed there was much to watch. Wagons attached to horses with goods piled high, carriages and their riders, bicycle riders, red buses. To this ordinary traffic there were now added trucks filled with German soldiers, soldiers on motorcycles, and sometimes even tanks and artillery, testimony to the war that was still raging in the world.

On the opposite sidewalk we spied soldiers strolling, and we occasionally saw people entering stores. Above the stores, on the second floor of the houses outside the ghetto, we sometimes saw two little girls, standing like us by the window. I wondered if they watched us and what they thought when they saw us imprisoned behind the barbed wire.

One day we saw them eating red cherries from a brown bag, throwing the pits at passing vehicles. Talka swallowed at the sight of the cherries and turned to me:

"Luzer, I know that we're in the ghetto because we are Jews. But what have we done to the Germans that they should punish us? How are we different from those Polish girls who are free?"

I looked at my younger sister, now eight years old, at her big blue eyes, and I could find no answer. For I asked myself the very same question: what evil have we done to the Germans and the Poles who persecute us? How have we sinned towards them? We have always lived quietly and modestly. We worked hard to earn an honest living. Just what is so bad about having been born Jews? We are not murderers or thieves. Why then must we bear a badge of shame and be imprisoned behind barbed wire? But no one could answer. The adults asked the same questions, too.

Sometimes I would walk through the ghetto streets to its end at the river Mrozitzka, sit on the edge and let its flowing waters mesmerize me as I sailed away in my mind. I thought of the distant Land of Israel...of our cruel fate...we had missed our chance to receive certificates by only a few weeks... I thought of my empty spot at the "Mikvah Israel" school... I would sometimes ponder the vistas of Israel as they appeared in my imagination—a land flooded with sunshine, where summer reigned most of the year. I would think of the datepalm trees which I recognized only from the postcards we received from Israel. I imagined orchards overflowing with oranges, the blue sea, and the cloudless blue sky, in a land where there was no ghetto and no yellow badge. All this had almost been within reach. Only a few more weeks and we could have been so happy. But apparently fate had determined that we must suffer this cursed war. When it is over, I thought, we will travel immediately to the Land of Israel. And then we will be so much happier, for we will know how to appreciate the good of the land.

After returning from my flights of imagination on the river's edge, I would feel elated. I did not complain about the dry bread or the tasteless soup spiced only with black oil.

Father would be angry at me when I complained. He said we must thank God that despite the war and the ghetto, we were not hungry. "Hunger is the worst thing in the world," he declared. He had experienced hunger in the First World War and knew what it was like.

News from the world beyond the barbed wire was smuggled into us by the few Polish wagoners who brought food into the ghetto. We knew of Hitler's victory march through Europe. Germany's incredible power was supplemented by its allies, Italy and Japan. Such news was grim.

"Father," I once asked, "If things continue like this the Germans will conquer the whole world. If no country can stand up to them and stop their progress..." But my father was optimistic. He believed that sooner or later Hitler and his armies would be defeated.

"It's only a matter of time," Father said. "England is very strong and Hitler won't succeed in conquering her. I believe that America will also finally get involved and will not allow the Germans to continue unchecked."

The Polish wagoners smuggled white sugar, flour, real coffee, and even luxury items such as salami and cheese into the ghetto in crates beneath their wagons. The black market flourished, and whoever had money could buy to his heart's content.

We were not among those fortunate people. Our profits from the butter sales had already been exhausted. We used the money that Father received for his work in the big warehouse to buy coupons for goods.

The large workshop for sewing uniforms was working at full steam, and the Germans kept bringing more fabrics. By the rate at which uniforms were being sewn we understood that they were drafting more soldiers.

People who owned sewing machines were permitted to work at home. There were no schools in the ghetto, children were home and could also be put to work.

One evening I saw Father and another man carrying home a sewing machine. I ran towards them to help. Father said he bought the machine from a man who no longer needed it. After the other man left, Father turned to me and explained:

"I bought this machine for you, my son. Though you are still so young, in a war children grow up before their time. I had not planned for you to be a tailor, but these days we cannot know what is in store for us. One thing is clear, it is good to be listed as a tradesman. The work in the warehouses increases daily as the Germans need warm uniforms for the winter, and the Judenrat reached an agreement with the authorities that pre-cut pieces could be sewn in private houses. So I bought the machine and listed you as one who knows how to sew."

In exchange for the work, Father said, we would receive additional payment which would help improve our living conditions somewhat. He explained how unhealthy it was for me to wander around all day with nothing to do and how good I would feel to make a contribution to the family's well-being. Father looked sadly at Mother and Talka, and added:

"I must tell you that in light of Hitler's victories so far I don't think the war will be over very soon. More than a year has already passed and we cannot see the end. One thing is clear: winter is once again approaching." Now he turned to me in a whisper, as though apologizing:

"I wanted you to know, Luzer, as I have already told you, that I did not intend for you to become a tailor. All of this is only temporary, just for the duration of the war. I have other dreams for your future, two dreams, and when the war ends we will realize them, with God's help. The first dream is that we will reach the Land of Israel; the second—that you should study."

The next day Father brought home a large bundle of fabric, all of it pre-cut to be sewn into pants. It was my job to attach them. Father sat by the machine next to me and began teaching me how to sew.

The work was not difficult. I could work at my own pace since no one was supervising me. I loved to hear the rattle of the machine, to see the connected cloth moving ahead in a straight line. I enjoyed my work. It did not require deep thought, so I dreamt of the Land of Israel and of what the future held in store for us as I sewed.

My work did improve our situation somewhat; already with the money from the first payment we bought an additional loaf of bread, some coal, and a little white flour, from which my mother used to bake a marvelous cake. And Father was right—I once again felt uplifted that I was helping my family and filling a responsible role.

Every morning, after eating a piece of bread with oil or margarine, I sat at the machine and sewed. Even little Talka tried to help me, handing me the pieces of cloth which I was to sew together. Sometimes, when my Aunt Chandzia brought Abonik over, Talka would stand him on a chair beside the window and show him the world beyond. She pointed to the houses on the other side of the street, telling the boy, then three years old, about life outside the ghetto before the war. Feeling sad and helpless, I listened to the stories the eight-year-old girl told her baby cousin. She explained that before the war, the Jews had also walked freely on the other side of the street, without the yellow badge. Then there was no barbed wire and we could live wherever we wanted, ride the buses, and even go to the movies.

Little Abonik would listen to her words, suck his thumb, and look at the sights that Talka pointed out. But he seemed unable to understand much of what she told him.

Sometimes Talka noticed that the rattle of the sewing machine had stopped and that I was also listening to her. She would get angry, even embarrassed. The evil of the Germans brought her to the point of shame.

In truth the German's tyranny also made me feel ashamed. I was humiliated at the thought of how low man could descend. At the same time I remembered that before the war Germany was considered a land of culture and scholarship. Everyone admired any man who had studied in Germany. Even the simplest product was highly respected if it was imported from Germany—and it would inevitably be among the most sought after items. All this now became strange and surreal in light of the disgusting behavior of the German people.

In addition to my sewing work, I found another activity that helped in the house. One day my Uncle Eli, a policeman, gave me a bag of radish seeds.

"If you plant these seeds," said my uncle, "within one month real radishes will grow for you."

I decided to try it. Not far from the river I hoed a small piece of land with a fork. Then I made some indentations in the ground and planted the seeds. I carried water in a pan from the river to water the small plot of land. Time passed and I forgot about the whole thing.

One morning, I remembered the plot and the seeds. I decided to see if something had grown there. How great was my surprise when I saw from a distance that the entire plot was covered with green leaves! I was dumbfounded when I pulled out a bunch of leaves from the ground, and saw that at their roots a round radish was reddening, a real radish! I removed the leaves and washed the radishes in the water of the river. I tasted one—it was the most delicious radish I'd ever eaten.

My happiness knew no bounds. I hurried home with several radishes. In amazement and joy my mother, father, and Talka looked at what the earth had sprouted. It was a wonder. The little plot of land on the edge of the ghetto gave me a new taste for life. My uncle gave me seeds for carrots, parsley, and beets, and Mother gave me potatoes that had already sprouted "eyes," so that I could plant them too. Every three or four days I worked and weeded my plot of land. Talka also helped me. In addition to the tangible benefits we earned from working the land, we also saw this as training for our eventual immigration to Israel, where we would someday be real farmers.

Mighty singing and the din of heavy marching awakened us early one morning. We all ran to the window. Over the edge of the blanket that covered the window we saw soldiers marching. Masses of soldiers in magnificent uniforms and sparkling boots, armed with rifles, covered the entire breadth of the street as they marched. Strong and confident of their power, they filed past to the beat of the echoing marches. The windows trembled from their famous "goose step." Red flags emblazoned with black swastikas were hoisted above them. The marching continued for hours, and following the troops came the heavy clatter of tanks and artillery chains on the machinery dragged by horses and motorcycles. We thought the road would sink under their weight. I had never seen so many soldiers and such heavy weaponry. From that day on for several weeks this sight was common, day and night.

Rumors infiltrated the ghetto that Hitler had broken the non-belligerence pact with the Soviet Union and had sent soldiers to conquer Soviet Russia.

My father's optimism was again strengthened. "Now Hitler will break his neck; with all his power he will not be able to conquer Russia. His end will be like the end of Napoleon. He also was not satisfied with all of Europe and wanted more and more. The Russian frost will defeat the German army just as it defeated the French army."

A Second Winter in the Ghetto

Another summer and fall brought us into the heart of winter, the second winter of the war: cold mornings, a shortage of coal, raging winds and snow. The ghetto's food supply decreased and its quality declined daily. The little sugar that we received—which at first had been white—later became yellow, then a deep brown. The monthly ration of meat, about a quarter of a kilogram per person, was horse meat. We did not touch it. We hadn't eaten meat since the outbreak of the war. "With the exception of meat," said Father, "we must eat whatever we receive: the food with which we will get through the war is permitted for it is a matter of life and death. And you, children, must eat so that you will grow and have strength." Father was also among the few in the ghetto who did not work on Sabbath, to the extent that this was possible. Not working that day meant not only losing his portion of food, but it also posed a very real danger. Nonetheless, he took the risk. Fortunately, Yasha Zagon of the Judenrat did not register his weekly absence.

During the winter I did not visit my plot of land on the river bank. It was desolate and covered with ice. I missed the few vegetables which had brought life to our souls, as well as the activity of working the land.

Ever since the Germans opened the Soviet front, they pressured us to produce more and more uniforms. In the big warehouse they were now working in two shifts, but ghetto conditions worsened from day to day. Peoples' money and property were nearly exhausted, and black market purchases occurred much less frequently.

The tyranny and acts of terror began to leave their mark on us. The head of the Judenrat, Fishka Ika, had grown in stature in his own eyes, and he began to rule us with a heavy hand. He took money and jewelry from the wealthy and then, in order to curry favor with the Germans appointed to work in the ghetto, would give them some of this stolen property, saving a good part of it for himself. The chief of police, Servin Perlmutter, who also hoped to get rich at the expense of his tortured neighbors, helped him.

The desperate conditions, the reductions in food, and the crowded living conditions also affected us. Typhus broke out. Dr. Warhaft was afraid of an epidemic so he quarantined all typhus patients. He worked very hard to prevent the spread of the disease. For as long as he could, Dr. Warhaft refrained from informing the Germans about the epidemic.

One morning Dr. Warhaft was called to Gestapo headquarters. With a heavy heart and fearing that word of the typhus epidemic had reached the Germans, he appeared before them.

Indeed, the Germans already knew about the illness. But they did not punish the doctor. They did not even reprimand him. The opposite happened—they spoke to him kindly and said that he had been mistaken by not immediately reporting the outbreak of the disease, as they would have been able to help him in administering injections and other medications. But now they had a different proposal. Since the German doctors had never seen a case of typhus—they claimed it was caused by the filth and lice, which were typical only of the Jews—they, the German doctors, wished to study the disease while helping the patients. They had, therefore, decided to transfer all of the patients to a large hospital in Germany. There they would receive the appropriate treatment and the spread of the epidemic in the ghetto would be prevented.

With a lowered head Dr. Warhaft listened to the Germans' accusations about the filth and lice which appeared, they said, only among the Jews. An image of large numbers of people, including children, in a single apartment, without toilets and running water, appeared in his mind's eye. But this lasted only a split second. Fear attacked him. The smooth words of the German doctors caused his throat to tighten and lit a warning light in his head. But Dr. Warhaft recovered quickly, raised his head, and explained why he had not yet reported the illness. There were only a few incidents of the disease, he said, and he had not wished to bother the Germans. Everything was under control. He told them that he still had enough medicine for the few patients. His staff had nearly succeeded in stopping the disease. In fact, a number of the sick had already recovered and been sent home. In his opinion there was no need to transfer the few remaining patients to a different hospital. All he needed was a new supply of the few medications which had been exhausted so that the remaining patients could recover.

One of the doctors, a high officer, impatiently interrupted Dr. Waarhaft and retorted that his stories of the patients did not interest them; and furthermore, the typhus patients found in the hospital would be transferred from the ghetto within a few days. He specified the date on which they would come for the patients, and by motioning with his hand towards the door let Dr. Warhaft know the meeting was over.

With a heavy heart, the doctor left Gestapo headquarters. He was inexplicably afraid of handing his patients over to the Germans. He brought his suspicions before Yasha Zagon and a handful of men from the Judenrat who were prepared to do anything to help their fellow Jews. They decided not to deliver the patients to the Germans, and Dr. Warhaft called the patients' families. He told them of his visit to the Gestapo and that he had decided to send the patients home. The doctor promised that he would continue to look after the sick and would make daily housecalls. He also gave instructions concerning the type of treatment required, and the need for total quarantine—even if this meant that the rest of the household would have to cut back beyond their ability. He distributed the rest of the medicine among them and asked that they maintain absolute secrecy. In the hospital only a few dying patients remained, those whose situation left no room for hope.

Dr. Warhaft waited in fear for the day the Germans would come to take the patients away. They arrived on the appointed date in the darkness of night, before dawn, in a large, closed truck. Armed soldiers jumped out, and burst wildly into the hospital. Amidst blows and kicks they took the dying patients, who were unable to stand on their own feet, from their beds. They dragged them to the truck, and, like unwanted packages, threw them inside. The nurse who was on night duty asked the soldiers if they would wait a moment so that she could call the doctor. In answer to her request she received a slap in the face followed by a threat to put her in the truck too if she bothered them anymore.

The removal of the patients was performed quickly. When Dr. Warhaft arrived at the hospital early in the morning he was amazed to find it empty; instead he found Nurse Rosenberg weeping and tearing her hair out. The manner in which the dying people had been treated stunned the doctor. Despite his apprehensions about the Germans, he had not imagined that they could behave so brutally with dying patients. Tears flowed from Dr. Warhaft's eyes. All of the ghetto was in a state of shock. People walked around in tears, unable to understand what had happened.

After that the hospital remained empty. We didn't dare hospitalize anyone, no matter how desperate the situation. Dr. Warhaft and his aides took it upon themselves to go from house to house attending to the sick, with a devotion which worked miracles. Two people died of typhus, but all the remaining patients recovered and the epidemic was halted. Nevertheless the number of deaths in the ghetto increased steadily because of malnutrition. There were already two cases of death by starvation.

One hundred and fifty young men were sent for two months to the Strikov region to work digging turf. They returned to the ghetto beaten and thin as skeletons. They reported that the Germans were liquidating small ghettos. Healthy people were transferred to the larger ghettos, while the old, the sick, and the children were separated from their families. No one knew where they were sent.

The Judenrat received an order to give the local authorities an exact list of all of the ghetto residents, making note of their ages. The atmosphere of fear could be felt everywhere. A few weeks after the list was delivered, all of the elderly reported to Gestapo headquarters. My grandmother was one of them.

I know few details of what happened that day. But what I do know will not let me rest as long as I live. Grandmother's son Yankel escorted her to the gate of the headquarters. Hours passed and she still had not returned. We waited for her, worried. For hours we walked near the building hoping to see her. My mother almost went out of her mind.

Towards evening Grandmother appeared with Yankel. We

were all waiting in the apartment of Chamota's parents; we ran to the door. Grandmother was unable to walk on her own. Yankel almost carried her in his arms. I looked at her, confused and shocked. Was this really my grandmother, the same woman I had seen that morning? Could such a change take place in a person in one day? She appeared shrunken and shriveled.

"Grandmother!" I cried, but at that moment she fainted. She regained consciousness, but when we attempted to undress her and put her to bed, she let out a horrifying scream.

"No! Don't undress me!" She held onto her clothes and would not allow anyone to touch them, finally falling asleep, completely dressed.

Only on the following evening, while I was lying in bed, did I hear my mother tell Father about the terrible day that the elderly had endured. My grandmother wouldn't talk, but my mother heard the story from our neighbors, an elderly couple. They told her what had happened in the Gestapo building on that day.

The old people were taken into a giant hall where they were ordered to undress. They refused, as men and women were together. Then German soldiers entered the hall, with rubber clubs in their hands. They hit the frightened old people on their heads and tore off their clothes. They stood them up naked in a line and ordered them one by one to approach a table. Two officers behind the table checked each person, turning him or her around and even looking at their teeth. If the people tried to cover up their private parts they were whipped. One of the officers noted precisely all of the details concerning each subject: name, age, address, and "quality of the merchandise." The second officer, meanwhile, stamped the subject's chest and backside.

But this was only the beginning. The Germans were looking for amusement. They brought ice water to the hall and poured it on the floor, forcing the naked old people to run. The soldiers laughed as those who stumbled and fell or fainted were forced up with cudgel blows or by ice water poured on them. Afterwards they ordered all the old people to stand in pairs, man and woman, man and woman.

More I would not, I could not, hear. I pulled the blanket over my head. I was ashamed that human beings could descend so low. My rage almost drove me mad. I was ready to run to the street and attack the first German soldier I saw, to grab his throat and choke him. At the same time I realized how helpless I was. Like a wounded dog I lay beneath the blanket and sobbed well into the dark night.

A Spring Without Tidings

Another winter passed. Again we could feel the warm breeze. But no one took the time to think of the weather. The people of the ghetto had changed since the day the old people were tortured. Their heads turned downwards now and their voices were lowered.

A new type of merchandise appeared in the big warehouse. Wagons arrived with used uniforms, torn and full of holes, sometimes also drenched with blood for us to repair and patch. This gave us a breath of hope. Whispers passed from mouth to ear: they are bullet holes and it is the blood of wounded soldiers. The Germans, with all their incredible power, can be wounded. God is beginning to punish them for their abuse of the Jews. If they lose and the war ends, and if we can only stay alive—our goal will be the Land of Israel.

Father, whose optimism had been flagging, was somewhat encouraged: "Apparently God wishes to save us. We will see that Hitler's luck is turning, like I said! He will break his neck on the Russian front."

Among the uniforms to be repaired that Father brought me from the large warehouse were the coats of officers; on the collars and sleeves pure silver ribbons designating rank were sewn. An idea occurred to me: when we have an army in Israel, we will also need such symbols. On the piece of paper attached to the bundles of uniforms, only the number of coats was listed, there was no mention that there were officers' uniforms in the bundle. I decided to cut the silver ribbons from the collars and sleeves. I then cleaned the jackets with a wet rag and a brush. I let only Talka in on my secret, and she also helped me. We turned many officers' coats into the coats of ordinary soldiers. We hid the precious ribbons between the oven and the wall—a treasure for the Jewish army, if it would some day arise.

One day we saw that in the giant yard close to the river they had started to build a large apparatus from wood. The strange construction quickly took the form of a gallows—for ten people. I was seized with trembling. We had no idea who were doomed to be hung. A rumor spread that the Germans had been told of food smuggling in the ghetto and of the black market. The Germans demanded ten smugglers from the Judenrat in order to put them on trial. The pleas of the delegation of the Judenrat, headed by Yasha Zagon, claiming that there were no smugglers in the ghetto, were to no avail. The Germans announced that if ten people were not handed over to them, they themselves would choose people from the community, and instead of ten they would take twenty people. Fear descended over the Judenrat. After a night of deliberations they decided to supply the Germans with ten victims. They chose people who were handicapped from birth, such as Lemel, the water-drawer, Mindzia, the insane woman, a half blind beggar, a hunchback, a person with a limp, two people sick with tuberculosis, and others like them.

Every person in the ghetto, without exception, was ordered to be present at the scene of the execution of the sentence. In a proclamation plastered on the walls of houses it was written explicitly that anyone found hiding at home would be killed on the spot.

To this very day the spectacle remains etched in my memory. A large group of men from the Gestapo stood near the gallows. At their side were the Jewish police, the members of the Judenrat and their leader, the *Judenalteste* (Jewish elder), Fishka Ika. The police brought in those who had been sentenced to death. They marched haltingly, their hands tied behind them. Some of them did not understand what was happening or where they were being led. The people of the ghetto stood frozen in their places until the insane woman, Mindzia, began suddenly to sing loudly. She sang a Yiddish lullaby, *Shluf Mein Kind* (Sleep, My Child). Hearing the song, everyone wept silently.

When the condemned reached the gallows, Fishka Ika stood up at the podium and delivered a speech in German. Fishka announced loudly that these people were receiving the punishment they deserved because they had hidden property from the Germans, and that some of them had had the audacity to smuggle food into the ghetto even though the Germans took care of us and provided us with plenty. All this, he went on, was at a time when they were in the midst of a difficult war. He was sure that the punishment would serve as a lesson to the people of the ghetto and would deter them from doing such things again.

The speech was over. The victims, some of whom had begun to understand what was about to happen, began to wail and scream. Only the insane Mindzia continued to sing. The sentenced were taken by force to the long bench.

Even before the hanging rope was wrapped around the neck of the first victim, I grabbed Talka's hand—she was standing beside me trembling from head to toe—and ran with her toward our home.

For two days it was forbidden to take down the corpses

from the gallows, so that everyone would see them and take note. For two days the corpses of ten innocent people swayed in the wind.

A Surprising Meeting

Only a few weeks had passed since that horrible day, and once again proclamations were plastered on the walls. Jews were ordered to report to the yard, this time for a census. We stood five people to a row throughout the yard, and the tremendous area held everyone. I stood beside my parents. At my side was Talka, who held my hand. I looked around. I recognized almost all the people of our town. After all, I was born and raised here.

Now we all stood pale and frightened, not knowing what lay in store for us. Women held their babies in their arms. Parents held their children's hands. Beside my parents stood my friend Dutzik and his family, and behind us in the second row, my friend Beinish with his family. Only two and a half years had passed since the outbreak of the war, when we were mischievous children busy with games, looking for practical jokes. Now everyone's face was serious and severe: nothing of the light of childhood remained. Like me, they had contributed to their families' livelihoods by performing all kinds of tricks and disguising themselves as Polish peasants. With the closing of the ghetto they worked alongside the adults on sewing machines.

Opposite us stood my grandmother and at her side was her youngest son, Yankel, with his wife, who held their baby close to her heart. Yankel was a handsome man, taller than his brother Avram, who stood on the other side of his mother. Standing like this they looked like their mother's bodyguards. But we all knew it was impossible to guard and protect someone in the presence of Hitler's armed soldiers.

My Uncle Avram no longer walked around with his pistol at his hip. Jews and Poles were forbidden to carry weapons.

Next to my Uncle Avram stood my best friend, Sholek, with his family. We had been very good friends, but since our confinement in the ghetto we hardly saw one another. Each of us was busy with his work and with worries about the immediate future.

Although technically spring had arrived, snow had fallen the previous evening and the day was cold, gray and cloudy. The hours crawled by, time stretching out because of the chill and our anxiety. Armed German soldiers wandered around the center of the yard. We had no idea what they were waiting for or what was awaiting us. The wind began to blow and the chill increased. Even though we were dressed in warm clothes, the cold penetrated to our very bones. Every once in a while a baby burst out crying.

A strange stir suddenly passed through the gathered crowd. Two black limousines reached the edge of the yard. Out of them stepped a number of German officers, handsome and tall in their magnificent uniforms, a few in green uniforms, and the others in black. On their arms was a blood-red band, upon which was a swastika. They wore tall, sparkling, black boots and hats imprinted with the image of an eagle. The officers in black differed from those in green by the emblems on their hats: the image of a skull with crossed bones, the symbol of death.

Absolute silence filled the yard. Even the babies stopped crying. Everyone seemed to sense the upcoming danger.

As though appreciating their own value, the officers marched upright. At each one's hip was his pistol; in his hand, a whip. The officers surveyed the crowd, passing from one to the next, while the soldiers walked behind them. They scanned the frightened faces with a look of contempt. Every once in a while one of them would strike someone's head with his whip or kick someone if it seemed to him that the line was not straight enough.

Suddenly I saw one of the officers in black, the tallest and youngest of the group of officers, point to a bearded man in the last row. With wild laughter and lashes from whips the man was pushed out of the line to the middle of the yard. Helpless, I watched what was happening. I knew the man only slightly. Over the years, on my way to school, I had seen him return from synagogue with his tallith bag under his armpit. He was a quiet and modest man.

Terror-stricken, we watched the pranks of the army officers. The old man was ordered to bend down on his knees and jump like a frog, while loud laughter and kicks from the German boots accompanied his movements. I clenched my fist. If it were not for my parents, if I were here alone, I would run to the man's aid, hit and kick those handsome soldiers, especially that tall one, and spit in his face. But I quickly realized how foolish my thoughts were. Who was I against them? I would not even have time to leave the line before the rifles of the soldiers would have shot me dead.

There was still more abuse. After the frog hops, the old man was ordered to jump on one leg and then on the other. He stumbled and fell, but the soldiers hit him with the butts of their rifles and forced him to get up. Then they started to pull out the hairs of his beard, until the man's face looked like one big bloody wound. The old man, who at first had not made a sound, now let out horrifying screams. I heard crying and moaning everywhere. My father mumbled a prayer. Talka's face was covered with tears, while my mother, white as a ghost, was close to fainting. Finally, they pushed the old man, dripping blood and almost unconscious, back to his place in line. The officers, the tall one at the lead, continued their survey as though nothing had happened. Now they were coming closer to us.

Suddenly I felt my knees give way, my breathing stop. On the blonde officer's forehead, between his left eye and his hat, I saw a red scar. "I know that man," the thought ripped through my brain. That is Gereck! That scar is my work, from the stone I shot at him. Now he is a Nazi officer. As he came closer I could make out the *Volksdeutsch* (Polish citizen of German descent) emblem on his sleeve. Unwittingly I squeezed Talka's hand.

"Zezka! What's happening to you? You're trembling. You're hurting me."

I loosened my grip. This is the end, I said to myself. If Gereck recognizes me he will kill me. There is no doubt that he will kill me right here on the spot. Would that he would kill me immediately with a shot of his pistol. But he would not do that. He would torture me first. He would pay me back for the stone that I, a Jewish boy, had stamped on his forehead, and for the scar which would remain there for all his life.

"God!" I prayed silently. "I hope Gereck puts an end to my life immediately, and if not, give me strength to withstand the torments. I just don't want to break down." I saw Gereck in my mind's eye, tearing out my fingernails, gouging my eyes. My whole body was trembling. Then another thought froze my blood: what would happen to my parents? What would happen to my mother when she wasn't able to watch them tormenting her son? What would happen to my father, my sister Talka and all of the family?

But maybe Gereck would not recognize me among this whole crowd? Almost three years had passed since then. Then my mind somersaulted and I was sure that I was deluding myself. Gereck would identify me without a doubt. If I had stood in the fourth or fifth row my chances would have been better. But now it was too late to move. The Nazis were already close, very close. All I could do was lower my eyes. I tried to convince myself that if he didn't see my eyes he wouldn't recognize me.

Out of the corners of my lowered eyes I followed the edge of Gereck's boots. They came closer and closer and stopped next to me, right in front of me. This is my end, I thought deep inside. A whip touched my chin. He raised my head slightly. Gereck stood opposite me. He looked at me from above. He was handsome in his black uniform. The black hat with the symbol of death accented his fairness. Our eyes met. I looked right back. I no longer had anything to lose: Gereck had recognized me, and my fate was sealed.

Gereck continued to stand opposite me. He measured me from head to foot. For a moment he turned his stare from me and moved it to the faces of my mother, father, and sister. And again he returned to me. The other officers and soldiers suddenly became impatient: Why is he standing there glaring at that Jewish boy?"

I imagined his intentions. He was thinking what death to choose for me, perhaps which tortures. Gereck continued to stand in front of me and every second seemed like an eternity. Suddenly he turned around, and with rapid steps walked to the black car. The other officers and soldiers hurried after him.

I remained standing in a state of shock. I knew that Gereck would return. He would not exercise restraint in avenging an insult perpetrated by a Jewish boy. He must want to play cat and mouse with me—letting his victim escape, in order to catch him again. Even after the black limousines had disappeared from the horizon, I knew that Gereck would return.

But Gereck did not return. I never saw him again.

The Expulsion

The cars had long since disappeared from the yard, and the Jewish police had given the order to disperse, but I could not move an inch—I remained frozen in my place. My parents and Talka also remained standing, pale and horrified. They did not understand why this officer had stood opposite me for such a long time, and what he wanted from me.

When we finally started home, my father turned to me: "Tell me, please, have you ever met this Volksdeutsch? Do you know him?"

"Yes, Father," I stuttered. "But now I cannot talk about it, I don't have the strength. Another time I'll tell you."

At that moment Talka fainted. When she regained consciousness, her first words were: "Zezka, that was Gereck, wasn't it? I was so afraid that he would kill you."

Three days passed before I managed to tell my parents about Gereck, three days in which I walked like a sleepwalker, unable to believe that Gereck had not taken revenge. My parents were shocked.

"I did see the scar on the officer's forehead," said Father. "But it did not occur to me that this was the work of my son. We were lucky. Only with the help of God were we saved from his hands. There is no other explanation."

My meeting with Gereck left its mark upon me for many days, but, as usual, we did not have much time to digest what was happening to us. Event followed event. A rumor spread that they were about to liquidate our ghetto and transfer us to another place. The Germans had decided to make Bzezin *Judenrein* (Jew-free).

The blow was severe. We did not know where they would transfer us or how the transfer would be carried out. Spring was already well under way, but we did not appreciate its beauty, for who knew what tomorrow would bring. Every day that passed without change was a lucky day bringing us that much closer to the end of the war.

But changes did come, and the war was still far from its end.

On the walls of the houses was plastered a notice ordering

all mothers and children, babies just recently born and children, age 10 and under, to report to the yard on May 14, 1942, at 6:00 a.m. The order also included all the old people who had been stamped.

Mother held onto us. We were prepared to leave our homes and move anywhere, to leave everything here if necessary—if only they would not separate us. We recalled the stories of the one hundred and fifty boys who had been sent to work outside the ghetto. We knew the small ghettos had been liquidated and the healthy people sent to work in the ghettos of the large cities. We remembered the stories of the old people, the mothers and children who were sent to unknown places.

Our immediate family breathed a sigh of relief. The order did not apply to Talka who was already ten and a half. But our sigh of relief was cut short quickly. In fear we remembered Grandmother, whose body was stamped, and Mother's two sisters and their children, Chandzia with her five-year-old son Abonik, and Sarah'le with her three-year-old son Pinchase'le. We anxiously thought of Yankel's wife with her baby, who was only a few weeks old. The list seemed endless.

In the evening we went to Chandzia's house, where Grandmother also lived. There we found all of the family members who would have to report.

The policeman, Eli, my Aunt Sarah'le's husband, calmed everyone: "There's nothing to worry about. Everyone is moving to the Lodz ghetto, and in that ghetto there are many children." He had heard that the children in the Lodz ghetto received special treatment, that Chaim Rumkovsky, the Judenalteste, took good care of them. There were even schools in the Lodz ghetto, and two orphanages supported directly by Rumkovsky. The orphans received more food than the adults.

"But, if everyone is to be transferred to the Lodz ghetto,

why do they need to separate husbands and wives, fathers and children? Why can't everyone travel together?" asked Chandzia. For this too Eli had an answer: "These are days of war, and it is possible that the Germans do not have the appropriate means of transportation for everyone." Eli continued to calm us all. He said, "The Germans are indeed cruel to the Jews, but not to women and children. Even they understand that the elderly, mothers, and children need more care."

In amazement, I listened to my uncle's words: Did he really believe what he was saying? Or did he just want to comfort those who were sentenced to deportation or perhaps even himself?! His wife and child were among them. Had he forgotten how the Germans had transferred the dying patients and what their attitude had been toward the old people?

To reinforce his words Eli added that the people who remained who were able to work would have to help liquidate the ghetto, package the prepared merchandise, and clean up. After that, they would also be sent to Lodz. Separation from the family would not last any longer than a few days. Meanwhile we must get ready for the journey and prepare bags, preferably knapsacks. We must pack only things which are most necessary for the mother and child. According to Eli, it was worth packing things for the rest of the family as well. And he had one more piece of advice before everyone departed: all of the members of the family must try to stay together so that they can help each other.

Eli's words were some relief to those present. His words seemed logical. Lodz was only about eighteen kilometers away from Bzezin, and a few days' separation for the families was not a tragedy.

Feverish work began in all of the homes. We sewed sturdy bags in which to pack the most important items. My mother took out strong sheets and blankets to use in making the bags. From strips of fabric folded four times we sewed straps. My sewing machine was now very useful.

The day on which the mothers with their children and the elderly were to report, arrived. In the morning twilight, even before the darkness dispersed, a miserable walking convoy passed through the streets: mothers with babies in their arms accompanied by their husbands, dragging bags and bundles; old people accompanied by their sons and daughters. The wailing of babies, who had been awakened from their sleep, also accompanied the convoy. In contrast to the gloomy mood of the walkers was the appearance of their clothes: they, especially the children, were all dressed up in fancy clothing. Everyone wanted to take their finest things with them. Many even wore two dresses, one on top of the other, two shirts, two pairs of pants—anything, so as not to carry too much in the bundles.

We also accompanied our dear ones even though we had said our good-byes the previous evening. In any case we couldn't sleep that night, and before dawn, we got up to be with them a little longer.

The whole family went together. Avram supported his mother on one side, and my mother wrapped her arm around her on the other. Chandzia held the sleeping Abonik in her arms and her husband, Chamota, carried the packages. The moment Talka arrived, Abonik woke up completely and asked to walk. Talka took his hand.

At their side walked Chamota's sister, Bela, with her son, Arush, and her husband, Yehuda. My Uncle Yankel walked beside his wife, Fela, and carried their baby. Behind them walked Sarah'le, my mother's younger sister, with her son, Pinchase'le. Sarah walked unaccompanied by her husband, the policeman, Eli, who had had to report to the yard earlier, in the middle of the night. My father took Pinchase'le, barely walking and crying bitterly, in his arms, while I took the boy's little bundle from my aunt. The convoy was completed by Bela's second brother with his wife and four children.

Although we were well into the month of May, a bitter chill stung the air. The wind blew and the skies hung low with gloomy clouds. This accentuated our sadness.

I heard Talka encouraging Abonik. She told him that they were traveling to the big city, Lodz, where there were very tall houses, and that in a few days we too would arrive there and would all reunite. But Abonik did not want to wait a few days. He wanted us to come with them: he wanted Talka to come now.

Near the yard the Jewish police were already waiting, and they allowed only those who had been called to enter, while all of their escorts were ordered to return home. The men were forced to return to work.

The separation of wives from their husbands, and of children from their fathers was heartrending. Everyone sobbed even though we thought that the separation would last for only a few days.

We returned home in silence. My mother cried bitterly.

The wind grew stronger, and the skies darker. Before we reached home rain was pouring, turning quickly into a flood. We were close to home, but by the time we entered, running as fast as possible, we were soaked to the bone. We shuddered as we imagined our loved ones in this stormy rain. My mother's silent weeping got louder: "Lord of the Universe, why do you punish us so? How did my mother sin, that she should suffer so much? And what was the sin of Yankel's baby and the little children? They will surely catch pneumonia. They might even die."

Father tried to calm her, saying that the soldiers would not make them stand in such rain. He tried to explain to her that the families of the police were among those gathered, and beside the yard was Stark's courtyard with the big building which had been appropriated. Surely they would bring every-one into the building. But Father's voice was not the least bit convincing.

It was true that all of those gathered were brought into the building, but not while it was raining. Only in the late afternoon were they allowed to use the building for shelter. Until then, babies remained with their mothers and the elderly under the open sky. The mothers tried to shelter their children, but to no avail: the rain soaked them down to the bone and penetrated their shoes. It seemed that even nature had turned her back on them, pouring her wrath out.

When the rain stopped after about two hours, the pale sun which peeked out from between the clouds was not enough to warm and dry the trembling people. Hour after hour they stood outside with their babies crying bitterly. Even the Jewish policemen in the yard were prevented from approaching their families by the German soldiers.

Around two o'clock in the afternoon a black car arrived, from which German officers jumped out with ease and elegance, pistols in their holsters and whips in their white-gloved hands. Members of the Judenrat, with the Jewish elder Fishka Ika, arrived simultaneously at the yard. The officers surveyed the gathering with a quick glance and ordered the old people to move to the other side of the yard and organize themselves in rows. Parallel to the row of elderly, the Jewish police were ordered to arrange rows of mothers who had two or more children, and on the third side, rows of mothers with one child.

Fishka Ika was ordered to identify who was pregnant, and they were to join the women who had more than one child. Since Chamota's second sister had four children, the police-man Eli hinted to his wife that she should make sure that all of the members of the family moved over to the side occupied by women with more than one child. He wanted them to do everything they could to stay together. Only Grandmother had to move to the the old people's side. Chandzia held onto her mother; she refused to let her go alone. Eli separated them gently, took Grandmother by her arm, gathered up her bag, and helped her cross to the other side. He whispered to Chandzia that this was just a temporary separation, only for the purpose of a count. Eli also promised her that he would make sure that Grandmother returned to her daughters. Grandmother herself was indifferent, and Eli was not sure whether she understood what he had said. But before Eli managed to position her a blow of the elegant officer's whip landed on his head.

"*Donnervetter* (Damn it)," yelled the officer. "Can't you walk any faster with that old rag? What are you thinking? This no time for a leisurely stroll!"

Grandmother's bag fell as a result of the blow, but the officer prevented Eli from picking it up. It remained lying in a puddle in the yard.

Eli had not yet managed to return to the yard, when he saw that same officer approach Fishka Ika and ask him if he had put the pregnant women on the side with the mothers of more than one child as he had been ordered. The German's face reddened when Fishka Ika answered him in a stutter that with all the commotion he had forgotten to do so. The man from the S.S. raised his club, and without any consideration of Fishka Ika's high position, struck his face. Trembling and shocked, all of those gathered stared at the blood flooding the face of the Jewish elder.

The German officers had apparently run out of time, and the officer who had orchestrated everything barked an order at the German soldiers and the Jewish police to put everyone inside the building without delay. The old people and the mothers of more than one child were put on the bottom floor; the mothers who had only one child were put on the upper floor.

Amidst shoves and blows from rifle butts the people were taken into the building. In all of this chaos, Bela decided to move with her son Arush to the side with mothers with one child. After the room filled, the S.S. soldiers bolted the door and stood guard in front.

All of this was told to us by Eli. He reached us in the evening, broken and exhausted. When we asked him what had happened, he started sobbing. I looked in awe at the strong young man in the policeman's uniform who was crying like a little boy.

"I didn't even have time to part from my own wife and child!" he yelled. "The way they left them standing for hours in the rain, transferred to the rooms, bolted and guarded in the rooms, I don't like any of it. Who knows where they will take them. And what will happen to them." With his clenched fist he suddenly hit his head: "Who knows if I will ever see them again?" My mother, who was also frightened and broken, tried to calm him. "Everyone is being transferred to Lodz," she said. "We will all meet soon." But this was no help. Eli refused to be comforted.

The following morning we heard that some of the mothers had returned, among them Bela. We hurried to her house, but stopped dead in our tracks as we approached. On the front steps sat a woman, and we asked ourselves: is that Bela? Could she have changed so much in one night? Just yesterday she had been young, with dark hair and a good-natured smile that lit up her face. Now we saw a woman with a mad look in her eyes, and hair that was wild and graying. Her face was scratched and bleeding, her eyes red and swollen. She was not crying now—it seemed that the source of her tears had been exhausted. Only every once in a while a chilling moan escaped her throat. She did not answer our questions. Where was her son, Arush? Where were Grandmother and the others? Why had only she returned? Where

were Chandzia and Sarah'le? She kept sitting silently while
we all stood around her.

Only towards evening did her husband, Yehuda, get her to
come into the house, and then her stream of tears flowed and
her frightened screams burst loose: "They killed my Arush!
They threw him out the window!"

She began again to rip at her face and tear out her hair as
she sobbed. Much later she gave us other details.

Everyone was taken to the big building in Stark's courtyard. To her great misfortune at the last minute, in all the
chaos, she had decided to break away from the other members of the family and move to the side with the mothers with
one child. When she reached this part of her story she once
again tore out her hair and screamed: "Why did I do that? If
I had not done that my child might still be alive!"

The room into which they were put was filled with cans of
paint and ladders. Despite the crowded and dirty conditions,
the blows, the pushing and their detention, the mothers all
breathed a sigh of relief. They would finally be able to take
care of their children. They undressed the children, who
were trembling from the cold, hugged them, tried to warm
them next to their bodies, and dressed them in the dry
clothes which they had in their bags. The wet clothes were
wrung out the window and hung on the ladders to dry. They
took out of the bags some of the food they had prepared for
the journey and fed it to their frozen and hungry offspring.

Bela found a place by the window where she sat with
Arush. After she had dressed him in dry clothes and hung
up the wet ones, she sat him down on the windowsill with
bread and salami. Arush ate with a hearty appetite. Only
now, when she watched the boy eating did she wonder where
Yehuda had obtained the salami for them. Salami was a rare
and precious treat which could not be found anywhere in the
ghetto. But suddenly, before Arush had finished his food, he

began to cry and vomit. She held his head so that he would vomit out the window. The boy continued and complained of stomach pains. With great difficulty she managed to calm him. He fell asleep in her lap. Bela laid him down carefully on her coat, which she had spread out on the floor. It grew dark. There was no electricity in the room. Some of the children slept in their mothers' laps, and some, like Arush, slept on the floor.

Bela stood by the window. Outside it was already dark—a heavy darkness, without moon or stars. She thought of the horrors that had taken place that day. She was so sorry that she had separated from the rest of the family, but she comforted herself that in the Lodz ghetto they would reunite. They might even meet on the train before they arrived in Lodz. She was still thinking of all this when she heard two muffled bells from a distance. It was two A.M. In the darkness she suddenly saw two small lights which very quickly got closer and bigger. At the same moment she heard the sound of traveling cars.

"They're coming to take us!" Bela screamed into the room.

"Quiet. What are you yelling for? You'll wake the children!" came a reprimand from the other side.

She hadn't had enough time to identify the woman scolding her when the door of the room suddenly burst open to reveal German soldiers with flashlights.

"Quick!" they yelled, "Hand over your children immediately! Give us your stinking shit!"

The children woke up crying. The mothers began to scream. They hugged their children, ignoring the blows striking them; they struggled with the soldiers and were dragged away from their children, holding onto them with all their strength; they cried and begged, pleading to be allowed to go with their children. But the soldiers were stronger than the mothers. They separated them from their children and shouted: "You will stay here to work, you are strong and can still be of value. Such is not the case with your trash. We don't need them!"

Bela pushed the crying Arush to the wall and stood in front of him, hiding him with her body. But a German soldier saw this. He pushed her aside, slapped her face and wrestled with her.

Bela stopped telling her story. A strange sob came out of her throat, and her eyes bulged out of their sockets. We all stood petrified, unable to make a sound. A long time passed before Bela continued.

"The soldier grabbed Arush and threw him out the window. The last sound I heard was his voice crying: 'Mama!....'"

Bela became silent. She stared at us strangely, and then crumpled up.

I bit my lips to make sure I wasn't having a nightmare. Bela seemed like she was out of her mind. Suddenly she raised her head and her gaze was pleading: "Do you think Arush is still living? Perhaps he is only wounded? Maybe he only broke a leg? Will they treat him? Will they take him to the hospital? In the Lodz ghetto there are good hospitals. I think that Chandzia and Sarah'le will look after him..." Then she began to cry bitterly: "Why did I separate from them? They weren't separated from their children. I also could still be with my Arush!"

It was difficult to calm her. All of us were stunned. Suddenly Talka burst out in horrible screams: "They threw Arush out the window! And the other children too! They killed them! They must have also killed Abonik!"

Father hugged Talka and tried to calm her: "It isn't possible that they just threw the children out the window. The children had done no wrong. Surely they had opened blankets under the windows so that the children would not be injured. They must have thrown the children out that way in order to get them evacuated more quickly." Father's voice broke. I looked at him. Tears were streaming from his eyes. Talka was not calmed. Her screams stopped, but not her crying.

The one who was calmed was Bela. She searched for any thread of hope. She wanted to believe that nothing bad had happened to her son even though with her own eyes she had seen her child's end. She turned to Father and asked, "Do you really believe, Yoseph, that they spread out blankets? Certainly it could not be otherwise. They couldn't possibly have just taken children and thrown them out the window. You're undoubtedly right. Soon we will travel to Lodz and I will find my son."

The Liquidation of the Bzezin Ghetto

We stayed in the Bzezin ghetto for only a few more days. Rumors spread that they were transferring us to the Lodz ghetto. In the large warehouse they were busy packing the German army uniforms, but aside from that no one was working. This was our most miserable time since the outbreak of the war. People withdrew inside themselves and inside their houses. No one spoke to anyone else. The streets were empty of people.

Before leaving the ghetto I wanted to go with Talka to the shore of the Mrozitzka River, to watch its running waters, to see the place where I had grown vegetables, to look out once again over the meadow. But hearing about children being thrown out the window had taken away my desire to do anything, even to say goodbye to the places in which I had spent my childhood. I stood beside the window and looked out at a small cloud sailing through the sky. I was jealous of its freedom to go anyplace it wanted. No one could forbid it to be free. Thoughts pulsed through my head, one after another. All of the values that I had learned, all the good and beautiful that I had grown up with—everything collapsed within me. I was full of complaints against the Creator of the Universe: "What evil, Lord of the Universe, did those little ones do? What were the sins of Arush, and Abonik, and Pinchase'le, and the others?" Below, on the other side of the window, beyond the dark blanket that covered it, beyond the ghetto, was ordinary traffic, with people free just because they had not been born Jews.

Some children had been permitted to remain in the ghetto: the Jewish policemen had their families, members of the Judenrat headed by the Jewish elder, Fishka Ika, all retained their children. The German officers responsible for the ghetto had promised to protect them until the end of the war.

Fishka Ika proposed to Dr. Warhaft that he and his wife stay with them in the ghetto. He promised them special conditions: plenty of food, good wages, a license to leave all their furniture in their house and to live there without disturbance. He tried to persuade the doctor because he was the only one left in the ghetto. In the Lodz ghetto and some of the others, Fishka said to him, there were plenty of doctors. There he wasn't needed as much as here.

But Dr. Warhaft rejected all the proposals. The people who remained in the ghetto, he said, were young and healthy. He felt obligated to go with the masses. No one knew where the Nazis were sending them. He and his wife would go with everyone, their fate was his fate. And as for money, said Dr. Warhaft, he himself did not need it. If there was a lot of money in the community treasury, it was only proper to give some to everyone being sent away. Dr. Warhaft's aggressive request earned the support of the members of the Judenrat, and influenced Fishka Ika to give 10 marks to each person.

Father called me to help pack our belongings, effectively cutting off my thoughts. The next day we were to leave the ghetto. Mother was still busy baking and cooking. From all of the flour which remained in the house she baked several kinds of little breads and cooked all the potatoes in their peels. She divided this food and a little bit of sugar among the four of us. That last night none of us slept a wink.

Early in the morning we dressed in as many of our best clothes as we could, layer upon layer, so that we would have clothes to change into when we arrived at any place. With packs on our backs and bundles in our arms we left our house. Below on the street there was already a mass of people, arranged in two rows of fives on both sides of the street. Everyone was laden with bundles. S.S. soldiers and Jewish policemen stood among them. Congestion and screams, curses and kicks, everyone pushing everyone else: these were the conditions. German soldiers tried to establish order with their cudgels, which waved and landed occasionally on someone's head. The Jewish police moved the people from side to side, in whatever way they were ordered by the Germans. They tried to count those being sent away. In contrast to the Germans, the Jewish police were not hitting the people, but rather, tried to support them. Occasionally a policeman would be whipped for such an act.

Father, Mother, Talka, and I held one another's hands. To be together, only to be together was our hope. The convoy advanced a few meters and stopped, advanced about two steps and stopped again. Thus we continued to move and stand intermittently. We stood more than we walked. The route seemed endless: hours, an eternity. People bent down under the burden of their belongings, sweating beneath all of the clothes that they had piled on themselves.

Our family too, pale and sweaty, barely crept along. My mother and Talka looked like they needed a wall to lean against, any kind of support. This was the longest day of our lives. Only towards evening did we finally arrive in the train station in Galkuvek, a distance of six kilometers from Bzezin.

We breathed a sigh of relief when we could see the train in the distance. We were so exhausted we did not even notice that it was a cattle car. All we wanted was to remove the burdens from our backs and sit down, to find something upon which to prop our bodies. But when we got closer to the train we saw that the train tracks were on a big hill. In order to reach the cars we had to drag ouselves and our belongings up the hill. Dumbfounded and terrified, we stopped, but the soldiers whipped us on. Occasionally we heard shots. People began the climb, throwing bundles as they went. Old and young alike fell and rolled down, got up and climbed again. My father supported my mother, and I pushed Talka upwards. The Jewish policemen also supported people and pushed them. Right beside me there was a policeman half-carrying a woman. A scream slipped out of my mouth: it was my Uncle Eli. I saw that he was supporting Bela, whose child had been thrown out the window.

"Luzer, quickly, undo the band on my sleeve," Eli called to me. "I am going with you. Maybe there, in Lodz, or in some other place, I will find my wife and our son."

Before I had time to undo the band, an S.S. soldier appeared next to us. "Hey, policeman! Get down quickly to help others up. Quickly!" he barked at Eli.

Eli was forced to go down. But before he did he managed to whisper to me that on the way he would throw away his hat so he could get on the train with those who remained.

However, things did not work out for Eli and he did not get on. We were put into the last car because all of the other cars were already filled to the brim. We were pushed inside the car. The doors were closed and bolted. We're being treated like dangerous prisoners, I thought.

Even before the door was closed, we heard a volley of shots, followed by another and then another. We all trembled. Had they shot all of those who couldn't fit into the train? No one spoke a word. It was forbidden to think such things. It simply could not be. Who would kill people just because there was no room for them on a train?

Just then I remembered something that had happened to me when I was a schoolboy. The shop teacher had instructed us to bring an empty box of matches to class. Mother gave me two half-full boxes so that I could concentrate all the matches in one of them and take the empty one to school. I filled one box with matches and threw away the rest.

Mother scolded me: "We could have used them. One doesn't throw out something that can still be used!" The sentence repeated itself now and echoed to the sound of the clatter of the train wheels. But, God, those were only matches. These were living people, flesh and blood.

Years later, I was told by Poles that all of those remaining, for whom there was no room on the train, were indeed shot. And not only they, but also our Jewish elder, Fishka Ika, his family, all of the members of the Judenrat and their families, and the Jewish police were shot. Before this they were forced to salvage all articles of value from the ghetto apartments and bring them to a collection post. Afterwards they were ordered to clean the entire ghetto area and dig a big pit. Then to the last man, they were shot, and their corpses put into the pit, which they had dug, as it turned out, for themselves.

Chapter Two

In the Lodz Ghetto

The train continued its journey. We knew that travel time on a train from Galkuvek to Lodz was only about half an hour, but hours had already passed and we were still nowhere. We had no idea where we were being taken. The train stopped occasionally, switched tracks and traveled in the opposite direction. Night fell. Many of the travelers fell asleep on the floor of the car, leaning on their bundles. Talka also fell asleep with her head on Mother's knees. By the moon's dim light, which penetrated through the small barred window, we saw Talka's face smiling in her sleep. Our hearts were wrenched at the sight. It had been so long since we had seen a smile on her face. Why should she smile now, of all times? There was something amazing about it.

Suddenly Talka began to shout in her sleep. "Abonik! Abonik! You see that I have come to you. I told you we would meet! You are here too, Ahrele? You weren't wounded? Then it's true that there were blankets spread out below, that they didn't just throw you out of the window for no reason at all?

We were so worried about you! Also your mother..." Her words were cut off in the middle.

Talka suddenly sat up. Her shouts had awakened her. Confused, she looked around. At first she could not believe where she was, and when it became clear to her, she began a horrible wailing. We had never heard her cry like that. My mother embraced her, sat her on her lap and rocked her as though she were a baby. We all tried to speak soothingly to her, saying that soon the dream would come true and that she would meet Abonik, Ahrele, Pinchase'le, and the others. It was difficult to calm her. She cried for a long time until she finally fell back to sleep in Mother's lap.

The journey lasted the entire night, the train stopped only towards morning. We could hear the doors being opened in the nearby cars. Finally our car door was also opened. Afraid, we looked out. This was not a station. There was no sign telling the name of the place. All around us we saw desolate fields.

But we did not have much time to wonder where we were: Jewish police entered the car. On their heads were hats with a rounded visor and a yellow line around them, and on their left arm was a band with the star of David. They told us: "Jews, you have arrived in the Lodz ghetto."

And so we were, after all, in Lodz. But there was no time to think. We were ordered to hurry and descend quickly from the train, for it had to continue on its way.

The policemen arranged us in groups of five. The German soldiers did not intervene this time. They got on the train, which soon pulled away.

Before we even had a chance to get ourselves arranged we saw a woman run out of her row, grab the sleeve of one of the policemen, and call to him in a trembling voice: "Mr. Policeman! Where are our children, where can we find them?"

It was Bela.

The policeman asked in amazement which children she meant.

"Our children!" Bela shouted, "The children from the Bzezin ghetto! They arrived here three days ago! My boy is Arush. Three days ago they arrived."

The policeman replied that no children had arrived here from anywhere. But when he heard the woman wail he tried to calm her, saying that perhaps they brought the children at a time when other policemen were on duty.

Bela and two other mothers whose children were also taken, ran from policeman to policeman, crying, screaming, and pleading. The policemen stood perplexed while hearing these horrible stories about how the children were taken away. They did not understand why the children had not arrived with their parents, why they were separated. In any case, no one had seen children in the Lodz ghetto. One policeman made a suggestion: in the Charnyetzkiego prison, which was now a transit camp for the Jews, there were more people from the small towns. Although he had not seen any children among them, perhaps something could be learned there. The mothers were somewhat calmed as they latched onto this new hope.

Meanwhile, we who had evacuated Bzezin, had begun to walk towards the ghetto. After a short distance we could see thick barbed wire fences with patrols of armed German soldiers around them. The gate to the ghetto was opened, and we were taken inside. We passed a giant cemetery which stretched out to our left but we still could see no houses. Finally we reached some small houses in the heart of desolate fields. We were taken into the houses, which contained many rooms with beds: one next to the other and one above the other. Beside the wall stood wooden planks three stories high, called *pritchot.*

The police explained to us that this was a temporary

station, that we would remain here only for a number of days until we could move into the apartments of people who had been evacuated from the ghetto and transferred elsewhere. They explained to us that these beds were built especially for us, since only a month ago these were classrooms for the academic high school.

I found it hard to understand these things. Why was it necessary to evacuate people from their homes in the Lodz ghetto and then bring other people in their place? I received the answer within a few days when we moved to a permanent apartment.

Meanwhile, we settled down on the pritchot, Mother and Talka on lower ones, Father and I on the upper. "The most important thing is that we have a place to put our heads, to rest a little," sighed Mother.

I put my pack down on my bed and went out to explore the area. All the other houses around us were organized exactly like ours: rooms with beds. Again they told us that our living arrangements here were temporary, until they transferred us to permanent apartments, and this place would again be a school. I hoped that we too, the children of Bzezin, might be sent to study. Talka and I could go back to school. We had already lost so much time.

From a nearby house the fragrance of cooked food reached my nostrils. It turned out that there was a large kitchen which supplied food to the students. The odor reminded me how hungry I was. Soon we heard the voices of policemen who ordered us to arrange ourselves in rows to receive soup. For this we had to take pans and spoons out of our packs. Amidst noise and commotion, but with the strict supervision of the Jewish policemen, rows were set up beside the tremendous pot which had been taken out of the kitchen. Women dressed in white aprons, with white kerchiefs on their heads, distributed the soup from a big ladle. The soup was very watery, with only two or three cubes of potato floating in it. It was intended more for drinking than eating, but it was tasty. We all needed the dish to warm our insides.

After I finished eating my portion of soup, I climbed up to bed and fell asleep immediately. I don't know how long I slept, but a loud cry woke me. Frightened, I sat up. Beneath me, on my mother's bed, sat Bela with her husband, Yehuda. Crying and screaming, she told my mother of her attempts to find Arush. She said that after she had received a bed, she had put her belongings on it, and immediately went to the Charnyetzkiego prison hoping to receive some information about Arush. Policemen guarded the gate to the prison, and prevented her from entering. The police explained to her that no children at all had arrived there. Some people in the camp had arrived from Bzezin, but none of them were children. A policeman grabbed Bela by the hand when she tried to push inside despite the prohibition.

"Miss," said the policeman, "at Charnyetzkiego you can go in, but it's impossible to get back out. Before you decide to go in think hard if it's worth it to you. Your son, Miss, is not there. We don't know where they sent the children from Bzezin—but they did not come to the Lodz ghetto. The people here now will not remain in the Lodz ghetto either; they will be transferred to another place." Then the policeman blocked the entrance gate with his body and pushed her away.

Bela continued walking around the barbed wire which surrounded the prison, in order to look in and search through the fence. In the giant yard in front of the prison building, many people were roaming about. The policemen arranged them in lines to receive food. There were only adults there. She recognized many people from her town among them. Suddenly she saw her husband Yehuda standing next to her parents. She called out their names. Only Yehuda left the line and came close to the barbed wire fence. He told her that he had lost her by the train when he had helped her parents climb the hill to the train cars, and he had then been put into the car with them. He had looked for her but after not finding her, he decided she must be in a different car. Even after they arrived at the Charnyetzkiego transit camp he had not seen her, and he was surprised that she was in a different place, outside.

Hearing this, Bela ran again to the gate and pleaded with the policeman to let her in, for her husband and parents were there. To her amazement the policeman was once again opposed.

"It would be better, Miss, if your husband got out of there rather than you go in," he said.

"How can he get out?" asked Bela, "He's waiting with my parents for the soup that they are handing out."

The policeman's face reddened, and showed his impatience: "Leave your parents. Take my word for it, they'll never get out of there. Tell your husband that he should give up his soup and find a way out." The policeman, pointing with his hand as if accidentally to a distant corner, turned his back on Bela and marched away.

Bela ran back to the place where she had seen her husband and repeated what the policeman said. She tearfully pleaded with Yehuda to try to get out of the camp. Yehuda gave up his soup and began to walk to the place the policeman had pointed out. The two of them walked alongside the fence, Bela outside and Yehuda inside. While walking Yehuda stepped on a piece of rusty sheet metal, stumbled and fell. The metal covered a deep pit which ran under the tangled barbed wire. Without hesitating, Yehuda crawled into the pit and passed under the barbed fence. He came out on the other side of the camp dripping with blood, his clothes torn. From there they came to our house where I found them sitting on my mother's bed.

Bela continued to cry and blame herself for what she had done when she moved with her son from the line with Chandzia and Sarah'le. If she had not done this, she too, like them, would now be with her child. Her cries and screams mounted as she again recalled that the children had not come to the Lodz ghetto.

My mother tried to calm her. "There is nothing you can do. It's impossible to turn the clock backwards. Perhaps the children were moved to a special camp; certainly Chandzia and Sarah'le will also protect Ahre'le." My mother tried to encourage her, but her voice lacked conviction. It was already night when Yehuda got her to bed.

We remained in those little school pavilions for three weeks. Our daily portions of food included only one helping of watery soup and a dry piece of bread. This was insufficient, but fortunately, we still had in our packs the food we had brought from Bzezin, which helped us withstand the oppressive hunger.

Here, in our transit camp, we could already feel the exemplary order which reigned in the Lodz ghetto. Coupons were distributed for portions of bread and soup. Food distribution was orderly and fast. Policemen guarded the lines to make sure of that.

Everyone told stories about Chaim Rumkovsky. They would tell of his "iron hand," his dominance, his involvement in everything despite his advanced age (he was 70 years old). They also spoke of his marriage to a young woman of 26 or 27.

Clerks began to count us and make precise lists of our first name, family name, age, and profession. I was angry at my father for listing me as a tailor, an expert at sewing military uniforms, three years older than my real age. I wanted to study, to be registered in a school, not sew.

However, very quickly I saw that my father had been right.

There were no more schools in the Lodz ghetto, and the small pavilions which had served as a high school had been turned into a *resort* (workshop) for straw shoes.

The clerks gave us books of coupons for rations—portions of food distributed once a month—and coupons for a loaf of bread which was given to us once a week. We also received money to pay for the goods. Ghetto money, like the Polish money that was used before the war, and like the German marks that the Nazis had introduced after their invasion of Poland, was printed on fine paper, with Rumkovsky's picture on one side and a Jewish star, Rumkovsky's signature, and the date and place in which the money was printed on the other. Rumkovsky's face on the bill, with an abundance of white hair on his head, looked like the portrait of a poet or some other very important person.

I was curious to see Rumkovsky, the so-called "king of the ghetto," the "president," the "Jewish elder," and I did not have to wait long. One day we sensed something different among the police. They informed us that Rumkovsky would come visit us. We stood in the soup lines and suddenly the man arrived in a carriage. To one side stood a contingent of clerks and police. Even in the distance his white head stood out. When he reached us he jumped out of the carriage with the agility of a young man. He was indeed a unique figure: a head taller than most, his white hair complementing his tanned face, a vigorous face expressing decisiveness and a powerful will. His manner of dress was also special. The Jewish elder wore a short sports jacket, riding pants, and high, sparkling black leather boots; clothes which gave him the appearance of power. But not only the appearance. This man was very powerful inside the ghetto; there was nothing he couldn't do. He could pardon or punish. For a small infraction, like stealing food, he could send a resident anywhere and separate him from his family. It was in his power to transfer a man from hard labor to an easy job or vice-versa. His power was absolute.

He arrived to greet us and I could see him with my own eyes. First he looked around, then immediately began a speech. His voice was strong and authoritative. He promised us places to live and work. "You are men with trades, and you can contribute much with your work," he began. "With fruitful and devoted work we are not helping our enemies, as many think. With such work we are helping ourselves. The work here is a guarantee for our lives. In exchange for work we receive sustenance. Food is not plentiful in the ghetto, but those who work well will receive an extra bonus. Remember my words! Work is our weapon, our hope!"

Rumkovsky's speech was over. He once again glanced at his surroundings, turned on his heel and jumped quickly into his carriage which waited behind him. We saw the carriage drive away as the white upright head of the "king of the ghetto" stood out from inside it. I don't know what happened to me at that moment, but when I looked around and saw that there were only Jews here, even policemen among them, I was filled with a certain feeling of confidence.

The pavilions in Marisin, the transit camp, began to empty out. Families were taken to permanent dwellings. The police served as guides. Soon our turn arrived. A policeman had us take our belongings and follow him. We left behind the fields of Marisin and arrived at the center of the Lodz ghetto. I looked around in disbelief and disappointment. This is the great city, Lodz? From my visits before the war I remembered the broad, busy streets upon which trollies, carriages, and buses passed noisily. I remembered the tall buildings with their stores and shop windows displaying fancy clothes, furs, shoes, toys, and more. I remembered the masses of pedestrians who streamed by endlessly. Now it was as though I were seeing a different city: small and miserable one or two story houses, narrow streets, no trees or greenery. Everything was gray and sad. The only vehicles that I managed to see were wagons full of coal or potatoes being dragged or pushed by people with leather straps or ropes tied around their bodies.

The sidewalks were also empty of people, and when a figure was finally seen, it was usually a child.

"Everyone is at work during these hours," the policeman who escorted us explained.

I nearly choked when I looked at these children. They were so thin and lean: their legs were like narrow sticks, barely able to carry the thin body and large head which were so out of proportion. Further on we passed by a lot from which people were dragging bags with coal.

"You will also receive a ration of coal so that you will have some way to light your burner," said the policeman while pointing to the lot. At that moment a pale, thin, fair-braided girl of about 13 left the lot, bent under the weight of a bag of coal. I thought: why is a girl like that allowed to carry such a heavy bag? Before I had a chance to organize my thoughts— that perhaps she had no father or brother who would do this work—the big sack slipped from her shoulders and all the coal scattered on the sidewalk and the street. The girl stood at a loss. Tears flowed down her cheeks. I wanted to hurry to her aid, but the policeman pushed us on. He had to return soon and he was in a hurry. I again turned my head towards the girl who now knelt on her knees and gathered the coal. People left the lot, each one bent under his or her burden, but no one helped her. I had still not gotten over the sight of the crying girl gathering coal, when a strange figure came toward us. He looked at us with protruding, fearful eyes under which were very swollen bags and protruding cheek bones. But the most frightening thing about him were his legs—legs so swollen that they looked like two tree trunks barely making progress.

"That is a *klapsedra* (an obituary announcement)," said the policeman. "That's what we call those who are swollen from hunger," he continued. "These people do not divide their loaf of bread over eight days, but finish it in two or three, while they fast until the next distribution. They don't hold up very long and soon die." The indifference with which the policeman spoke proved that he was accustomed to such things, that they were daily occurrences.

Before we arrived at our new home, we ran into a long line in front of a store. "This is the line for meat. Once every month or two every person receives 100 grams of horse meat," the policeman continued to explain. "The meat has still not arrived, but the children, who do not work, stand in line from early in the morning, in order to help the adults receive the staple. The amount of meat is not enough for everyone and those who come too late have to come back another day."

I looked at the line. Indeed, only children stood there. The situation here was in no way similar to what we had known in the Bzezin ghetto. And I had thought there that nothing could be worse.

Our Fifth Home

The policeman took us to a rather large house, three stories high, at 16 Volborska street. We received our new apartment on the third floor. The policeman used a pair of scissors to cut the tape on the door, a sign that the apartment had been out of bounds until now, and opened the door to a long, narrow room. It was in horrible disorder: pieces of clothing and kitchen utensils were thrown around on the floor. There were crumpled sheets on the two metal beds pushed against the wall. On the third bed in the middle of the room there was a ragdoll, a sign that a little girl had lived here. Everything testified that the people who had been sent from the house had left in haste.

A heavy feeling passed through us all at the thought that we were now taking the place of people who had been expelled to who-knew-where. Who were these people that we should be taking their beds, their utensils? Were we in some way guilty? We also were expelled from our house; this was our fifth home. Did we have any guarantee that we would end our wanderings here?

"I hope that this is our last home until the end of the war," sighed my mother. "I haven't the strength to wander anymore!"

"If only it will be so!" added my father.

After the policeman left, my mother began rearranging the house. Talka helped while Father went to get the monthly food portion.

"Tomorrow we must report to work," said Father. "Therefore we had better take care of everything today." "Yes," my mother added, "for there is nothing to eat in the house."

I was responsible for acquiring the weekly portion of bread and coal from the courtyard. Despite my desire to get the bread so that we could eat a slice of it, I decided to run to the coal yard first. I was still obsessed by the girl gathering the black stones. I hurried to help her but when I arrived there I saw only a spot of black dust and tiny bits of coal scattered on the sidewalk and street.

The line was not long since these were working hours for most of the ghetto residents. In a short time, I returned home with the heavy bag of coal on my back.

It was almost evening when I came home with the bread from the bakery. Father was already home, a fire was burning on the stove, and mother was peeling potatoes to make soup from them. We all hoped that this would indeed be our last home.

The following day Mother, Father, and I had to appear where we had been assigned to work: Mother at the straw shoes workshop; Father, who had sworn that he was a warehouse keeper and not a tailor, was placed in a resort for carpentry; while I was sent to a sewing resort for young people. Talka, who was still young, only ten and a half years old, had to stay alone in the house.

Night came and we all lay down to sleep. Talka slept with my mother since there was no fourth bed. Now I heard my mother as she spoke to Talka comforting her that it would not be too bad to stay alone in the house, that she could keep sleeping after we had gone out to work, that she should take a slice of bread and eat, that we would return early from work—and most important, that she had nothing to be afraid of here, as there were only Jews inside the ghetto.

In the Workshop

Very quickly I realized that I had gotten the best work place. The hall manager said that since I was an expert in sewing uniforms, I would be responsible for the work of the twelve girls at the sewing machines. He led me to the edge of a large hall in which the workers were arranged in ten rows, each of which had twelve sewing machines. The workers were young women, some of whom looked like little girls. He introduced me to them and said that I would be their supervisor. The girls stopped their work and looked at me curiously, while a feeling of discomfort overcame me. "Who am I that I should supervise these girls my same age?" I also knew that my expertise was no greater than theirs. I hesitated. I wanted to turn to the manager and tell him that I was not an expert, but rather a simple seamster who sewed cut fabric. Then I remembered that my father had listed me as an expert, adding three years to my age. If I told the truth, they would ask me why my father had given incorrect information. I decided to keep still.

I was disturbed by the fact that I was to oversee the Jewish girls so that they would work well for the Germans. Then I recalled the words of the king of the ghetto, Chaim Rumkovsky, who said that by our work we were helping ourselves, that the work was the guarantee for our life and that in exchange for it we received food. At that same moment I decided that I would try to help these girls as much as I could, but I would also see to it that their work was performed properly.

The manager noticed my surprise that the girls were sewing thick white pants rather than army uniforms. He explained that these were also army uniforms for the winter, so that the soldiers would blend in with the white snow. These uniforms were apparently intended for the Russian front.

My work in the resort was not difficult. I received packages of cut fabric to divide, distributed the fabric to the girls who worked in assembly line fashion, and afterwards, gathered the finished product, organized the bundles, listed the quantities, and transferred the prepared merchandise to the department which handled finishing. I would also walk around among the machines, replacing broken needles and taking out threads that had gotten caught inside the machines. I wanted the girls to have the feeling that I was prepared to help them. But this took time.

In the beginning, they were suspicious of me, and when I got close to any machine, they would stop talking and start sewing faster. I did not know quite how to act. I couldn't tell them not to fear me so I said nothing. I believed that with time they would learn to know me.

Despite the noise of the machines in the hall, the first day in the resort passed rather quickly, even pleasantly. The only thing that bothered me was the thought of Talka who remained alone at home. Once in a while I would say to myself that the day must be passing dreadfully slowly for her. Close to ten o'clock I felt the hunger begin to gnaw at me. The tasteless coffee substitute sweetened with saccharin and the dry piece of bread that I grabbed before going to work did not last very long. But when I saw that the other workers in the hall continued to work with the same amount of food, I tried to shake off all thoughts of food.

At twelve o'clock I heard a bell ring. As though in response to a magic wand the machines fell silent all at once. The girls got up from their places noisily and happily. Everyone took a pot and spoon out of her bag and ran to the hall on the bottom floor. I walked after them. It was very crowded in the stairway. From every floor, men and women were hurrying and pushing with pots and spoons in their hands.

Below, in a large hall on the ground floor, behind a portion of wall next to the large windows, were women wearing white aprons and white kerchiefs, doling out soup with a big ladle, one ladle-full per person.

The smell of the soup made me painfully aware of my hunger. I remained on the side and watched. I saw that the young people stood in a separate line and received soup from a smaller ladle. They worked fewer hours than the adults so they received less food.

I watched the people who had already received their portion of soup. I saw them stirring with the spoon in the pot to count how many cubes of potato they had received. I heard exclamations of joy from those who had been given an additional cube. In amazement, I watched a few of them who swallowed their soup with a wild appetite directly from the pot before they had even walked away from the line and who now stood as if amazed that their pot had emptied so quickly. On the other hand, I saw people who tried to eat slowly in order to extend the eating time.

One girl from my group came up to me and asked: "Why aren't you eating? Didn't you get coupons for soup from the manager?"

"I have no pot or spoon," I answered.

She handed me her pot and spoon. "I already finished my soup. You can use my utensils today. But tomorrow you'd better bring your own pot and spoon from home."

"What luck you have!" called the girl, who introduced herself as Estherka, when she saw the large number of potato cubes floating above the mix.

The soup we received was similar to that in the Marisin transit camp. It was more for drinking than eating, but it tasted wonderful. Perhaps it just seemed that way because of my hunger. My heart shrank when I thought of my sister Talka, who remained alone in the house and was not provided with any soup.

After a half hour break we returned to the hall to work. At one-thirty the five-hour work day for youths had finished. In the streets many children hurried back to their homes. In their hands were not bags with schoolbooks, but pots.

Talka did not complain about her hours alone, but was glad when I came home. She showed me how she had put the house in order, straightened the sheets, and swept the floor. She insisted that I tell her in detail everything that happened to me from the moment I arrived at the resort. I felt uncomfortable when I told her about the hot and tasty soup we had received. Sadly, I looked at my little sister who had long ago stopped asking the questions which certainly still bothered her. Even at her age she already understood that the adults had no answers to her questions. She had also stopped mentioning Abonik since she heard Bela say that the children of Bzezin never arrived in the Lodz ghetto.

Suddenly, Talka sighed like a grown-up. She repeated what mother had said upon entering this apartment. "Zezka!" (Recently she had gone back to calling me by that name.) "My biggest wish is that this will be our last home until the end of the war." I could tell she wanted to add something but stopped herself.

"I believe that it will be so," I answered my sister, though a feeling which I did not understand prevented me from really believing it.

Potato Peels

It was already dark when my parents came home from work. Father returned first and seemed extremely tired, but when we asked him if he worked very hard he shook his head no. Mother did not complain either and only mentioned the long way that she had to walk to and from work, as well as her concern that Talka remained alone for so long in the house without food. Talka calmed her and told her that she had gotten up late, was busy for a long time setting the house in order, and when the hunger bothered her she sucked a sugar cube from those we had brought from Bzezin. She even reminded Mother that I had returned home early.

Mother, despite her fatigue, peeled some potatoes, and, with a little flour and a lot of water, made a soup which we ate for supper. The soup was very watery, but it was still important for us to eat something hot before going to bed. Some of the soup Mother reserved for Talka to have as a meal the next day.

The days now began to settle into a pattern, each day much like the others. Our parents got up early in the morning, particularly Mother, who had to walk a great distance to her work place in Marisin. I would leave last and, while walking, I still had time to look around me, to think about the masses of adults and children hurrying to work.

My place of work was pleasant. Only the thought that we were working for the Germans disturbed me. The days passed by quickly and the work was not difficult. Since I was not tied down to a machine, I was free to wander around the workshop and meet new people.

One evening, when my mother was peeling potatoes, our

neighbor from across the hall came to visit us. She and her family had arrived in the Lodz ghetto from Berlin about half a year before. She said that in Germany also the Jews had lived in quarantine since the outbreak of the war. But in Germany they did not go hungry.

The neighbor instructed Mother how to divide the monthly rations and the weekly bread so that there would not be days without food. She told of acquaintances who hadn't done so and had died of starvation as a result. While she was talking our neighbor looked at my mother's hands peeling the potatoes and suddenly she asked Mother what she did with the peels.

"What do you mean?" Mother asked in surprise. "I throw them away. What else?"

"Throw them away!?" the woman cried out. "If you do that then you have never felt real hunger."

The neighbor told of many people who had died here of starvation and explained to Mother that potato peels were valuable in the ghetto, that doctors distributed coupons for them, and that long lines stretched out in front of the kitchens in hopes of acquiring them.

We all stared at her in amazement.

"How can one eat peels," asked my mother, "especially from potatoes that are completely rotten?"

"You can make a *babka* (cake) from them," the woman replied. "If you want I can teach you how to prepare it. It's very simple: you wash the peels and grind them in the meat grinder, add a little flour and salt and place the mixture over a low flame. When the babka is ready and chilled, you cut slices from it and take them to work." She explained that if you prepare the babka immediately after receiving the ration, you can eat a little sugar or jelly with it and then you hardly notice its bitterness. "I know it's tasteless food," she said, "but it fills the stomach a little, and makes it possible to spread the distributed portions throughout the month. There's another type of babka, made from the crumbs of artificial coffee that we receive. But the babka from the coffee crumbs is good only if you make it right after the distribution of the ration, because it is so bitter that, without a little sugar, it is impossible to even put it in your mouth. You'll learn to eat these foods," said the woman. "It disgusted us in the beginning too, but slowly we got used to it."

After Mother finished peeling the potatoes, she moved the peels to the side. Despite our neighbor's explanations, Mother was embarrassed to offer them, but the woman herself asked Mother if she was going to try to use those peels.

My mother gave the woman permission to take the peels. "I guess we still don't know what real hunger is," Mother said to her. "We have certainly been hungry before, but we still haven't reached such a level of hunger that we should eat potato peels."

The woman grabbed the peels, as though afraid that my mother would have second thoughts, and with a few words of thanks, hurried away.

Life in the Ghetto

It quickly became clear to me that not only was my workplace the best, but that I had been extremely lucky. Compared to my parents' hard work, my own was child's play.

One day I happened to visit Father's workplace and was astonished to see him doing backbreaking labor. This happened towards evening. After a clear, warm day the sky clouded over and rain began to fall. Talka was worried about Father, who had left for work dressed in only a light shirt. I took his coat and hurried to the resort in which he worked. In the distance I could see people carrying heavy boards as they trampled in mud, completely exposed to the rain. When I came closer I saw to my amazement that my father was among the workers. He was actually bent under the weight of the boards. I ran to help him, but he scolded me for having come. He did not want me to see him like this. He asked me not to tell Mother and Talka what I had seen and explained that he did not always work so hard. But I did not believe him and was convinced that this was his daily work.

With a heavy heart I returned home. I did not tell Mother and Talka about Father's work. I did not want them to feel this heartache as well—my own was quite enough. Mother also tried to hide the difficulty of her work. The distances which she had to cover to reach her work and to return from it wore her out. And once, when I saw her peeling potatoes, I was shocked by her hands. My mother's delicate white hands were now swollen and scratched, covered with blisters and blood clots. She tried to hide them from me.

"Mother, what happened to your hands?" I asked anxiously.

"Nothing at all," she replied falteringly and with a sad smile.

"Mother, how did that happen?" I implored.

"It's as I explained to you, my son," said Mother, "I'm still not used to the hard work. That doesn't mean that I work so hard," she tried to correct herself after seeing my worry. "The work is not difficult, but the straw that we sew with is very hard and it wounds our hands. It's very difficult to insert the needle into it. From this straw we make shoes for the German army. In the winter on the Russian front they use straw shoes instead of rubbers. But please, don't call Father's attention to my hands. He has a hard enough time without having to worry about that." Actually, I think he noticed Mother's hands before I did, but said nothing. Father used to put his head in the palms of his hands, and sit that way, immersed in his worries, for a long time.

Mother still continued to send Talka to our neighbor to give her the little bits of potato peels. Hunger had already affected us for we were unsuccessful in dividing the bread over eight days and the total ration over the month. Sometimes hunger made sleep impossible, but even so we could not bring ourselves to swallow a piece of the babka our neighbor brought us occasionally. We would then vow that next time we would be more careful in dividing up the food, but all our decisions and vows were made in vain.

One day, after weeks of work as a supervisor over a group of girls, I was called to the director's office. I was surprised and a bit afraid. I knew from experience that my group was no slower in its work than the other groups. His invitation therefore came as a surprise; but my surprise was several times greater when the director handed me a book of food coupons.

"These coupons are a food bonus for two months," the director said. "All the supervisors receive them. Until now only adults received them, but we managed to get the bonus for the youth as well. I am sure that this addition will help you and your family."

I took the book of coupons and quickly left the director's room. I was overcome with shame that I, the youngest and strongest in my family, had received the coupons. My work was inestimably easier than my mother's and father's. But the feeling of shame passed quickly, and I was filled with happiness. The addition was indeed meager: only a little bit of flour, a little sugar, and sometimes an additional kilo of potatoes. But under these conditions every little bit was tremendous.

On my way home I entered a store and bought the items with the first coupon. Talka's face beamed at the amazing sight, and my parents were beside themselves with happiness.

But even this addition did not keep hunger from our door. My father continued to observe the Sabbath and did not work on that day. On the days that he did not work he did not receive a portion of food, of course. Father was lucky that in the Lodz ghetto, as in Bzezin, his work supervisor overlooked the fact that he did not appear for work on Saturdays. Father also used to get up before sunrise every day in order to put on his *tefillin* (phylacteries) and pray. This too took away from his rest.

Only a few weeks had passed since our arrival in the Lodz ghetto and our appearance had already changed. Talka's face, which had long ago turned pale, now looked transparent, while her blue eyes appeared darker and larger. Since Talka did not receive soup, we always tried to leave her a larger slice of bread. She was reluctant to eat it and even got angry at Mother each time she brought her the remnants of her soup.

Mother and Father seemed to have shrunk. Their clothes were all too big, and they both began to complain of pains in their feet. Mother's feet were particularly swollen. My own pants had also become too big for me and my mother had to take them in.

The Gypsy Camp in the Ghetto

One night I heard the story of the Gypsy camp in Lodz. On her very first day of work, my mother's co-worker told her about the Gypsy affair—how they used to hear indistinct sounds, a sort of distant music, blended with wild laughter. And every once in a while a scream would pierce the tumult, a scream which was impossible to identify and the likes of which she had never heard. Everyone stopped work at the sound of it. After the screams they heard applause and wild laughter, enough to drive one mad.

The workers in the resort knew that at some distance from the workshop, at the end of Bzezinska street, a number of tall buildings had been set apart from the ghetto with barbed wire to serve as a ghetto for Gypsies, and that truckloads of Gypsy men and young and beautiful Gypsy women were taken into this camp. From that day on cars would come with German soldiers who used to hold wild orgies in the Gypsy camp. I did not know the meaning of the word orgies, but I imagined that it was something horrible.

The Gypsy men were ordered to sing and play music while the Gypsy women had to dance naked before the soldiers, who were so cruel to the women that their screams carried a great distance and curdled the blood of those who heard.

One night when I heard Mother telling Father about this, I put a blanket over my head because I couldn't stand it anymore. I tried to think of something else but I couldn't. I tossed and turned for hours, unable to fall asleep. An old picture suddenly appeared in front of my eyes, also one of Gypsies, but completely different.

It was during our summer vacation in the village. A rumor had spread that Gypsies were on their way and we children ran to the road to see them coming. And indeed we saw a column of slowly advancing wagons covered with cloth draped over arched poles. When the Gypsies reached the forest, they set up camp. We continued to watch them from our hideout. We saw men with dark faces and black hair jump out of the wagons. After them came the Gypsy women, children, and even dogs. The Gypsy women in their colorful dresses began to take out all kinds of utensils from the wagons. Noise, tumult, and barking dogs were everywhere.

But the most beautiful picture, which remained in my memory, was of the nights in which the Gypsies sat around the campfires singing songs, some merry, others filled with sorrow and longing. We saw a few of them in their embroidered white shirts with ballooning sleeves, passionately playing their violins in accompaniment to the songs. The sight of the men wearing an earring decorating one ear amazed us. We saw the Gypsy women, whose hair was dark and long and whose eyes were beautiful and black, dancing and clapping their hands, playing tambourines. They looked like giant flowers in their colorful dresses, long earrings, necklaces, and long red dresses with their skirts blowing in the wind.

In my imagination, that of a little boy, I was very excited about their free lives: the children did not have to go to school, and they lived in the midst of nature wandering from place to place without suitcases or packages. Everything was attached to them—their houses and belongings, always on the go, like circus people. Wherever they found a place that touched their fancy, they camped.

But now the enemy had imprisoned them too in a ghetto within a ghetto. And who knew what was happening to them. Other pictures came to mind: I saw the old people of our town falling naked on the icy floor, and German soldiers pressing giant stamps on their flesh. I saw children being thrown out of windows. And I saw my grandmother and Abonik.

My mother's voice awakened me: "Luzerke, get up, you'll be late for work. You must have had nightmares last night, for you yelled in your sleep, and you're soaking with sweat."

All that day in the resort I wandered around in a daze. I could find no peace for myself and I couldn't calm down. In the soup line I asked Esther'ka if she had heard about the Gypsy camp. She looked at me with a strange gaze and blurted: "Of course I've heard. Everyone in the ghetto knows of the German soldiers' cruelty to the Gypsies." Then she told me the whole story.

This camp, which existed for only two months, was well hidden. It was destroyed even before you arrived in January, 1942. Our gravediggers had to gather corpses that were strewn about along with musical instruments. Among them were the bodies of naked Gypsy women and detached limbs. Not one of them remained alive. After disinfection, the area of the camp was returned to the ghetto. The Jews were given the job of taking apart the barbed wire fences, and cleaning and painting the rooms in order to remove any bloodstains which remained. The whole ghetto was in a state of shock. The first two people from the ghetto who entered the camp, Aryeh Printz, the guide from the resort for straw shoes, and the photographer, Mendel Gross, trembled at the sight of the German writing that the Gypsies had left on the walls of the houses—writing which testified that many of the Gypsies in the camp had already left their wandering life and were educated professionals, even holders of academic degrees.

Within a few days the appearance of the houses had changed. The place turned into one more resort, and no reminder was left of the Gypsy camp.

My Sister Talka

That day, on my way home from work, I did not hurry as usual, even though I knew my sister Talka was waiting for me. I walked slowly and thought about the German people. Could it be, I said to myself, that God created the Germans to look like human beings but without the normal human emotions? Otherwise it was impossible to understand their actions. But I quickly rejected that thought. It was unreasonable to think that they were created without emotions. They also had families, wives and children, parents who got sick and died, and those cruel and vulgar Germans most certainly walked in mourning behind the coffins, in tears. And in addition to that they also had pets, dogs and cats, that they fed and perhaps even caressed. Questions on top of questions raced through my mind, but I found no answers.

I quickened my pace so that Talka would not remain alone at home much longer. But Talka did not notice that I was late. The rumor about the Gypsy camp and its terrible end had not reached her. As always, she received me happily. This time she had something to tell me that she made me promise never to tell our parents. At first, she was embarrassed to reveal her story to me. Filled with curiosity, I looked at my sister and solemnly promised to keep her secret.

Talka excitedly showed me the rag doll we had found in the apartment. The doll's appearance was different from when we had first seen it. The doll now resembled a boy, and instead of the dress in which it had been wrapped, it was now dressed in pants with suspenders.

"This is Abonik," said Talka seriously. "And now you understand, Luzer, why I am not bored staying alone in the house. I sewed the pants myself so that they would look like Abonik's pants. When you all go out to work I sit Abonik on the bed and talk to him. He knows everything," she continued in that same serious tone, "everything that has happened to us since we escorted him to the gathering point where we were separated from him. He watches when I make the beds and sweep the floors. He waits for me when I bring water in the pail from the courtyard. He keeps me company whatever I do. It's a shame that I can't take him with me when I go to stand in line. I'm embarrassed to take him with me, because people don't know that it's Abonik. They think it's just any old doll, and wonder why a big girl like me is still playing with dolls. It's a shame," my sister added, "that Abonik knows everything about us and we know nothing about him, where he is or what he's doing. But after the war, when we all meet, Abonik will tell us everything. He will be a big boy then and will know a lot. He will certainly be happy that I made a doll of him so that he could be with me, even though he is so far away."

I turned away. I did not know how it happened but suddenly my face was flooded with tears.

A few days later Talka's world expanded even more when she met Chana'le. Chana'le lived one floor below us. One day, when Talka was going downstairs, she noticed a head peeking out of a half-opened door, watching her as she walked by. This head, with black curls and dark eyes, belonged to little Chana'le. Talka stopped and asked the girl what her name was.

"Chana'le," the little girl answered, "and I am three-and-a-half years old."

"And who is with you in the house?" asked Talka.

"No one. I'm already a big girl," she added with pride, "Mother is at work and Father is in the army."

From that day on Chana'le, the skinny little girl, was a guest in our home. When I returned from work, I saw her sitting on the bed with the doll, Abonik, in her arms. She knew who Abonik was — Talka had told her.

"After the war," my sister Talka promised Chana'le, "Abonik will return and you will get to know him."

"After the war, my father will also return and you will get to know him too," said Chana'le.

Talka's attitude towards Chana'le was different from her attitude at the time toward Abonik. From the first moment my sister met Chana'le, she was very protective of the baby whose mother was forced to work entire days, leaving her alone and whose father had not returned from the army. Talka wanted to make up for the injustice done to her.

Once, when I came into the house, I saw Talka giving her a piece of bread from her own portion. I acted as though I hadn't seen, but in my heart I thought: Dearest Talka! You are our shining light!

Chana'le's mother was happy. This was the only happiness the young woman had known since the outbreak of the war when her husband was drafted into the Polish army and did not return, leaving her alone in the last months of her pregnancy. She entered the ghetto with a very young baby, raised her by sharing with her the meager portion of food she received at work and by leaving the baby alone in the house for long hours at a time.

I saw the woman when she came in to get her daughter. A young woman, who was so terribly thin that it was impossible to know her real age. Her cheeks were sunken and among her black hairs sprouted locks of prematurely gray hair.

The "Bnei Akiva" Youth Movement

One day Father returned from work with good news. "Today I met a friend from the *Mizrachi* (Israeli emigration movement). I knew him before the war. He even visited us once in Bzezin," Father told us excitedly, "and just imagine, from this man I learned that here in the Lodz ghetto the pioneering youth movements have extensive activities. The young people meet and make plans to immigrate, to make *aliyah* (literally: to go up) to the Land of Israel at the end of the war. How wonderful it is that they have the strength to organize. This also gives us hope and strength to get through the war which must end someday."

Father told us that the *Hashomer Hadati* and *Bnei Akiva* (similar to the Mizrachi) movements were also here and that he had their addresses. Then he urged me to go there. In his opinion, joining this organization would make me happy. "My only regret is that Talka is still too young and cannot also participate," he said sadly.

I felt my breathing stop from so much joy. Here, in the Lodz ghetto, Zionist activity? Here, youth organizing and making plans to make aliyah to the Land of Israel? If that was the case, then we were lucky to have arrived in the Lodz ghetto!

Talka's eyes also sparkled when she saw my happiness. She did not think about the fact that from now on I would be away from the house in the evenings as well.

The following day, the time in the resort passed by in anticipation of the evening. I felt uplifted. After Mother returned from work, I hurried to the address my father had given me. The apartment belonged to the Rosen brothers. Their parents were no longer alive. Their mother, Esther, had been sent away in the middle of the night, and the father, Yaakov, had died of starvation. Only the three brothers, Chaim, Isaac, and Avram, and the sister Dvorah lived in the apartment which they now used for the benefit of the movement.

After climbing three flights of stairs, I knocked excitedly on the door. There was no answer. I heard voices inside. I turned the doorknob, pushed open the door and gazed upon a wonderful sight. In a very big room were dozens of boys and girls, some of them standing. But most of them sat on the floor in two circles. One of the girls, Sarah Stern (I later found out that she was the leader), was giving a talk.

I quietly passed by those who were sitting and found a place by the window. Sarah spoke about the land of Israel. She told of the pioneers and educated youth who had left their studies, comfortable homes, and beloved parents and had immigrated to Israel to rebuild it. She spoke of the pioneers' difficulties, the terrible heat which they were not used to, the swamps, the mosquitoes, the malaria which had taken many victims, and the lack of water. But none of these obstacles had deterred them and they had not returned to the diaspora and their comfortable homes. She also spoke about the problems of the exiled Jews, and of the need to build a homeland for the people.

After her, Yitzchak Zacharyash spoke. Yitzchak was a handsome young man and, when he spoke, fire burned in his eyes. He told of the kibbutzim, harrassed by Arabs who plotted against the Jews and did not let them work in the desolate areas. He spoke of the situation in the days of the British Mandate governing Palestine when it was forbidden to build houses and occupy territories. But the pioneers had found a solution for every difficult situation.

"We, too," he said, "will follow in the footsteps of these courageous pioneers, and with strong hands we will help build up the desolate land. Now, when we are sealed up in the ghetto, we understand more than ever before how important it is to have our own homeland."

I felt my heart overflowing. Why, these were also my father's thoughts and those of my whole family, who dreamed of aliyah to our holy land!

Someone motioned to me to come closer to those sitting in the circle. The group crowded together and made room for me. One girl, Zehava Urbach, began to sing. Soon many voices joined hers and the singing, which was at first quiet, slowly mounted until it was a mighty wave. All of the songs they sang were filled with longing for the distant and so-beloved Land of Israel. I already knew many of these songs, but not all. When I heard the words of one song—"There in the land which was the delight of our fathers, we will realize all our hopes," I felt goosebumps all over.

When the singing ended, Yitzchak Zacharyash once again got up and began to teach the group a new song. I repeated along with everyone the words of the song, line after line, and joined in the singing. The melody was sad but still gave us hope that we too would finally reach the land of our fathers. To this very day I still remember the words of the song: "On a starless night, starless night, we will go up to the homeland, to the homeland./ You are a mother to me, you are a brother to me/ You are my outstretched arm . . ."

After this song the group turned to a boy named Shaia, whose eyes were blue and cheerful, and they asked him to sing a solo. He sang a song in Yiddish, also filled with longing for the Land of Israel, where the sun was always shining.

For a short time I forgot all of my troubles and tragedies. When I left there I felt like I was carried on wings all the way home.

My mother waited for me with the little bit of watery soup she had prepared for dinner, which everyone else had already finished. I was not hungry that night. I did not even remember that ten hours had passed since I had last eaten the soup in the resort.

Excitedly I told my family everything that had happened. Everyone sat quietly, listening to my words. Talka's eyes welled with tears.

From then on I hurried to 18 Zidovska Street to the Rosen brothers' apartment. Twice, and sometimes three times, a week we gathered there. Sometimes, however, we would gather in the house of the sisters Mala and Bronka, or in other houses.

It was not long before I knew everyone and everyone knew me. These wonderful young people were prepared to help anyone in need, even though they themselves were needy. When they heard that someone was sick, they took food from their own mouths to give the sick person.

I became particularly friendly with one boy my age, whose name was Eliezer Zelver. He was alert, bright, and courageous. From then on we were known in our group as the two Luzers, but in order to distinguish us he was called Lazer and I was called Luzer.

Eliezer Zelver told me about his family. His mother struggled daily to divide the food rations among her four children, the youngest of whom, Yankush, still did not work. His father and baby sister had died since the outbreak of the war. I recalled little Chana'le and in my heart I thanked God that our family was still whole and together. In those days in the Lodz ghetto, despite the heavy hunger and the separation from my grandmother and other relatives whose fate we didn't know, we could be somewhat happy because we were still together. We didn't dare tempt fate by talking about it. Although we didn't know it then, not much time would pass before we, too, would separate.

The Big Child Hunt

Even though only four months had passed since our arrival in the Lodz ghetto, it seemed like an eternity. Hunger
was the reason for this. Waiting an entire month for the
distribution of rations, waiting throughout each long week
for the bread distribution, and waiting through creeping
hours for soup distribution stretched out time.

Only about four months had passed before the beginning
of September, a time that I will never forget. That was the
week of the child hunt.

One day, returning from work, I saw new decrees plastered
on the walls of the houses. We received all of our official
information from these decrees. I came closer, even though
from far off I could read the German words which virtually
shouted from the walls:

"Beginning tomorrow there will be a curfew in the ghetto
which will last several days. Ghetto residents will be forbidden to leave their homes. Anyone disobeying this order will
be shot. Obviously, the work in the resorts will be discon-
tinued." From bystanders I learned that a rumor was spread-
ing that parents would have to hand over their children ten
years old or less. We did not hear where they would be taken.
Policemen with lists in their hands would go from house to
house and take the children.

I felt my knees give way and everything began spinning
around me. The sight from Bzezin came up in front of my eyes.

The rumors about the children spread rapidly. Panic seized
the ghetto: "What does it mean to hand over the children?
Hand them over to whom? Where will they take them? What
do they want to do with them?"

People, particularly those who had small children, ran
through the streets madly, in a state of shock. I saw mothers
running and tearing out their hair. When I came home and
saw little Chana'le sitting on my bed with the Abonik doll in

her arms, I was unable to respond to my sister's welcome. I felt that if I opened my mouth, I would burst out crying or start knocking my head against the wall.

When Father returned from work, his face was white as a ghost. With clenched fists he told of Rumkovsky's speech in the Balooty Square.

"That disgusting old man tried—although through tears, it is true—to convince parents to hand over their children in sacrifice. What does that mean, in sacrifice? What do they want to do with the children? Better that we parents should be a sacrifice to the children. What does he understand, that childless man, about children? Have we returned to the time of Egyptian slavery? This is even worse than what happened in Egypt. These children are not babies who still understand nothing. We must hide them and not give them away!" cried Father.

"That's right," said my mother, "we must hide the children. But where? They will certainly search everywhere in the houses. But we have no choice. We must not give them." Then mother added: "What really happens to the children, where do they take them? Since they sent the children from Bzezin, we have heard nothing about their whereabouts. Every night, before I manage to fall asleep, I'm driven crazy by the thoughts: Where is my mother? Where are my sisters and their children?"

"It's also true that Rumkovsky loves children, even if he never had any of his own," my mother added thoughtfully. "Everyone in the ghetto knows that he always took care of children. It's a fact that he established two orphanages in Marisin. And what will happen now to those children, will he hand them over too?"

I told a frightened Talka, who didn't understand the conversation, about the decree. She sat down next to Chana'le, who understood nothing of all this, and hugged her as her tears fell upon the little girl's hair.

That very moment the door opened and Chana'le's mother

burst inside. Something was strange about her appearance, particularly in her eyes which darted about ceaselessly. Without a word she grabbed her little daughter and ran out of the room at a run.

"God," whispered Talka, "if they take Chana'le, her mother will go mad."

"I, I think that that has already happened," answered my mother through chattering teeth.

Even though our family would not have to hand over any children—Talka was already close to her eleventh year—we were shocked at the publication of the decree. That evening Mother was unable to prepare a drop of food, and we felt no hunger. None of us could fall asleep. We all tossed and turned, kept awake by our thoughts and horrible memories.

We spent the next day closed up in our house. On the next day I went downstairs and peeked into the street. It was totally deserted. A threatening silence prevailed broken only by occasional patrols of Jewish police. Our neighbor Mrs. Winogrodsky came to our apartment in a frenzy. Despite the strict curfew, hair-raising rumors had filtered through: trucks of German soldiers had entered the ghetto. First they closed off streets and entire areas. Then Jewish police and German soldiers broke into apartments to take the children away. They made a thorough search everywhere, taking out children, the sick, and the elderly, attacking and even shooting parents who dared hide their children.

"Is there no God in heaven?" screamed Mother, "And what will happen to Chana'le? We must help Chana'le's mother find a hiding place for her baby."

"Where can we hide her?" asked Father. "The Germans will look everywhere and find her."

"We must hide her anyway. Otherwise they will take her away for sure. We must go down to Chana'le's mother and think together."

Mother and Talka walked down one floor and knocked gently on the door.

"Chana'le's mother, it's me, Talka, with my mother. Open the door."

No voice answered us from within the apartment. Talka repeated her call. We heard quiet steps and the door opened. Chana'le's mother appeared at the entrance.

"Hello Ma'am, ..." Mother began speaking, but she could say no more. Her words stuck in her throat. Mother and Talka stood frozen in their places. Could this be Chana'le's mother? they asked themselves. Is this the young woman who thanked us politely every day because we took an interest in her daughter, happy that Chana'le found a second home with us? A strange woman now stood in front of my mother and sister. Her head was wild—but most frightening was her gaze. Her eyes looked as though they were covered with blood and rolled around and around. She looked at Mother but did not really see her.

"Chana'le," the frightened Talka tried to call inside the apartment, but no voice responded. It seemed that Chana'le was not at home. Suddenly, the woman pushed my mother from the entrance to her apartment and slammed the door shut. Mother and Talka returned home frightened.

"Poor woman," said my mother as her eyes filled with tears, "she did not let us in, she chased us away. The fear that they will take her little baby girl, the only soul left her in the world, has apparently driven her crazy."

"But where is Chana'le?" asked my mother, "What had she done with her?"

"Chana'le's mother has an aunt in the ghetto. Perhaps she found a hiding place with her aunt and Chana'le is there," Talka burst out. "I'm sure that if Chana'le were in the house she would have answered me."

Within a few days—days which seemed like years—we

learned where Chana'le was. Meanwhile two more days of tense, foreboding quiet passed by.

"And the Gates of Heaven were Locked"

In the early morning hours we heard a strange noise which got louder and louder, as though a storm was coming closer. And indeed, it arrived. First we heard an indistinct noise, but we soon also saw carriages and heard the stamping of horses, as well as screams and shouts.

Mother suddenly threw an alarmed glance at Talka, as though understanding only now that her thin little girl looked younger than her age. "Everyone knows that the police have lists of the children up to age ten," said Mother. "Here in the Lodz ghetto everything is managed with exemplary order and there is an exact listing of residents, but just to make sure I will take Talka's birth certificate with me."

We began to search feverishly for the certificate. Even after we found it, my mother did not calm down; she sensed danger for her daughter. She dressed Talka in two layers of clothing so that she would look fuller, and with a piece of pickled beet left over from the last ration, colored Talka's cheeks to give them a fresher look.

The noise outside continued to get louder. Soon we heard the Germans shouting "Raus! Alle raus!" (Outside! Everybody outside!)

The shouts were now accompanied by the steps of heavy boots in the stairway, hard raps on the doors with rifle butts, and break-ins of the apartments. These were not Jewish policemen, but German soldiers. They burst into our house too, and amidst screams, kicks, and blows, herded us all out of the house and into the courtyard.

In the hallway during all the commotion I ran into Chana'le's mother. Her face was covered with a strange smile, a smile that did not budge even when a whip landed on her head to get her to move faster. Chana'le was not with her.

In the courtyard the Jewish policemen arranged us in rows. Everyone in our family held each other's hands so that they would not separate us.

Two German soldiers dragged an old Jew who had lain sick in bed and hadn't the strength to walk from an apartment on the ground floor. They dragged him to the well that was in the courtyard. One of the soldiers put the old man's head into the opening of the well while a second soldier took out a pistol from his holster and shot him in the back of his neck. The old man remained sprawled out on the well, dripping with blood.

All this happened in a moment, right in front of the horrified eyes of the old man's two sons and all of his neighbors.

Why don't they run to their father's help? I became angry at the old man's sons who remained immobilized, afraid that the Germans would kill them. My anger immediately subsided and turned to fear, when I saw that one of the sons was trying to break away while his brother and a Jewish policeman held him back by his shoulders.

"We must not let him. He can no longer help his father anyway. They'll kill him too."

Before we had a chance to recover from the atrocity we had just witnessed, a different German soldier appeared in the courtyard entrance. With a victorious look on his ugly face, he pushed ahead of him a little boy about six years old whom he had taken out from some hiding place. The soldier pushed the boy to the wagons standing at the gate in which children, crying and calling for their mothers, sat guarded by soldiers holding bayoneted rifles.

I saw the boy who had been taken out of his hiding place, his eyes torn wide open and his mouth gaping in a scream.

The boy's mother broke out of the row and attacked the soldier, at which time a second soldier shot her.

I wanted to shout out to God, to plead to him and ask him to help these little innocent children, but the word God did not leave my mouth. As I saw the polished German soldiers in their gallant uniforms, well-fed and well-armed, passing among the rows of tortured Jews and evaluating them as though these were not people but worthless merchandise, I raised only a clenched fist towards heaven.

Helpless, we now saw Chana'le's mother, who was only skin and bones, taken from her row and pushed towards the wagon in which several old people also sat. Chana'le's mother held her head high and smiled. This strange smile, which had been on her face since we had seen her in the stairway, and her restlessly racing eyes, reminded me of something horrible, something that gave me the chills. This was exactly the way the mad woman, Mindzia, had looked when she had gone up to the gallows in Bzezin.

I didn't have a chance to finish my thought before the contingent of German soldiers reached us. One of them gave us a quick glance, grabbed Talka by the shoulders, and took her out of the row. Immediately my mother shot out of her place and grabbed the soldier's sleeve.

"Mister soldier!" she turned to him, "My girl is already close to eleven years old. She is ten and seven months. Here, please take a look. This is her birth certificate." The soldier stared at my mother, furiously removing her hand from his sleeve. With a look of disgust he shook his sleeve and pushed my mother away. But Mother continued to run after him, waving Talka's birth certificate and announcing that her daughter was already almost eleven years old. The soldier lost his patience. He stopped again, grabbed the certificate and, without even glancing at it, tore it to shreds, crumpled up the pieces in his fist, and threw them into the street. He once again grabbed Talka's shoulders, which were trembling in fear, and pushed her toward the wagon. My mother continued running after them and begging that they either return her daughter or take her too. My mother did not let up even after the soldier knocked her to the ground. She got up and continued running all the way to the wagon. She grabbed it even though Talka was already on board. The German soldier now grabbed Mother and pushed her into the wagon too.

That whole time I stood motionless in my place, as though someone had hammered nails into my feet, as though the horror that was taking place before my eyes had nothing to do with me or with people who were more precious to me than anything in the world, as though it was not I who only a few moments before had been angry at the sons of the old man who didn't run to their father, even at the cost of their lives. Suddenly I felt the blood rushing to my head. Thoughts flooded my brain, jumbled one with another: I will sneak up and jump the soldier who pushed my mother and I will strangle him. Just so long as I strangle him before the others shoot me. No, not that. I will jump on the wagon and go with Mother and Talka, came the second thought. I was all ready to do that, when at that moment my father literally collapsed at my feet.

All of the thoughts disappeared from my head. I could not leave my father now. We must not let the Germans find out what had happened. They would shoot him on the spot. I stood in front of him in order to hide him from them. I instinctively pulled the sleeve of our neighbor, Mrs. Winogrodsky, who understood the hint and stood with her daughter Rachel by my side. Luckily, the German soldiers did not come back to us. We were the last ones in the row. The hunt in our courtyard had come to an end and the wagons went on their way.

I bent down to my father. He was lifeless. I was choked with fear. Was he dead? Had I lost him too? Our neighbor calmed me. She said that Father had simply fainted, and we must pour water on him.

I ran to the well from which the sons had already taken their murdered father's corpse. Only a giant bloodstain remained. I filled my hat with water and ran back to my father. When I poured the water over his head, Father opened his eyes. He looked around, shocked, at his surroundings, seeming not to understand and then closed his eyes again. He let out a terrible sigh.

"My wife, my daughter, where have they taken them? I will never see them again. God, take me too!"

With the help of the Winogrodsky family I took Father up to our apartment and lay him down on a bed. I was in shock, unable to think or do anything. I sat beside my father, who lay with his eyes closed. His prayers about my mother and sister pierced my heart like knives. I wanted to say something but could not. Like Father, I also felt that Mother and Talka had been taken from us forever.

I don't know how long I sat like that next to my father before I looked down at the floor, where the Abonik doll was lying. Suddenly an idea flashed in my head—Uncle Avram! Uncle Avram's brother-in-law worked as a policeman in the prison on Charnyetzkiego street!

I quietly left the house and went in to the Winogrodsky family. I stopped for a moment in disbelief upon seeing the father with his son standing and praying. I asked Rachel if she would keep an eye on my father for a short while.

"Where are you going?" she asked, terrified, "It's forbidden to go out in the street. Do you want them to catch you too? Then what will happen to your father?"

I did not respond but quickly left the room. I ran through the empty streets. The wagons with the children and old people, as well as the trucks of soldiers, were no longer anywhere to be seen. The day's hunt was apparently over. Breathless, I knocked on the door of my Uncle Avram's apartment. His wife opened the door.

Uncle Avram, who had been widowed from his wife Pola, had remarried. His new wife was the sister of his friend to whose apartment he had moved in the Bzezin ghetto. I now stood before my new aunt. She looked at me in fear, as though in disbelief. My face must have revealed what had happened to me that day. She screamed.

"They took Talka?"

"Yes," I answered, "and Mother, too."

My uncle, pale as a ghost, came to the door and grabbed my arm. "Let's go!" he said.

His wife pleaded with us not to go into the street during the curfew, but to no avail: "They'll catch you too. It's forbidden to leave the house. They'll shoot you!"

Running wildly we passed through the lifeless streets. It had already begun to get dark when we reached Charnyetzkiego prison.

"I don't want you to come with me," my uncle commanded. "Stay at a distance so they won't see you." I stood behind the wall of a ruined building. Nearby, I saw my uncle walking up to the policeman, who was surprised to see him, and I heard Uncle Avram's confident voice say to the policeman: "Call Policeman Fogel, please!"

A second policeman came out and yelled at my uncle: "Are you crazy! What are you doing here now? Get out of here quickly before they arrest you!" But my uncle did not move. His back straightened even more.

"Don't shout before you know who is standing in front of you," said my uncle in a restrained voice. "I was sent here by order of the president Chaim Rumkovsky to deliver an important message to Officer Fogel."

The two guards looked my uncle over thoroughly. Only his firmness convinced them.

"Wait here," said the first. "I'll go call him."

I remained hiding behind the wall of a ruined house. My uncle waited beside the gate, but when time passed and Fogel had still not appeared, I decided to walk around the outside of the prison, hoping to see my mother and sister.

The tremendous yard behind the barbed wire was filled to the brim. The old and the sick were lying on the ground. A few people were walking around. I didn't see my dear ones among them. I continued to walk around the outside barbed wire fences. On the other side of the yard I saw many children sprawled out on the ground, sleeping. A few lucky ones sat with their mothers who had been taken with them. I will never forget this picture of children, cruelly torn from their parents, imprisoned behind barbed wire fences.

Suddenly I felt my heart flutter and my knees give way. Among all of these, near the prison building, I saw them—my mother and Talka. Mother sat on the ground with her head in her hands. Talka lay beside her with her head on Mother's knees.

I began to call to them, to shout in their direction, but they did not hear. They were too far away, and it was too noisy. In despair I decided to go back to my uncle. Just then my mother got up from her place. She began to walk in the direction of the bathrooms. On the other side of the barbed wire I ran in the same direction, calling out her name. In disbelief, thinking she was hallucinating, she raised her head. When she saw me her frightened eyes opened wide.

"Why have you come here? It's dangerous. Go back to Father!" she yelled. Then she began to tremble and almost fell. At that moment I would have given many years of my life to run and support my dear mother, to soothe her. Instead, because of the barbed wire fence separating us, I had to watch her cry like a little child in need of help.

All I could do was tell her that Avram was here and that maybe he would manage to arrange something. When I saw how that spark of hope changed my mother's face, I was sorry I had said anything for I was probably planting vain hopes. Her pain would be even greater if we failed to get them out of there. With a heavy heart I left and returned to my hiding place behind the ruined wall.

I saw Avram standing with the policeman Fogel a few meters away from where I was standing and, although they spoke quietly, I heard every word.

"There is no way to take anyone out of here," I heard Avram's brother-in-law say, "and there's also no guarantee that they are even here. Most of the wagons went directly to Marisin, where the people were loaded on cattle cars. Only the wagons with the children who were caught later, after the train had already departed, were brought to the Charnyetzkiego prison, and they will be sent away early in the morning. Meanwhile, as you can see, the children are yelling and crying. Many of them are so young they don't even know their names. Nobody made any lists so it's impossible to check on your sister and her daughter. Here there is only chaos."

Hearing this, I ran out of my hiding place: "Uncle Avram!" I yelled, "Mother and Talka are here! I saw them!"

"What? What are you doing here?" asked Fogel in surprise, but Uncle Avram excitedly cut off his words: "You see, they are here. You must get them out. Now is the time. You must get them out immediately."

"But how?" Fogel was dumbstruck. "They won't let me. No one leaves Charnyetzkiego."

"No one leaves, but they will leave," my uncle declared, "even if I pay for it with my own head. Blame me if you have to."

"No," said Fogel, "let's think rationally about what to do."

"You know," Uncle Avram interrupted him again, "you are an officer here. Bring them to the gate and tell the guards that the Jewish elder, Rumkovsky, ordered that they be returned home. They called you after I said that I was sent by him."

"It won't work that way. They won't let me take anyone out of here without a written order," said Fogel.

"Then go to your office and write whatever order the guards need," said my uncle firmly.

"Yes," said Fogel, more to himself than to my uncle, "that's an idea. In the room belonging to Gertler, the commander of the Zonder-Commando, on the desk, there are forms with Rumkovsky's signature. I will have to sneak in there in order to take one of them. That's the only way they will be able to leave."

"I'm counting on you," said Avram, "and hope that with God's help you will succeed."

Fogel turned to us: "I will do all I can. Now, go." He turned towards the gate and went inside. I saw the guards salute him and I was filled with hope.

We did not leave immediately, but wandered around a bit more. Night had already fallen by the time we each turned homeward, filled with doubts and a heavy heart. I walked in the dark streets of the ghetto and did not know what to tell Father. If they were not let out, I thought, if Fogel did not succeed in his mission, Father will collapse again. I was happy to find Father sleeping when I entered the apartment. Or, at least, it seemed to me he was sleeping. He opened his eyes and stared at me in confusion. He asked no questions and I told him nothing.

I sat by the table, put down my head, and fell asleep. I don't know how long I slept, but an embrace around my neck awakened me. It was Talka. I jumped up and rubbed my eyes. I screamed: "Father! They're back! Mother and Talka have come back!"

Father didn't believe his eyes. He thought he was dreaming. He got up from his bed and looked around him as though he were not seeing his wife and daughter, but rather creatures from the underworld. Father burst into tears, and Mother clung to him while the two of them sat and cried for a long time. It was four o'clock in the morning. At the sound of the crying and the screams of joy our neighbors came in—the family from Germany and the Winogrodsky family. They also stood and cried at the sight of the miracle which had taken place. The return of Mother and Talka momentarily wiped out the horrifying sights we had seen in our courtyard that day.

Intoxicated with joy, I ran in the middle of the night to Avram's house.

"Mother and Talka are back," I called to him from the entrance, "Thank you for everything you did." "Not I," said my uncle. "You, you Luzer, you did it."

The manhunt continued another three days. The Germans combed the remaining streets of the ghetto until they had completed their despicable work. For those three days we completely forgot that we didn't have even a crumb of food in the house. We were half afraid to believe that our whole family was still together.

The manhunt lasted nine days. At the end of that time the curfew was removed and everyone was ordered to return to work.

Only afterwards did we learn more details about the atrocities that had taken place in the ghetto. We learned that the children of the two orphanages under Rumkovsky's protection, whom he had seen as his proteges, were taken first. They had fought and struggled not to be taken from the ghetto. Many of them jumped from the windows and were killed on the spot. A few of them escaped to the cemetery where they could hide among the tombstones, but many were later found there, sprawled lifeless. Hunger and cold had ended their lives.

Every third or fourth family was hit in this horrible hunt. Many workers were missing from my parent's workplaces. In my youth hall, as the girls sewed uniforms for the German soldiers, their tears wet the cloth. The mother of Rachelka, who sat at the end of the first row of sewing machines, was taken because she was sick and unable to work. Her two daughters, Rachelka and her sister, had been giving her part of their meager portion of soup. Mina, from the second row, lost her seven-year-old brother, the only living soul left to her. She had tried to hide him, covering him with all kinds of clothes, all to no avail. The Germans overturned the crate and found the boy. Roozka's sewing machine also remained idle. I was told that Roozka refused to separate from her nine-year-old sister and was permitted to go on the wagon with her.

The distress in the hall was tangible. Through the clatter of the machines, I heard an occasional sigh. I could see silent weeping. No one spoke with her neighbor or looked at one another. The same atmosphere reigned in the street. People slipped by like shadows, clinging to the walls of the houses.

About four days had already passed since the end of the hunt, but we could not free ourselves of its horrors. It was particularly hard for Talka, who stayed home alone while we were at work.

That day, when I returned from work, Talka said: "I miss Chana'le so much. We don't even know if her aunt succeeded in hiding her, or if they took her too."

Talka repeated her words that evening too, when our parents returned from the resorts.

Mother stopped in the middle of the room and said suddenly: "Talka's right, she is definitely right. Because of all our own troubles we forgot to find out what happened to

Chana'le. Who knows where she is and what happened to her. And who knows what will happen to her when she finds out that they took her mother."

"Good heavens," continued Mother, "why didn't I think of that before? If she is still alive, we will find her and take her in with us. She is used to us; she loves us, especially Talka. I am sure that her aunt will also like this. She won't have to leave the baby alone."

Talka's face lit up. She told Mother how wonderful it would be if she could take care of Chana'le, that she would play with her and encourage her.

"She'll be happy with us!" Talka concluded.

I looked at my sister. It had been so long since she looked like she did now. Her pale cheeks blushed and her eyes sparkled with a special shine. I feared that she would be disappointed after getting her hopes up, so I had to say: "Don't make any plans yet. The Germans might have taken her too."

"That's true," said Father. "We must first find out what happened to the little one and where her aunt lives. It seems a little strange that her aunt hasn't shown up yet, in order to return the girl to her mother. After all, she can't know that the murderers took her mother too. Who knows?" he added, "Perhaps the aunt was taken along with the little one."

Tense, we all went downstairs to Chana'le's apartment.

As soon as we opened the door, we were met by a horrible stench from the direction of the bed. Mother, pale as a ghost, ran to the bed and hastily began to throw the sheets on the floor. At first we saw nothing. Only after she lifted the mattress did she let out a terrifying scream.

We all ran toward her. And what we saw I will never forget.

On the bedsprings lay Chana'le, lifeless. Her eyes were wide open, as though ripped open in terror. Her mouth was open too, caught in a scream that she never let out or, perhaps, in a desperate attempt to grab a little air before suffocating.

I stood frozen in place, my blood drained. But I immediately felt a certain strength pass through me. I grabbed Talka, who stood trembling like a leaf in the wind, and hurried back with her to our apartment.

The Miracle that Happened to Talka

For many days after finding Chana'le's corpse, Talka had been mute. She did not answer our questions and just wandered around the apartment in a daze. We were afraid to leave her alone in the house, for fear that she had gone mad. Each day one of us stayed home from the resort. We did not know what to do. This situation lasted until the day I met my friend Eliezer Zelver.

Since the days of the hunt we had not had a meeting of the movement. Everyone was still in shock from that tragedy. Eliezer told me that they had succeeded in hiding his little brother Yankush, but his aunt's three children had been taken.

I told him all that we had been through, about Chana'le's death, and the shock this had caused Talka—such a shock that she had stopped speaking. Eliezer was very moved by my words and murmured, "What a miserable people we are ... what a miserable people." And suddenly, without saying goodbye, he turned and walked away.

The next day I stayed home with Talka. In the afternoon someone knocked on the door. At the entrance stood Eliezer Zelver. He came in and sat on my bed. Talka was standing by the window, looking about with glazed eyes.

"You know, Luzer, why I have come?" Lazer began loudly, looking over at Talka. "My sister Surtzia teaches a group of girls reading and writing, a little arithmetic, Bible, and Hebrew. She teaches about ten girls Talka's age. Of course,"

Lazer continued, "since the hunt she has not gone back to teaching them. But yesterday, after I told her about your sister, she decided that tomorrow she would go back to teaching. She wants Talka to join the other girls."

After these words were spoken, I saw Talka turn her head in our direction. She did not say a word, but I thought I saw a spark of life in her eyes.

And indeed, it was true, and not just my imagination. When Eliezer Zelver left our house Talka turned to me and began to speak. My happiness knew no bounds. "Luzer, I want to study. I want to know how to read and write." Then she became silent, and tears flowed from her eyes. When she spoke again, she said, "I want to study, but I'm embarrassed to go there. All the girls must already know a lot and I don't know anything."

I caressed my sister's head and soothed her. I told her that the other girls had also only just begun to learn and that they didn't know any more than she did. Purposely lying to her, I swore that Eliezer had told me this. I advised her to go and find out for herself. I also promised to help her do her homework. I knew how much Talka yearned to read and write.

"If I only knew how to read," she had said before the hunt, "I would read Chana'le all kinds of stories from the books we found in the apartment."

Talka, who was close to eleven years old, was almost completely illiterate. She was supposed to start school when the war broke out on the first of September, 1939. Even the spring before, our house was excited over this. In June Mother bought her the uniform she was supposed to wear in the Polish schools: a black, shiny apron-dress with a white collar, a dark blue pleated skirt with a white shirt for holidays, and a beret with the school symbol. All our uncles and aunts competed by bringing gifts to the new student. Talka was so happy with all the gifts that even during summer vacation she could not part with them — we had to take them with us to the village. Every night Talka would fall asleep with her school things by her bed — her book-bag, her school-boxes, and her black apron-dress with the white collar that was hung on the back of her chair. But she never got the chance to use any of them; when we returned home from vacation, the war broke out. And when our house was bombed, Talka's school equipment was turned to ashes.

All the horrible things that had happened since then prevented Talka from studying. In the Bzezin ghetto my mother tried to teach her the letters of the alphabet and to write her name, but that effort was also aborted. Only now did we understand how badly Talka wanted to learn. The word "school" was magic to her, one that worked a miracle and freed her from depression and muteness.

Mother and Father could not believe their eyes at the sudden change in Talka. Talka began to study hard. The next evening, I went with my sister to the Zelver family's apartment. Surtzia, Eliezer's sister, welcomed us with a heart-warming smile. Surtzia was a young and very delicate girl, and despite the unbearable circumstances of the ghetto she gathered a number of little girls together and gave them her strength and time. Surtzia was aware of everything that had happened to Talka and treated her very gently.

A new era began for my sister and for us as well. From then on she was entirely absorbed in her studies. In her quiet voice and with a smile on her face, Surtzia tried to bring a little lightness into the heavy atmosphere that prevailed. She introduced the new pupil to the other girls and asked Talka just to sit and listen awhile.

After the lesson, when all the girls had left, Surtzia remained with Talka and taught her to write words, each day a few more words, in print and script. For homework, Talka was to copy the words over and over in her notebook. She did this diligently, carefully protecting the notebook which we had found in our apartment. She tried not to use up the notebook too quickly, since it was impossible to buy a new one in the ghetto. In addition to writing in the notebook, she would practice words endlessly on every piece of paper she found. In this way Talka also learned arithmetic, Bible, and Hebrew. Her eagerness was boundless and we were no longer afraid to leave her home alone. She was so involved in her studies that she never noticed how quickly time passed. Each time I came home from the resort she would lift her head and ask: "What happened? Why have you come back so early today?"

Before long, Talka had caught up with the other pupils, and she even began reading books fluently. The first book, which she borrowed from one of the other girls, was *The Girl with the Goat*. I was very frightened when I returned home from work one day and found Talka crying, her eyes swollen. But, with her bashful smile, she reassured me; nothing had happened. She was crying because of the book she had read, because of the bitter fate of the little orphan girl, the heroine of the book, whose parents had died and who was taken home by an evil peasant woman. The orphan girl's only friend, to whom she could tell all of her troubles and whom she loved dearly, was the little white goat. I reassured my sister that she needn't be so sad. But this aroused in me an endless stream of thoughts. I asked myself, how could she get so upset by the troubles in the story when she herself had already experienced tragedies many times more horrible? I couldn't answer this question. Who can understand a human soul?

Talka clung to the world of books. She devoted her whole self to this world, and found happiness and satisfaction in it.

Sometimes I was jealous of her for this. I myself had no spare time to read. I had to perform all the hard chores around the house. My mother and father were so weak that they couldn't do anything when they got home from work, so all of the worries and errands fell upon my shoulders. After returning from the resort I had to bring two pails of water from the well in the courtyard and carry them up to the third floor, since our room had no faucet. Then I would run to the big kitchen on Dvorska street to stand in line for potato peels. We had been in the ghetto for such a long time, and our hunger had increased so much, that we no longer remembered the days when we could not eat the babka made from peels. Once a week I had to stand in line for our portion of bread, and once a month for our rations. The distribution of the rations took place in two locations: we received some items—after hours of waiting in line—in the grocery store, and the other things—a little bit of kohlrabi and potatoes— in the vegetable yard. Here too there were endless lines. They also would sometimes distribute one hundred grams of horse meat, which meant running to the butcher shop to obtain this rare item. And then there was the run to the coal yard once a month. I had to go there twice because the coal was so heavy, which meant, of course, standing in line twice. Inexplicably, every time I went to the coal yard I hoped to meet the girl with the braids, whom I had seen crying after her sack of coal slipped from her shoulders and scattered over the street. But I had not met her yet. Sometimes, after waiting for a long time, I was informed that the distribution for that day had ended or that there was nothing left and I would have to return the next day.

Talka tried to help me by waiting in line while I was still at work. But usually when I arrived Talka stood near the end of the line. She was little and weak and the others took advantage of her. She would take a book to read so that the hours of standing in the cold and wind would pass more quickly. When I think now of Talka's incredible achievements in her studies in such a short time, it seems amazing to me, truly unbelievable. I think she must have been extraordinarily gifted.

Several weeks after the hunt, our meetings resumed. Many of our members had lost their dear ones. For weeks they were unable to recover from this tragedy. Only after some time had passed did Eliezer Zelver notify me that Yitzchak Zacharyash and Sarah Stern had decided to resume the meetings.

After a while we even resumed singing Jewish songs. Those were moments in which we tried to believe that somehow we would exit from this dark tunnel and see the light beyond it. These meetings were like an injection of encouragement for us all.

Two Years

We remained in the Lodz ghetto for another two years after the hunt—two horrible cycles of autumn, winter, spring, and summer; two years of uncertainty about what would happen to us. My mother's and father's health had declined so much that they were unable to get up once they sat down. Their feet became more and more swollen, but they still had to drag them to their day's work at the resort. In the ghetto streets we once again began to see the klapsedras, the human skeletons with swollen feet who knew that only a few steps separated them from the grave.

One day my mother came home very agitated. She was barely able to get a word out of her mouth. She sat heavily on the chair. A long time passed before she could speak anything. She told us that she had seen her brother-in-law Chamota. She had barely recognized him. His feet were horrifyingly swollen, and his eyes looked like two narrow slits through his swollen cheeks. Mother nearly fainted on the street.

"Yes, Esther," said Chamota, "I have turned into a

klapsedra, and I am only thirty-two years old. Until now I had hoped that I might still see my wife and son. Now I know that I will never meet them again. I ask you, Esther, if you should meet Chandzia and Abonik after the war, don't tell them that you saw me like this—just tell them that I never stopped thinking of them and worrying about them. Tell them that I loved them very much." Mother told us that Chamota began to tremble and she supported him so that he would not fall. After a moment of silence Chamota went on to say: "But who knows if they are still alive? Until the hunt I still had hope, but since then I know that the Germans are capable of anything." He closed his eyes and said that he had only two wishes, and he would be happy if they were fulfilled: one, to see his wife and son once again, if only for a moment, and, two, to eat as much bread as he wished, without having to stop eating in order to leave some for tomorrow and the next day and another day—to cut from an entire loaf one slice after another, and eat until he was just plain full.

Neither of his wishes came true. A number of days after the meeting we found out that Chamota had died. The death rate in the ghetto had reached alarming proportions. The black wagon no longer traveled with one corpse; it was now piled with many.

We no longer mentioned little Chana'le. We did not speak of her openly. We were also afraid to do so, because of Talka. Even so, we knew that the affair of Chana'le's death still haunted us. Every time we passed by the door of her apartment, we felt our hearts ache.

Talka managed to obtain many books and continued to read voraciously. That took her mind away from the hunger and everything else happening around us. It took her mind off the seasons of the year as well; she did not even feel the cold. Every day when I returned from work, I found her sitting wrapped up in her worn-out coat, which over the years had become too small for her—its sleeves barely covered her elbows—half-frozen and shivering, but not even noticing. On the other hand, I once found her crying over the fate of *The Little Match Girl* who tried to warm her frozen hands by lighting matches. In her imagination she passed through wastelands and forests with the children in Henrik Sienkevitz's books, and she would forget that she was imprisoned in the ghetto. Together with Robinson Crusoe she sailed to a deserted island, and she participated in the sorrow in *Les Misérables* of Jean Valjean, who was pursued all his life because of the loaf of bread that he had stolen for his hungry little sisters. Her breath stopped lest the farmer in *The Good Earth* sell his daughter in exchange for a little rice.

Talka read many books—she really swallowed them up. Every day when I came home from the resort she would tell me what she had read. When I went to fill the pails of water, she would come down with me from the third floor and go up with me again, all the while reciting the stories. She told them so well that I too was drawn into the magic of her descriptions, and for a moment forgot where I was.

Despite the relative quiet of those two years, we still felt something very heavy hovering over our heads. We feared that this was the calm before the storm. But there was nothing we could do, so we preferred not to think about it. All we wanted was to live through each day.

One day Talka brought home a book called *Uncle Tom's Cabin*, and as usual, she told me all about it. I had learned of black slavery when I was a pupil in elementary school. Even then it had enraged me; but now, in the context of our experiences in the ghetto, these things aroused new thoughts in me. By what right did man trade another man, take him from his house, his mother, his wife, and his children as though he were private property, an object, merchandise? I remembered the Bible lessons my father taught me when I was a child. In ancient times the Torah had ordered that slaves be freed; and if the slave did not want to go free, he had to bear a sign of disgrace for the rest of his life. And since then, supposedly, humanity had marched forward.

While walking in the streets of the ghetto to work and back, or on the way to some line, I would think of the cruelty of the white man towards the black. And suddenly a thought shot through my mind: what about us, the Jews? Over us, too, a master has arisen who sees us as private property and who can do whatever he wishes with us. And this master, Hitler, succeeded in taking with him an entire nation, millions, whom he turned into predators. Abraham Lincoln had tried to end the injustices performed against the blacks and was assassinated for his mercy. Many followed his lead. Eventually, after a bloody civil war, the goal was achieved and slavery was abolished. Eighty years had passed since then and the world had advanced even more. A stream of new inventions had come on the scene, all designed to make life more pleasant and comfortable.

I asked myself what the concepts "enlightened man" and "enlightened and progressive world" meant if one wild man like Hitler could achieve leadership and spread a theory about racial superiority. And the plight of the Jews was getting worse from day to day. What we needed was a man like Lincoln, a fighter for freedom, who would shake heaven and earth protesting the horrors perpetrated against the Jews! Surely there must be such a man! Not only one but many. The world would hurry to our aid. The enlightened world could not be silent in the face of the horrifying injustices performed against the Jews. When the war is over, we will hear what the world and humanity have done for us. It is just that now we are closed in and ostracized from the world.

In the movement, during our meetings, in which the goal was to arouse in us, the youth, hope for a better tomorrow, the fear never let up that the days of the manhunt might be renewed at any time. Meanwhile, sickness and death in the ghetto were increasing.

The days were very long, but they passed. Thus we arrived at the summer of 1944.

The Last Expulsion

Nothing changed in the ghetto. Our complete isolation from the outside world continued, as did order within Chaim Rumkovsky's "Little Kingdom." An ordinary workday still consisted of waiting for the distribution of the soup, waiting for the distribution of the bread and of the rations, etc., the daily standing in lines in the hope of receiving a few potato peels.

And Talka remained immersed in her world of books. She was now reading Upton Sinclair's book, *Cataclysm in the Year 2000*. Both of us hated the hero of the book and were shaken by the tragedy that mankind had brought upon itself because of its inventions.

Every evening Mother and Father returned wearily from work, always accompanied by the troublesome thought: how much longer will we be able to hold out?

Twice a week there were meetings of members of the movement, where we obtained a little bit of encouragement and hope that the war would someday come to an end, that the current situation would not last forever. That summer, vague rumors reached us that Hitler's army had met with defeat on the Russian front and that the United States had joined the war against Germany. We did not know the source of these rumors or how reliable they were. Some said there was a radio receiver in the ghetto, but we didn't know whose or where it was. We were also afraid to speak of it: such a thing was likely to bring annihilation upon the entire ghetto.

Chaim Natan Widawsky's suicide was shattering. Widawsky

was known by only a small group of people as a source of news about the war. Only a few people knew where his information came from, but somehow this reached the ears of the Kripo (Criminal Police) and Widawsky was pursued for a long time. His close friends protected him by changing his hideout every so often. But he did not want to endanger them, so when the Germans got close, this man committed suicide. The same friends who had helped him hide provided him with the cyanide. Even without him, rumors still penetrated and spread. They might be cautious and vague but they kept us alive.

And in the movement? We felt that we had sprouted wings, were infused with new strength. We began to daydream of the defeat of the Germans, of the day when we could avenge all that they had done to us. At the same time we were aware that the Germans were still liable to cause us more trouble before their defeat. We talked of acts of resistance, although it was clearly impossible to stand empty-handed against tanks and machine guns, particularly when each of us had someone dear whom we would endanger.

We made plans to prepare hiding places for members and their families. We felt that something was about to happen. Father, Mother, and Talka also began to believe that a better time was just around the corner, and it was as though they too were infused with new life.

One morning, while we were still hopeful, we found giant posters on the walls of the houses informing the ghetto residents that the essential factories and resorts, and those employed there, were being transferred to Germany. Fear seized Mother and Father. I tried to calm them. "You have no reason to be afraid," I said. "This time will be just like the last, when they transferred us from Bzezin."

I pointed out that the messages on the posters, which seemed innocent and even believable, were very similar to those posted in Bzezin before we were transferred to Lodz. The posters said that the transfers would occur according to workplaces. Workers and their families were to gather at the resorts. From there we would be transferred to the transition camp in the Charnyetzkiego prison and then to the train station in Marisin. The posters detailed the things we would need in the work camp and warned us not to take more than twelve and a half kilograms. At the gathering place, everyone would receive an entire loaf of bread and a little bit of sugar for the trip.

"Exactly like our trip from Bzezin to Lodz," I repeated.

But despite the similarity in the announcements, my parents were not relieved. They both declared that this time they didn't believe the Germans and were deeply worried. They did not like my proposal to leave with the tailoring resort where I worked, which appeared on the list of essential resorts. Finally, father stated: "We will not budge from here!"

I looked at my father. With this firm decision it seemed that he had found renewed strength. I tried to convince him that it would be impossible to stay in the ghetto as the Germans would certainly appropriate all the buildings and evacuate the streets and any Jew found anywhere would be sentenced to death.

Father replied that he had heard that not all of the ghetto was being evacuated and that the important metal resort along with one or two others would remain. He was sure that there were many who would not go either, and we could all find refuge in hiding places. Meanwhile, perhaps, the Russians would arrive in Lodz and the war would be over.

"I won't discuss it," Father said stubbornly, "If they clear one street of Jews, we will move to the second street and from there to a third. We will hide as long as we can. And that's that!"

I heard Father's words, but I feared that my parents would

not have the strength to live in the stressful conditions of hiding, that we would have nowhere to hide, that we would be left without food. There were lots of possibilities, all unpleasant. I tried once again to convince him that they would not separate us now just as they had not separated us then when they took us from the Bzezin ghetto. "If then, when Talka was ten years old, they didn't separate us," I said to Father, "now, when she's twelve, they certainly won't separate us."

But Father did not want to listen and it was impossible to convince him. "Talka looks younger now than she did then because she is so thin," he claimed, "and the thought that they might separate us terrifies me. I would rather die than have that happen."

"And where will we find a hiding place?" I asked Father, once I realized that his decision was firm.

"I've thought of that," he replied. "My friend from the Hamizrachi movement, who we prayed with on the High Holidays, told me that he had recently prepared a hiding place in his apartment and that there was room there for us too."

Father told me that behind the big room in which his friend lived there was another small room, the door to which he had hidden with a large closet. The man had closed the wall behind the closet with a thick wooden board which could be moved. Even when the closet door was opened it was impossible to see it since the back wall of the closet could also be moved.

"My friend suggested to me," continued Father, "that if we are not thinking of reporting for the transfer, we could go to this hiding place with one other family. I, of course, accepted his proposal. You will see. God will help us."

Then everything happened quickly. Chaos reigned in the ghetto which until now had been so orderly. The resorts were closed and people stopped going to work. All services stopped functioning. Filth and stench were everywhere. People could be seen running through the streets. Entire families, laden with bundles, hurried to the gathering places from which they would be sent to work camps. I did not believe that we would be able to hide from the Nazis, and I was jealous of those who were leaving the ghetto. I was sure that nothing could be worse than staying here.

We also were busy making preparations. Mother and Father took out the bags that we had sewn before leaving the Bzezin ghetto. Again, we packed them with our few belongings. Out of the corner of my eye I saw Talka casting embarrassed glances about her, and when she thought that no one was looking, she shoved her "Abonik" doll into her bag. Mother prepared some food from the goods that we had received in advance that we could store in the hiding place.

The Hiding Place

Masses of people flooded to the resorts. Others were walked in a convoy from the resorts to the prison on Charnyetzkiego street. And in the mornings, long convoys escorted by the Jewish police left the prison for the exit gate of the ghetto, towards the train tracks behind Marisin.

It was summer, but everyone was dressed as though it were winter, in layer upon layer of clothing, keeping with them as many clothes as possible. They were bent under their burdens, covered with sweat. When I saw many children walking alongside the adults, I realized that many had succeeded in hiding their children during the hunt after all.

After the initial flood of people, the convoys appeared less frequently, until they stopped altogether. The ghetto emptied out. Only a few people could still be seen slipping through the streets and they too disappeared after a curfew was announced.

On the morning the curfew was to begin, before the crack of dawn, we left our house, each of us carrying a pack on his back, while I also carried the pot of soup that Mother had cooked the day before. The street was deserted and we slipped through quickly to the apartment building. Out of breath, we arrived at the second floor, and carefully, according to the agreed upon signal, knocked on the door to the apartment of my father's friend, Yaakov.

The man opened the door quickly and received us warmly. It was hard to believe that next to this room, which looked disorderly, and behind the heavy closet in which there were actually a few clothes strewn about, there was another small room or, more correctly, a storage room. We entered the room. After the closet wall was moved back in place and we got used to the dim light in the little room, we saw other people sitting on their belongings or leaning against the walls. They moved their bags a bit to make room for us. It was very crowded, but we could hardly complain as the owners of the place had given up their own comfort in order to help us hide.

The only light that penetrated the hiding place filtered through the cracks in the boards nailed over a little window close to the ceiling.

Before we had even managed to settle in, we heard the first sounds from the street: huge trucks passing by, the clicking of heavy boots, screams, and orders in German. Occasionally a shot echoed through the air. The sounds came closer, then moved away, came closer, and then again moved away.

We sat hunched up, clinging to the wall and afraid to breathe. Every scream from outside and every shot made us tremble. The hours crawled by, and the heat in the room became unbearable. The day seemed to last an eternity. Only when day turned to night did the noise cease. The German soldiers made searches only during the day—we remembered that from the days of the hunt. After the noise calmed down, we dared to eat a little of our soup. Till then we had hardly thought about food. Our neighbors also nourished themselves with the bits of food they had brought with them. When darkness fell upon the ghetto, we left the hiding place and, like shadows, slipped through the streets to return to our apartment.

"We are lucky that the Germans leave the ghetto when it is dark so we can come back home to prepare something for the next day. What's even more important is that we can sleep in our own beds and straighten ourselves out a bit," Mother sighed.

We covered the window with a blanket, so no light could be seen from outside. Father burned a fire in the stove and Mother cooked soup for the next day.

"The food will last us another three days and no more," said Mother. She did not ask what would happen then.

The pattern repeated itself over the next few days. Every morning, before the crack of dawn, we stole into the hiding place, where we sat crowded and hot, hungry and fearful of every sound, lest they come to take us. And every night we had to slip through the streets to get home. At night we were afraid to fall asleep, in case we woke up too late and found that the day had brought the Germans back into the ghetto.

Mother was right. The little bit of food could barely be divided over three days. At the end of that time not a crumb was left in the house. In the darkness, I descended the steps in order to bring water from the well in the courtyard, but instead of going to the well I went into our neighbors' apartment. My eyes had already adjusted to the darkness. I examined the floor and searched in all the corners, but with the exception of a few pieces of clothing that were scattered in the empty apartment, I found nothing. The same was true in the apartment of our neighbor from Germany. I skipped

Chana'le's apartment because no one had lived there since the hunt, and I entered the rooms of the two brothers whose father was killed near the well. Next to the crate of coal I found two potatoes and a rotten kohlrabi. Intoxicated with joy, I ran home. Mother, Father and Talka did not believe their eyes; we would have soup for another day.

"God is still looking out for us," muttered Father.

During the day, as we sat in our hiding place, I wove a plan in my head. That night, I decided, when we returned home, I would go to the vegetable yard, only a few feet from our home, and I would look around. Perhaps I would find something edible there.

When I went down with the pail to bring water, I again did not go to the well, but rather continued in the darkness to the yard. I was lucky that the night was not too dark. By the light of the moon I felt through a pile of rotten vegetables which gave off a stench. I filled my pail with them and returned home with this booty. Despite the words of rebuke for my having endangered myself by wandering about alone at night, my booty was received with a joy that is beyond words. From then on, every night, I retrieved rotten vegetables and we were once again saved from starvation. We gave some of these vegetables to our neighbors in the hiding place whose food supply had also been exhausted.

Another three days passed. The noise from behind our hiding place got louder and closer. Searches were now being made on our street. We heard the click of boots right beside us. In addition to the curses, screams and shots, we now heard strong banging on doors, with iron rods and the butts of rifles. We heard doors being broken down. We were afraid to move or breathe. Talka closed her ears with her fingers and she was overcome by a strange trembling.

Horrifying calls—"God! Hear O Israel!"—shook us. I was unable to sit like this. I moved my bag close to the window and stood up on it. Through the cracks in the boards I saw the house across the street where a group of German soldiers was escorting a Jewish family which had hidden in the basement.

I saw the faces of the German soldiers, wild with victory as they hit the heads of the Jews, who bent over in an attempt to hide their heads in their hands. I saw a German soldier grab a young girl's hair and drag her, and I saw another soldier kick an old limping woman, whose wounded leg was flowing with blood.

Father pulled me down from the window. "They might see you even through that crack," he said firmly.

Not much time passed before we heard heavy steps in our own stairway. We heard them breaking into the lower apartments. Our hiding place, which until that day seemed secure, suddenly became extremely vulnerable. The soldiers reached our floor. We heard bangs on the door of our apartment. Each bang made us feel faint. Then the door burst open and they entered the room. We heard them moving furniture, shouting and cursing and opening the door of the closet—but then they closed it. We heard them saying that there was no one here and going down the steps.

For a long while we sat paralyzed. We were afraid to move. Father was the first to recover. He lifted his hands toward heaven and thanked God for having saved us.

Room for Hope?

Our joy did not last long. In the evening, on our way home from the hiding place, we once again saw posters plastered on the wall of the houses. By the pale light of the moon I read that the ghetto would be reduced in size. This was announced in the form of a harsh warning with many exclamation marks directed to the people who had still not reported and were found on the streets that would from the next day on belong to the Aryan side. Our street was among those listed. These people still had a final chance to report with their families and their belongings to the Charnyetzkiego prison.

We stood frozen in our places. We felt the danger of death lying in wait for us. From what was written it was clear that if we stayed here one more day, we would find ourselves outside the ghetto.

We quickly recovered and broke out in a run to Yaakov's house, where our hiding place was. In the stairway we met the second family who shared our storage room. They too were on the way to their apartment. We told them to return to the hiding place, that we had an important message. The two families listened to the information about the transfer of our street to the area outside of the ghetto with great fear but, it seemed, also with relief. Then and there, the two families decided that they would report that night, and Yaakov, Father's friend, also breathed a sigh of relief.

"It seems that God Himself wants us to report, for we have done all that we could. We have no more strength to sit starving in this hideout, trembling at every little noise."

The members of the second family also prepared themselves for the journey, and it seemed suddenly that a tremendous weight was removed from their hearts. For them, too, this was God's will.

I was almost sure that we too would finally reconcile ourselves to our fate. Nothing could be worse than being hunted. But Father once again would not concede.

"We will not willingly report!" he declared with finality. "We will keep hiding. I don't care about the difficulties, the hunger, or the fear. Everything is preferable to being separated."

Mother's pleas that she had no more strength for this kind of life were to no avail. Also useless were my explanations that this time the situation was different, that there was no intention of dividing the families, that Talka was already a big girl, twelve years old, and that all of us would go together. Father stood his ground and claimed that he did not believe the promise of Bibov, the German responsible for the ghetto. It was he who opened his speech on Balooty Square with the words "Meine liebe Juden" (My dear Jews) and promised that not a hair would fall from our heads.

"I would rather die," said Father, "than see them take someone from us."

I began to resent Father's stubbornness. With open jealousy I looked at the two families who were preparing to report. In my mind's eye I could already see the soup and bread they would receive in the prison and my mouth began to water.

We had no choice but to look for another hideout. That night we left our fifth house, with our belongings on our backs, and went first to the fields of Marisin and then to the large cemetery of the Jews of Lodz, where we found a place on one of the tombstones. The cemetery was good to us for two days. The fear that we would be caught faded slightly. We believed that the Germans would not search among the thousands of crowded tombstones. At night we slept on the soft ground around a big tombstone, and during the day we were protected from the scorching sun by its shade. By the light of day we could see other figures slipping from tombstone to tombstone, trying to find a little bit of shade. During these two days we finished what was left of our food: seven uncooked potatoes, which we cut in thin slices and chewed very slowly so that they would last as long as possible.

But the cemetery could not protect us from the rain. On the second night of our stay there, a steady rain poured down and wet us through to our very bones. Mother burst out in tears as she shivered from the cold: "I'm so jealous of those who are lying here *under* the stone!"

"For that there is always time," my father replied angrily. "Now we must think about another hideout." And he immediately added, "The parents of my friend from the Bzezin ghetto, Laibele Ziman, live on the corner of Dvorska Malinarska street. Laibele told me about a hideout that they set up in the attic. He said it was one that even a magician would not find. If we just get there, I'm sure they'll let us in," Father concluded.

I looked in amazement at my father, who had been so weak lately but who now seemed to be filled with a renewed strength which spread to the rest of us. At night, wet and shivering from the cold, we followed him to Dvorska street. We passed by buildings that were completely empty. On the street corner we noticed the little house in which my friend Eliezer Zelver had lived. The window to his apartment was smashed; it was obvious that no one lived there now. My heart ached when I thought of my good friend, his family, and his courageous sister Surtzia, who took in girls and taught them to read and write—Surtzia, thanks to whom Talka was introduced to the world of books and values that the Nazis had tried to suppress.

All of the ghetto streets seemed desolate, as did the four-story house towards which we walked. The apartments on all the floors were broken into, and the top floor also seemed deserted. But Father went up the steps leading to the roof, knocked on a thick wooden wall, and called out a name. There was no answer.

With his head bent, Father started back down. Suddenly we heard the voice of a man who told him to go into the apartment below and wait. To our amazement, a wooden board that fit into the ceiling was moved aside and a ladder was let down. We all climbed up, and then the ladder was also pulled up and the board returned to its place in the ceiling. We now found ourselves in a small room, or more accurately a small wooden cell, dark and windowless. Only a little bit of light penetrated through the cracks in the ceiling and the floor. The area of the little room was about four square meters, too small to fit all of the people sitting inside it. Later I counted and found that there were ten people, all crowded together to make room for us too.

Once I got used to the darkness I saw that my friend from school in Bzezin, Melech Appelion, was in the room. He was here with his sister. My friend, the only youth in the group, had supplied food to the others in the hideout, as I had done in our previous hiding place. Like me he went out at night and looked in the deserted apartments for anything edible. I now joined him, and the two of us managed to cover great distances in search of remnants of food in the deserted and broken stores. We quickly adjusted to the darkness of the night, which gave us confidence. At night there were no Germans in the ghetto.

When it was dark, the women would go down to the apartment and cook, while the men were responsible for getting fuel, lighting a fire, bringing water, and after the meal, making sure that not a trace was left that could give us away. All this activity took place at night. With the crack of dawn we would go up to our cell and pull up the ladder. The men would pray silently, and the long day began. We would sit pressed up against one another in the strangling heat and congested air, trembling in fear at any sound we heard outside.

The days crawled by, each day longer than the one before. We had long ago lost track of their number. We occasionally heard familiar sounds: a truck passing by, the heavy steps of soldiers' boots, screams, orders, and curses. Then we would try to make ourselves even smaller and hold our breath. It was impossible from our cell to see anything that went on in the street. We could only guess, according to the noise, which street the Germans were patrolling. And the noise from the searches grew ever closer.

The more time passed the less food we found in our scouring. One night we did not find a single crumb. We stood in an open store and the thought that we would come back to our starving companions empty-handed filled us with despair.

We were just about ready to return when my foot stumbled onto a hook sticking out of the floor. I bent down and pulled it. A square cover, part of the floor, remained in my hand, while beneath me was a pit, a sort of cellar. I called my friend and the two of us jumped down. The cellar was filled with moist leaves and when we took out some of them we saw that these were beet leaves. Even though they were moldy, they were still in good condition. This was new food, which could last us for many nights. We knew that we must take only enough for one meal. We could not leave any sign in the apartment that people had been there, and it was also forbidden to bring anything to the hideout whose odor might give us away.

The beet leaves that we brought and the satisfaction of knowing that we would have food for the coming days energized the hungry and depressed people. The men went down to the well in the courtyard to wash the leaves, and the women made a fire and filled pots with water in preparation for cooking. The soup tasted bitter but its warmth was good for our shriveled insides. Before dawn, after hiding all signs of our night activity, we went up as usual to our cell.

Outside, it was already light but I was attacked with stomach pains and had to go down to the bathroom in the courtyard. Before I reached the ladder to the hideout, I glanced through the window to the street. What I saw was shocking. Along the entire length of the street an incredible number of German soldiers were progressing in three rows covering the width of the road. They looked ready for battle, with steel helmets on their heads and sub-machine guns in their hands.

I hurriedly lifted the ladder and moved the board that closed the opening to the ceiling. My heart beat like a hammer, but no one felt what was going on inside me. I didn't tell anyone what I had seen. I knew that the Germans were now breaking into all of the houses; our house, too.

Everyone sitting in the hideout felt that the Germans had come to search. All around us there were already echoes from the heavy footsteps of the soldiers' boots, from shouts and curses, from the breaking down of doors and the smashing of windows, all accompanied by shots into the empty apartments. We sat crumpled up. Only by using our senses could we tell on which floor or in which apartment people were found. Then we heard the Germans coming up the stairs. They were now in the apartment we used at night. Had we left any sign? It was better not to think, just to hold our breaths. We believed that in a little while it would pass, that they could not uncover this hiding place.

From their footsteps we knew when the soldiers had reached the stairway bordering our cell. We heard them talking. There were two voices. Our hair stood on edge. They evidently did not see that there was a little room on the other side of the wooden wall for they began to go back down. We heard one of them say: "There's nobody here, this whole building is empty." We almost breathed a sigh of relief when we heard the juicy summarizing curse of the second soldier: "Goddammit, I'm sick and tired of searching for those filthy Jews!"

As he cursed he let loose his ax on the wooden wall. The strength of the blow smashed some of the boards of the wall, and we found ourselves out in the open, right in front of the German soldiers' eyes. We remained motionless. The German soldier also stood momentarily surprised. He had expected nothing like this. But his surprise lasted only a second.

"Hans!" he roared. "I found Jews! Call everyone!"

In a second the stairway was filled with soldiers running at us. We were quickly bombarded with blows from rifle butts. They kicked and shoved us down the stairs. Laibele's old father was bleeding from his head. I saw Melech's sister slip and fall down the steps. Talka helped her get up, and for this she was also hit. I myself managed to protect my head a little with my knapsack, which I had succeeded in taking with me.

The soldiers' blows did not stop even when we were already outside, but continued until we were transferred to the Jewish police.

Chapter Three

Auschwitz

After that, everything happened quickly. Beside the Jewish police stood several other families who had also been caught. We were sent with them to the prison on Charnyetzkiego street, where we stayed only one night. Early in the morning, after we were given bread for the trip, the long convoy made its way to Marisin.

We left the gate of the ghetto, which we had entered just two years and three months before; a period so short, yet so horrible and long. After we had walked a great distance we saw a train that was waiting for us. It was a locomotive and many cattle cars. The chaotic screaming was indescribable as the soldiers forced us into the cars. As each car filled up the heavy iron door was closed, reinforced with an iron rod placed along its width and even locked with a big bolt. In addition to all this, on the steps of the car stood two German soldiers carrying bayoneted rifles.

After we had entered a car and the heavy door was closed behind us, we breathed a sigh of relief because they had not separated us. We would travel together. There was only one small window set high up in the car, close to the ceiling. This window was so heavily barred that daylight barely filtered through. The suffocating heat was unbearable. We crowded together in a corner of the car. I put my bag under my mother's head. Talka sighed because she had not had a chance to take her bag containing the Abonik doll. I wanted to comfort her, but didn't know how.

Finally the train began to move. Two long, deafening whistles were the sign that we were on our way. Only the Germans knew our destination.

The stifling heat let up a little at first, but I nonetheless felt pressure in my head. So we were caught anyway! I thought angrily about my father and all the unnecessary suffering we had undergone in our hideouts. We could have saved ourselves all that suffering and left with everyone else.

The clatter of the tracks seemed to speak to me and mock me, driving me out of my mind, with what seemed like hostile words repeating themselves over and over:

"You were caught! You were caught! It was all worthless! There's no hiding from the Germans. You were caught! See, you were caught!"

In one more day I would discover that my father had been right and that all our suffering in the hideout had been worthwhile. Every hour and every minute had not been in vain.

But I would only know this on the following day. Meanwhile I was in a daze, as though everything that was happening now had nothing to do with me, but was just happening around me and I was looking on from outside. The fear that we would be caught had evaporated. We no longer had to fear every rustle.

The train continued on its way, sometimes faster, sometimes slower, sometimes standing still and then again starting up. When the train stopped, the air became unbearably stifling. I wanted the train to go on and on. Nonetheless it was good to feel my mother's warm hand, to hear Talka's steady breathing as she slept, and to lean on my father's back.

The car became darker and darker. Night descended upon the world. Quiet. I thought everyone must have fallen asleep. Only the train continued in its monotonous and mocking voice: "You were caught! See, you were caught!"

I must have fallen asleep, too, because I was abruptly awakened by a thunderous, deafening noise. When I opened my eyes, sunlight was filtering through the dense bars of the little window. The train stood still. Before I had a chance to wonder about the meaning of the horrible noise outside, the iron door of our car was pulled aside, and a group of oversized men, dressed in some kind of pajamas and equipped with thick clubs, burst in. As they screamed "Raus!" and hit people on their heads, they pushed everyone towards the opening. In vain I tried to grab my knapsack, in which were the last remnants of bread we had received for the trip. The knapsack disappeared under the legs of people who trampled over it, who then trampled over one another.

It wasn't until I was pushed to the opening of the car that I sobered up. I must protect my parents and my sister. Where were they? We must be together. We must not, God forbid, lose one another. From the open door I saw a sea of heads below, thousands of people, the victims of cudgels waving above them.

For a short moment I managed to see Talka holding onto my mother's dress, when they were near the tall steps. I couldn't understand how they would get down. Then I saw them being pushed, almost flying out of the car, and then I lost them. They were swallowed up among the masses. I no longer saw them. I pushed and I jumped. Someone was holding onto my sleeve. It was Father. We both tried to make it to where Mother and Talka had disappeared, but German soldiers and the men dressed in the striped pajamas cruelly pushed us back. "Men to the right! Women to the left!"

We heard screams from every direction. Once again we tried to edge our way to the opposite side, but our efforts were frustrated by the flow of people pulling us to the right side and the blows raining upon our heads. A blow that landed on Father's shoulder chafed my heart, but also brought me back to reality. I now knew that we would not be able to get to Mother and Talka, that we would not be able to find them among these incredible masses. I decided to just look out for Father. We must stay together. He was the only person I had left. We were pushed along with the current.

"Luzer," I heard Father groan, "Luzer, this time we lost them forever. I sense that I won't see them again, that I'll never see them again."

I didn't answer him. I was seized with fear. How could I comfort him, when I also felt the same way? I also knew that I had lost Mother and Talka forever, without having had a chance to say goodbye.

From the moment we left the train we set foot on another planet. Auschwitz: a strange world of whose existence even God apparently did not know, for did he not destroy Sodom and Gomorrah in fire and sulfur?

Auschwitz was something special that escapes definition. Strange creatures ran about, hungry, with shaven heads, dressed in rags, and barefoot. Concepts like mercy and pity were unknown here. Instead of beauty, there was only ugliness; instead of love, hatred. Fear and death, cruelty and suppression, reigned here.

Not much time passed before I began to learn the rules of this planet. They weren't hard to learn. Life itself taught us, and whoever did not learn quickly suffered the consequences. That's what happened to my father. He absolutely would not and could not learn the laws of life in Auschwitz.

Meanwhile, we were new to the place. The current pulled us

along together with masses of others. We passed through the gate with its notorious inscription: "Arbeit Macht Frei" (Work makes you free). We walked along a wide street bordered on both sides by tall barbed wire fences. After we passed the gate we were arranged in fives, accompanied on both sides by fat, overgrown men, equipped with thick clubs. Every once in a while one of these clubs waved and landed on one of our heads, a blow accompanied by a roar: "Faster!" Warning signs with symbols of lightning were attached every few meters to the barbed wire fence, announcing that high voltage passed through the prickly wires. To illustrate this warning, sooty figures had been attached to the fences. Barefoot figures with shaven heads, dressed in rags, ran along the fence and shouted something at us, but we could neither hear nor understand them.

If I had not felt my father's grip on my arm, I would have thought that this was a horror movie invented by some madman, or a nightmare. I don't know how long we walked, but the long way ended next to a large barrack. One group of people was taken inside, and then a second group, which included us.

A number of German soldiers stood beside a table heaped with gold jewelry. Everyone had to hand over any valuables he had with him. People emptied their pockets and took watches off their wrists, but this was not enough for the Germans. The *kapos* (overseer prisoners) thoroughly searched people's bodies, and woe unto him who still had something of value. Two soldiers with pliers and flashlights in their hands searched people's mouths. If they saw a gold tooth or crown, they would pry it out using excessive cruelty. In some cases all the man's teeth were knocked out and his mouth left toothless.

After Father handed over his watch and after the search made of our bodies, accompanied by blows, we were pushed to another barrack, where other kapos waited for us, equipped with shavers. We were ordered to undress, and they shaved not just the hair on our heads but every hair, even around our most intimate parts. Degraded and naked as on the day we were born, we were pushed towards a kapo who sprayed us from a pump with disinfecting powder, while another kapo threw at us pieces of clothing which were nothing other than black rags. These rags came as something of a relief—at least we had something with which to cover our nakedness.

I put on two pieces of clothing, supposedly pants and a short coat. The pants were short and very wide. I had to leave them unbuttoned and tie the two ends in order not to lose them. The coat was also very wide and very long. It occurred to me that my body must have looked ludicrous. It's too bad I don't have a mirror, I thought to myself. Even Mother and Talka would certainly not recognize me. With the thought of the names "Mother and Talka," my heart sank. How could I not have thought of them all this time? They must have also gone through these degrading procedures. Remembering those two names so precious to me drove me nearly mad, but the sight of Father once again brought me back to reality. If it weren't for the horrible situation in which we found ourselves, I might have burst out in laughter. Instead I felt my face become wet with tears. Father looked like a real scarecrow, his head was shaven and his clothes hung upon him like on a hanger. And so, I thought to myself, in a moment's time we have been turned into those strange creatures whom we had seen running along the electrified barbed wire fence.

We were taken to one of the large barracks that stood in a line, separated from the next by a few meters. In the dim light of the barrack into which they pushed us I could see wooden planks, pritchot, next to one another and above one another, filling the walls up to the top. Only the middle of the barrack was divided by a kind of stage built with red bricks. After a while I was told that the building had been a horse stable before the war. There were countless planks, but none of these planks belonged to any one person—or two, or even three. The kapos compressed countless people on each plank, each time shouting "crowd in!" as they used their cudgels to back up their words. It was already impossible to breathe as there was so little space. They pushed about ten people onto each plank.

I sprang to a plank on the lowest level, and I dragged my father after me. It quickly became clear that this was lucky. While it is true that those on the lower levels received most of the kapos' blows, this was still preferable, especially for Father, when we were ordered to climb down each time we heard a whistle blowing for an *apel* (rollcall). The whistles were blown whenever the German officers felt like having a show.

Upon hearing the whistle and the word apel, many kapos burst into the barrack, waving their cudgels in every direction while letting out terrifying screams, and hurried everyone outside. People would start pushing and shoving on their way down. Those on the upper planks sometimes fell as they came down; others would trample them, while the kapos never stopped waving their arms and clubs.

The apel was a distinct genre of torture. We had to kneel while the kapos walked among us making sure that no one dared lean on his behind. Anyone caught doing that would be dealt horrifying blows. Standing on our knees was so difficult that every once in a while we would hear a body fall over faint. Father was unable to hold out. Whenever I saw the kapos drawing away, I would support him. Time stood still and the officers, accompanied by their soldiers, walked slowly, feasting their eyes on the sight: a tremendous field filled with ugly creatures bending on their knees.

All we wanted to do then was return to our tenth of a plank

and lie down. We didn't care about the suffocating air, or the bodies pressing on us. We just wanted to set down our tortured bodies, to end this standing on our knees. But when we did, the hunger, the suffocation, and the thirst soon took their toll.

Because of the bodily torture and the frequent rollcalls there was no time to think. And this was exactly what the Germans intended—to destroy in us any ability to think.

Even the food they provided us involved tortures. In the morning each person received a piece of dry bread with honey. We used to seize this bread like wild animals. This food not only increased our thirst, which was great anyway, but lit a fire within us. We were desperate for any kind of drink, for a drop of water. We would go literally mad in the afternoon when they brought two giant vats with soup. The aroma of the soup drove us crazy. The kapos distributed the soup themselves, pouring it from the big vats into little pots, two for each plank, to be divided among ten people. Now began their big show. The thirsty people pounced upon the pots fighting each other all the while. Before the first person could bring a pot close to his mouth, his neighbor had already grabbed it and tried to take a big gulp which burned his insides. From his hand too the pot was stolen. While this struggle was taking place the thick and salty liquid spilled and those left hungry could only lick it up from the boards. The kapos tried to keep order, while in the doorway German officers appeared—once again to enjoy the show.

God, I thought, we have arrived in hell. I saw that only power ruled here, and I too grabbed the pot. After I managed to take one gulp that burned my tongue, I used my strength to keep the pot for Father, so that he too would get a taste of the soup. The drops of this soup only increased our thirst. Sometimes I tried to suck my finger, but it was always dry.

Hours passed before the kapos decided to give us water. They took us like a herd of cattle out of the barrack, and again the mad rush began. People pushed one another, knocked others down and trampled over them to the faucets. We barely had a chance to wet our lips before we were pushed on.

This same procedure was used when we were led to the toilets, which were nothing but a giant barrack lined with benches with holes. This barrack served as a sort of bathroom, but whenever we arrived there our bowels rebelled and seemed to refuse to obey us. At precisely the moment we were ordered to leave the bench in order to make room for someone else, it was as though they changed their minds and were filled with a desire to empty themselves, but now it was too late.

Tortures of the body and soul were our daily and nightly lot. We had long ago lost track of the days. This was a nightmare that did not end. Time was unceasing.

A Memory from the Past

Father's eyes became more confused and glazed each day. At first he could still run while I supported him. Now he looked around as though he did not understand where he was or what was happening to him. I sensed that he was beginning to lose touch with reality. I was seized with fear.

"God, protect my father," I would say to myself, "that I should not, God forbid, lose him too."

I didn't leave him for a moment. I would pull him by his sleeve and by his coat. With my elbows I cleared a path for him when we were run to rollcall, or to the drinking place, or to the toilets. I would grab the pot of soup and make sure that my father got a sip before it was taken out of our hands. Only then would I drink my own portion before passing it on to the others.

One night, when we could not fall asleep due to the torturous thirst and crowded conditions, as we were pressed up against one another, I heard my father whisper to me. "You know, Luzer, what I remembered just now? It's strange, but for some reason I just remembered that Sabbath long ago when you almost lost your life drowning. I didn't know why I was thinking of those happy days. But it's a fact, I remember them."

I felt a chill pass through my entire body upon hearing of things from such a distant era. Maybe this was a way to take one's mind off what was happening all around us? For a few moments I also immersed myself in the memory of that experience.

"Father!" I whispered, "You knew then what a sin I had committed and you didn't punish me, you didn't even say one word of rebuke."

I saw that Father, who occasionally cut himself off from the current reality, was again immersed in memories. The little light bulb hung from the middle of the ceiling barely lit the tremendous barrack, and even less the bottom planks that we lay upon. Even so I saw that tears flowed from his eyes when he heard my words: memories from a different world, where he lived as a human being, where he had a wife and children, his own house, his own bed. His words had returned me, too, to that day so far away, a distance of thousands of years.

It was a Saturday. A holy Sabbath day in Bzezin, where all together, we enjoyed the Sabbath rest. A winter sun sparkled on the carpet of snow that covered the courtyard in our house. In the house it was warm and pleasant. Father and Mother had retired to their bedroom for their Sabbath afternoon nap. Talka played with her dolls. It seemed to me like the sun outside was winking at me and calling me as it sparkled on the surface of the snow. I silently peeked in my parents' room and, when I saw that they were asleep, I returned to the dining room and quietly took my skates out of the closet drawer. I knew that I was disobeying, that it was forbidden to skate on the Sabbath, but the temptation was too great. All week I dreamt about skating and all week I was too busy and unable to satisfy my craving. So now I took advantage of the opportunity and left the house silently. I continued at a run and passed by our town's big skating rink. I must not let anyone see me, I said to myself. If someone sees me, the rumor will spread throughout the town that Yossel Zyskind's son, the grandson of Pinche Yakobovitch, went ice skating on the Sabbath.

With a throbbing heart I continued to run in the direction of the Mrozitzka River. The river was covered with a layer of ice. I knew that the ice there was thin and that it was forbidden to skate upon it. But near the river was a small lake where I had skated the year before. The layer of ice covering it seemed from the outside to be thick. I quickly tied my skates to my shoes and went out on the ice. My heart was filled with joy as I began to skate. Soon I'll return home and no one will see me, I thought to myself. I was happy skating. I felt as though I was flying through the air. I wanted to fly away and sing. Suddenly, boom! The ice beneath me exploded and I began to sink.

I'm drowning! My first thought was that this was my punishment for skating on the Sabbath. This was my end!

With all my strength I tried to stay on top of the ice, to grab hold of those places which had not yet broken, but each protrusion that I grabbed broke off in my hand. The ice water froze my arteries and made it difficult for me to breathe. I continued to grab pieces of ice and make my way towards the shore. But the ice kept breaking and my shoes and skates, as well as my soaked clothes, were heavy and drew me downward. I was close to the shore when I sank to my shoulders. Only my head was left out of water.

"I'm drowning!" I screamed, but no one was nearby. And suddenly I felt that my hand was touching something, a stalk and then another stalk. I grabbed them with all my strength and pulled my body to shore. The stalks did not break, and near the shore they were plentiful. The stalks saved me.

Agitated and scared, my clothes cracking from the frozen water, I knocked on the door to our house. My mother opened it. She nearly fainted when she saw me, but she immediately recovered. My dear mother, I thought now as I lay upon the plank, and I even remembered how she put her finger to her mouth and whispered that I was lucky that Father and Talka were still sleeping. She led me to the kitchen and removed my coat and frozen clothes. She went outside and brought a pan of snow, with which she rubbed my body and my frozen feet. She then dressed me in warm clothes and gave me a glass of hot tea. I told my mother everything that had happened, and she promised me that she would not tell Father. And, indeed, that's how it was. Only now, here in Auschwitz, on our plank, Father told me that he had heard everything, that he had really wanted to come into the kitchen to hug and kiss me but had stopped himself, for if he had come into the kitchen he would have had to punish me for the transgression I had committed on the holy day.

"You had already been punished enough," Father added after a moment. "On the following morning I went to the synagogue to say a prayer of thanks to God for having saved you."

A wave of warmth washed over me. I was so thankful even now to my father for reminding me of our happiness then—a happiness that in those distant days we did not appreciate, as we thought then that it was natural and just the way things were. It was good now to recall that happiness and to forget for a short moment our current plight, which was nothing but a chain of fears and terrors.

I suddenly felt a terrible thirst. For a moment I saw around me a lake filled with water. I saw that lake next to our river, and a question began to plague me—why did I not drink water from the lake then, lots and lots of water, even frozen water, why didn't I equip myself then with all that water? It surely would have quenched the fire scorching my body.

A sharp, deafening whistle, was heard beside me. "Raus! Outside! Rollcall! Quickly!"

Kapos with their clubs burst inside. People began to push from every direction. The bubble of memory from that other world was burst, and the reality of Auschwitz returned to us in full force.

My Meeting With a Kapo

After the rollcall whistles, when everyone had already left the barrack, the kapos would make thorough searches in order to make sure that everyone descended from the planks and went out to rollcall. They would reach even the upper levels, and if they found someone who was unable to stand on his own feet, they would get him up with the help of their cudgels and chase him to the apel. Only when their victim was unable to get up, despite their blows, did they transfer him to a special barrack which served as a sort of hospital called the *revier*.

Nearly every day, two or three kapos would come without their cudgels to our barrack, where they would announce in gentle language that if anyone did not feel well, or was really sick, they would take him to the revier. At the same time they would tell us that the sick people in the revier did not have to go out to rollcalls and that their plight was immeasurably better than that of those who lived in the barracks. Those who were in the revier just lay in bed and rested and, if it was necessary, they even received treatment.

Despite the weakness and illness of many of those in our barrack, in the beginning no one was taken in by the kapos' promises. Everyone felt that, here in Auschwitz, one could not admit weakness and survive.

Each day people got weaker and sicker. There were those who were struck with a high fever, stomach pains, and diarrhea, particularly the older ones among us. They could barely lift themselves off the planks. All that they wanted was to be allowed to lie down and rest. But even these people were not tempted by the kapos' offers. With failing legs they too would run to the rollcalls and stand nearly fainting on their knees until the end of the apel.

All this was only the beginning. After a few days people began to break. Illness overtook them and they became indifferent to their fate. They would turn to the kapos and beg to be taken to the revier. The kapos, with a special satisfaction on their faces, would lead them to that barrack, in which all the sick were concentrated. Father was getting very weak. Every day he lost more strength. I saw him fading like a candle. As soon as I heard the first whistle for the apel, I would hurry to get him up and support him. I always supported him from behind during the running, pushing him so that he would not lag behind.

One night during an apel, in which we knelt on our knees for a long time, I heard him whisper: "Luzer, I have no more strength. Were it not for my desire to stay with you, I would have turned to the kapos and asked that they take me to the revier. There they would let me rest, there I could lie down..."

His words terrified me. All along I had feared that Father might think such a thought. I still remembered the evacuation of the sick from the Bzezin ghetto. I remembered how the Germans had promised Dr. Warhaft that they would treat his patients, and how they had later dragged the dying patients from their beds.

"Father," I whispered, "Remember how the Germans treated the sick people in Bzezin?" Father heard my words and sighed.

"None of that is important to me anymore," he added. "I am fighting only in order to remain with you. But I already lack the strength to fight. All I want is to lie down, only that they should let me lie down." He wavered as though he was about to fall but I held him up. Only when the kapo was no longer near us did I loosen my grip.

Father's situation went from bad to worse. He was attacked with stomach pains and diarrhea. He became so miserable and depressed because of the diarrhea that I began to fear for his life. He once again proposed that he ask the kapos to take him to the revier. When I heard this I turned to him and nearly screamed: "No, Father, we must not separate! You will see that your stomach pains will stop, that everything will be okay after we get some soup to you."

Unluckily, that day the pot of soup came to us only after it was totally empty. I was at a complete loss. I felt how much Father needed a sip of soup, however salty it might be. I decided to leave the barrack and look for something. I didn't know where to go or what to look for. I could not go out while he was awake, so I waited for him to fall asleep. I got up off our plank and looked around. Once again, my eyes rested upon the shaven figures lying helpless on the planks, lacking any identity, each one like the next. It occurred to me that Father and I also looked like all the others. We also lacked identity. No one knew us here.

As I continued to look around, my eyes met the eyes of a youth who lay squeezed between a young boy and an old man. The boy's eyes reminded me of something from the old days. Before I had a chance to search my memory, I heard a whisper that shocked me: "Luzer! Is it you? You're here too?"

I now remembered the youth's name, I even remembered how our teacher pronounced his name: Aharon Gustinsky, my classmate. Aharon Gustinsky pointed to the youth that lay sleeping beside him: "Look, Luzer, Melech Appelion is also here. We met during the run and now we're sticking together."

A wave of warmth flooded my heart. Here, in Auschwitz, I met two friends from school, two partners from my happy childhood that was an eternity ago. Melech Appelion had even been with us in our last hideout in the Lodz ghetto. Together we had spent nights searching for food for our families, and we were together when we had been caught by the German soldier who had knocked down our hideout wall with an ax blow.

"I am here with my father," I whispered, "but he is very sick and the soup didn't reach us today. I'm going to look for something. Maybe I'll find something outside. Look out for my father. If there's a whistle for the apel while I'm gone I'll return right away."

"Stay in place and don't leave the barrack," said Melech Appelion, who had awakened meanwhile. "This is not the ghetto. You won't find anything here. Only some kapo might catch you and beat you for wandering outside. Luzer, it's very dangerous."

"I'll go anyway," I answered. "If there's a whistle for a rollcall, help my father down. I'll come back immediately, but I don't think there'll be a whistle; we just returned from an apel."

"Quiet!" screamed one of the figures, who had been awakened by our talking.

I quickly went outside. Between the barracks, which were a few meters apart from one another, I could see a few figures slipping by. What, actually, could one find here, I thought to myself, but I kept going. If I see a kapo with a club in his hand I'll enter the closest barrack. I continued by the barracks, peeking inside each of them. They were all the same. Each had wooden planks up to the ceiling, filled with the shaven figures.

I already arrived at the next to last barrack. After the last one there was a very high wooden wall. A strong smell of soup made me think that in the last barrack there must be a kitchen. But I didn't get there. A tall and robust man walked out of the next to last barrack, dressed in striped clothes, with a thick club in his hand. I was all ready to slip behind him and enter the barrack, when I heard his voice and stopped in my tracks. He was not yelling at me; he hadn't even seen me. It was the sound of his voice which stopped me. I know that voice, I thought to myself. No, I'm not mistaken, it is Dudu's voice. Dudu, who was a good friend of my Uncle Yankel. He used to come to our house. He knew me when I was still a little boy. He used to play with me. Could it be that he was now a kapo? Could that kind and cheerful boy have been made a kapo in Auschwitz? No, no, it's impossible, I said to myself. I stood paralyzed, stupefied. Maybe I was just hallucinating? But then the man turned his head to me, and a cry escaped my mouth: "Dudu! Is that you? Are you a kapo?"

The man turned to me quickly and our eyes met. For a moment I felt that Dudu recognized me. He came close to me with a leap and grabbed me by the neck.

"You filthy pig!" he roared, "What are you doing here?"

I felt my blood freeze, but I continued speaking to him: "Dudu! It's me, Luzer Zyskind, the grandson of Pinche Yakobovitch. Only Father and I are left from our whole family, and now Father is very sick. We didn't get any soup today. Please help us."

My words only angered the kapo even more. He did not ease off my neck but with a violent push took me out of the barrack, continuing to yell at me and waving his stick over my head.

"Get out of here, you filthy pig! I'll show you how to talk back to me!"

In a daze, almost fainting, I dragged myself from him.

God, this is it. This is surely what hell must look like, where good people turn into devils. I suddenly remembered my father who remained alone and was waiting for me.

"Sir," I began to beg. "Forgive me, sir. I was mistaken. Allow me to go, please."

By now we were already outside the barrack. The kapo continued to push me and wave his stick. I was seized with fear. What will he do to me? Suddenly I heard what was certainly a humane voice. It was Dudu whispering: "Luzer, you were not mistaken, it really is me. Forgive me, Luzer. Keep running in front of me as though I were pushing you. That's the only way we'll be able to talk. There's a law here in Auschwitz: if someone is being chased by someone else, and especially by a kapo, everyone else leaves him alone. Everyone knows that the person being chased will be caught and get what he deserves. So run, Luzer, run."

For a moment I thought that I was attacked again with hallucinations, but this was reality. Dudu's grasp was strong and he continued in his whispering voice: "This is the only way we can speak. Never let on that you know me, for that will be my end. Yes, I am a kapo. But I didn't want it. They broke me. They succeed in breaking everyone. There is no force that can oppose them. And I really tried, but in the end, they won. Luzer, this is the end of the world. You see the top part of the building peeking over this wooden fence? That is the crematorium. Those are the gas chambers. They are killing our people, our parents, our dear ones. Do you see the big chimney with the smoke rising out of it with sparks of fire? That's where the bodies are burned."

As though through a fog I heard his voice, which was now filled with tears. Dudu continued his story as he held my neck and pushed me forward: "The Germans chose the strongest and tallest among us. They took us to see how they kill people in the gas chambers. They forced us to watch through small glass windows how people were choking and quivering as they died. It was the most horrifying sight I had ever seen. I almost fainted. Everyone almost fainted. But they poured water on us and beat us until we watched again. It is impossible to describe in words what I felt. They said that our fate would be like this if we did not agree to be kapos. There were those who broke. I did not. I was prepared to die rather than raise a hand against my brother. But that was not the end. They did not let up. They hung us by the soles of our feet and hit us until we were senseless. Again there were a few that broke, they could take no more; I kept holding on. A four-day fast also did not break me. I asked God to be kind to me and kill me. He did not do this kindness for me. The thirst broke me. I could not go on. I thought that I was on fire, that I was going mad. I was in a very hot room. After the fast they fed us salty and honey-covered food. We were prepared to drink anything wet, even muddy water, but there was nothing. Behind an armored glass door we saw an open faucet with running water. We all acted like madmen. We screamed and pulled out the hair from our heads. We beat on the glass with all our strength. It would not break. But we broke. We all broke. I had no feeling left. I wanted only to drink. Not a single man succeeded in opposing the will of the Germans. I am jealous of those who were led to their death and did not have to experience the hell that I experienced. More than anything I hate myself. But one thing, Luzer: until now I have not hit anyone. I only yell and curse and wave my club."

"Nu, you filth! Get going already! You'll soon feel what I can do to you!" I felt a strong push. I didn't understand what was happening and lifted my head. Another kapo had passed by us. When the kapo was some distance away, Dudu continued:

"I will help you, but you must never come near me and

show that you know me. Now, pay attention. We will run a
little bit slower. I will bend down and take off my shoe, the
wooden clog on my foot, and I will raise it over your head, as
though I am going to beat you. Very soon some people will
walk by here carrying a large pot of soup for the last barrack.
Grab the clog from my hand, dip it in the pot, and take it out
quickly with the soup and begin to run away. The people carrying the pot won't be able to chase you, because they'll have
to keep carrying it. I'll begin to yell at you and chase after
you, and then for sure no one will interfere. You remember I
told you that there is a law here in Auschwitz that if someone
is being chased by someone else, others don't touch him."

I stopped in my place and turned my head towards Dudu.
He understood my amazement. He quickly bent down and
took from his foot a wooden shoe in the shape of a boat, big
and deep—all the while not easing off my neck.

"You filthy pig, I'll break your bones," he again raised his
voice and immediately continued quietly: "What are you
looking at me like that for? Maybe you want a bowl and
spoon? Maybe you forgot that you're in Auschwitz. You don't
know what a treasure you have in your hand. Here a clog is
worth more than gold. What am I saying? Here it is worth
more than human life. People would kill you in order to
have this treasure which can help you steal soup. You will yet
understand what it means to have your own clog," Dudu
continued. "Protect it like the apple of your eye. It's good
that you got such a wide coat, so you'll be able to hide it. And
one more thing, Luzer, make sure that your father does not
go to the revier, even if he is desperately ill, because that is
the end. From there, no one returns. From there the sick are
taken directly to the gas chambers. Don't stop, continue as
though you're running away from me and don't look at me in
disbelief. Everything I told you is true. Here they kill human
beings. This is a death factory."

Dudu sighed and continued: "It's too bad I met you. It is forbidden for me to get emotional. I am a kapo. That could mean my end. But I don't care any more. I will help you. Whenever you want something, come to me. Climb up to my plank, which is the highest one, just try to make sure no one notices. I have my own private plank, a whole plank just for me, and even a mattress. I have plenty of food too. That's my reward for my services as a kapo. Under the mattress you will always find a slice of bread that I will leave for the two of you, even when I am not there. Just make sure, Luzer, that you don't show that you know me and don't tell your father that I am a kapo!"

I promised him. Just then I smelled the strong odor of soup.

"They're coming closer with the vat. Take the clog and do what I told you," Dudu whispered. He stuffed his wooden clog into my hand and pushed me toward the vat, which was attached to wooden poles and carried by four men.

I did as he said. I quickly dipped the clog into the soup and began to flee with it.

"You miserable wretch!" I heard Dudu call, "I'll catch you, you won't get out of this alive!" He ran after me with his stick raised and I ran faster. Thus we arrived at our barrack and I disappeared inside it.

Excited and agitated I quickly went up to our plank, holding in my hand the clog with the precious liquid hidden inside my broad coat.

"Father," I whispered, "Father, look what I brought you."

But no answer came from the place where my father had lain. When my eyes adjusted a little to the dimness in the barrack, my speech was abruptly halted. Father's place was empty.

Father Leaves Me

Confused and enraged I turned to my friends Melech and Aharon who now lay close to our place.

"Where is my father? What happened to him?" I called to them.

My friends, who were also confused, told me that after I had left the barrack, two kapos had come in as they do every day, and they asked if there was anyone who did not feel well and wanted to be taken to the revier.

As though in a fog, my entire body trembling, I heard their words.

"Your father turned to me," Aharon Gustinsky told me, "and said that he asked you to forgive him, but he decided to go with the kapos to the revier. He was no longer able to cope with his illness, with his weakness. The thought of the whistle for the apel drove him out of his mind. He had no more strength left for anything. He had only one request: that God be kind to him and let him die in his sleep."

My friend repeated my father's words. "I wasn't sleeping when Luzer spoke with you. I waited for a chance when he would leave the barrack, for he would not have let me go." Then, my friend added, "and unfortunately, just after you left, the kapos arrived and your father saw this as a sign of God's will. We pleaded with him that he should wait for you, that he should go a different time, but to no avail. He only asked us to tell you not to be sorry, that this was better for both of you, that in any case he would not get out of here alive and your concern for him would only be a burden on you and kill you too. Your father also requested that you fight for your life. He said that it was clear to him that you could make it, that you are young and that therefore you must not give in, till the very end, so that you can leave this place and tell the world," Melech Appelion added.

I felt my head spinning, the clog with the hot soup that I pressed under my armpit, inside my coat, burned my flesh. I took out the clog and gave it to my friends.

"Eat this," I said haltingly. They looked at me and at the soup as though they didn't believe their eyes, as though I had fallen out of the sky.

"Where did you get that?" they asked in amazement.

"Eat it yourself, it's yours," they whispered.

"Don't ask where it's from. Just eat. Eat it all. I've already eaten." I jumped off the plank and ran outside.

"Where is the block that contains the revier?" I asked the figures wandering outside, but the figures looked at me with glazed eyes and shrugged their shoulders.

I raced over the distance separating our barrack from Dudu's and went up to his plank. He was there. Whispering, I told him what my father had done. He trembled.

"That's the end," he concluded. "From there, no one comes back. And maybe your father was right," he added after a moment, "your father could not have lasted in this hell. Think, Luzer, logically—what good would it do him to suffer another few days, or even a few weeks? Eventually he will collapse."

I cut him off and nearly screamed: "But you yourself said that from there everyone is taken to the gas chambers. And if my father had a supplement of food he would be able to hold out. He is still a young man!" I continued to yell without thinking about where I was.

"Quiet!" Dudu whispered to me. "You are not supposed to be here. If, God forbid, you are found here, they'll torture both of us to death. In fact," he added after a short thought, "all of us will meet our end here. We will all end up in the gas chambers, one a little earlier and another later, and maybe luck is on the side of those who finish earlier. There's another type of lucky person: the one who is sent to Germany to work in the factories." He looked at me and added, "You, Luzer, might have a chance to be sent there. Your father does not. They only choose young people and those who have not yet lost their human form. But who knows what happens to the people there?"

I didn't have the patience to hear him out. I had to get my father back at all costs.

"Dudu, what can be done?" I asked him, "I must get my father out of there. Help me! I am sure now, now that you will supplement our food, Father will recover. Tell me, where is the revier?"

"The revier is in block 24. But before that they take the people to a transition block, number 11. That's not far from your barrack. You won't be able to get your father out of the transition block either. The heavy door to the barrack is double locked. I have never heard of anyone leaving there. And perhaps when the soup is distributed the door will be open?" Dudu continued more to himself than to me. "In any case, you must get out of here quickly before someone sees you. You must be careful, Luzer, for you might lose your life." Dudu put a piece of bread into my coat pocket and immediately pushed me down. Before I even had a chance to reach our barrack there was a shrill whistle and shouts announcing an apel. I don't know how long we stood in this apel but it seemed to me that this was the longest rollcall during my whole stay in the camp. The things that Dudu had told me about the gas chambers and the burning of people only now began to be absorbed in my mind. I tried to convince myself that all those things could not possibly be true. I tried to think that such a thing could not possibly have happened to Mother and Talka.

I felt that if I kept thinking about it I would go mad and begin to scream and run wild. One thing was clear to me: I had to get my father out, no matter what. At the same time I was also angry at my father, that he had given into his weakness and had not tried to overcome the hardships. Why had he left me now, just when I had found someone who could help us. I believed that the little bit of additional food would bring back his strength and he would recover.

It was already getting dark when they announced the end of the apel.

Instead of returning to my barrack I ran directly to barrack number 11. But the barrack was locked with a heavy door. I walked around the barrack, putting my mouth close to the wooden wall, knocking on it and calling: "Father! Yoseph Zyskind!" I called over and over again but I heard no answer from inside.

I was near the door when I heard a weak whisper from inside: "Luzer, I am here."

"Father," I called into my hands which I placed on the boards of the barrack wall, "What have you done? Why did you go?"

"It was God's will," I again heard a feeble response.

"Father, I am going to get you out of there," I managed to say before I saw two kapos drawing near and had to take off.

Most of the next day I spent behind barrack 11, all the while clinging to the outside wooden wall that separated me from my father.

"Father!" I shouted and knocked on the wall, "Father, I am here!"

"Look out for yourself, my son," I heard Father's voice, "It is good for me here. I am okay, I am lying down."

I was afraid to move from there. I was afraid that if I left they would take the sick people to the gas chambers, as though my presence could somehow help. But the barrack was closed and the door was locked. No one came out and no one went in.

In the afternoon a miracle happened. I saw four people carrying two poles bearing a giant pot with soup. Behind them walked another two people with small pots for distributing soup, and after them were the kapos guarding the whole contingent. The moment the heavy door to the barrack opened I entered with these people.

Before my eyes had a chance to adjust to the dim light inside the barrack, I walked toward the place where, according to my estimate, my father was lying. I saw him right away. He was lying crumpled up on a plank and he was frightened when he saw me.

"What have you done? Why did you come in? You won't be able to get out of here."

Screams and shouts were all around us. The sick and starving people really went wild from the smell of the soup. Everyone wanted them to begin the distribution from their side. The kapos went to work establishing order. Taking advantage of the chaos, I grabbed Father's hand and pulled him after me. "Father, quick, run!" I called out to him.

Without saying a word, Father ran after me.

We succeeded in slipping outside without being spotted. I took Father back to our barrack. At the time I believed that I had brought him back to life.

From then on I wanted only to protect my father, to protect this last crumb of happiness that was left me. I told him how I had been lucky to meet Dudu. I did not break my promise to Dudu and tell my father that Dudu was a kapo. I told him that Dudu worked in the kitchen and that he would help us get a little more food. I took the slice of bread that I had received from Dudu out of my pocket and gave it to my father. Father refused to eat it himself even though I promised him that I had already eaten my portion. He broke the bread in half and forced me to eat half of it. He ate with such an appetite that I quickly realized that in block 11 they did not receive any bread at all. Aside from the soup that was given them once a day they didn't receive anything. I promised my father that from now on we would not be hungry again and that his health would improve because of it.

"Father," I said to him, "you will see that I will also get some extra soup." I asked him to hold on for me and not repeat what he had just done, that he should not be hard on me when I left the barrack to get food, that he should know that I am always near the barrack and the moment I hear a whistle for an apel I will return. I also told father about the gas chambers, but he refused to believe it. On the other hand, he also didn't believe that he would get out of here alive. He felt that he would die of hunger and suffering, that many would die because of the terrible conditions. This was, in his opinion, what the Germans intended. After the work that we did for them in the ghetto, they no longer needed us. But mass murder? Gas chambers? That he could not believe. His whole body trembled nonetheless.

Meanwhile, I thought of a trick we could use to get more soup. In order to do it I needed the help of my two friends. I instructed them to come down from their plank, so that my father would not hear us, and I laid out my plan before them. "We will wait by one of the barracks close to the kitchen," I said to them, "and when we see people leaving the kitchen with pots of soup I will approach the pot carriers as though I wish to help them. At the appropriate moment I will take the clog out of my coat, dip it quickly into the soup, and then run while you chase after me and shout, giving the impression that you want to catch me and punish me for what I have done."

My friends were very worried by the whole plan. They said that if a kapo was nearby he would catch and kill me. But I reassured them. I told them that I knew all about this. I reminded them of the soup I had brought them two days before, which I had obtained in the same way.

In the end they agreed. It must have been the memory of the soup from two days ago that convinced them.

In the afternoon we slipped close to the front barracks. We saw people coming out of the kitchen carrying vats of soup;

next to them walked kapos. This was a dangerous situation and made our mission nearly impossible. Only after they passed by with four such vats did the situation change. Beside the fifth vat walked people carrying small pots for distribution. I signaled my friends and took off in the direction of the fifth pot. I quickly dipped the clog into the boiling soup and took it right out. My hand was burned, but I paid no attention. I tore off in a frightened run. The people carrying the soup could not put down their precious cargo and chase after me. They made do with screams and curses. At that moment my two friends began to chase after me and shout: "We'll catch that scoundrel! We'll teach him a lesson! We'll break all his bones!"

As I had predicted, this satisfied everyone. Our trick had worked. I stopped next to our barrack and gave the clog with the soup to Aharon Gustinsky. He drank a little of the soup while Melech and I stood around him to hide him from the others. Then Melech Appelion and I drank. What remained of the soup, most of it, we brought to Father, whom we also hid from the other residents of our plank while he drank. Father was worried. He did not understand how we had obtained the soup. He warned me not to endanger myself and to protect my life.

The few sips of soup that we stole did not satisfy our hunger. But it was an important addition to our regular portion. And with the piece of bread that Dudu left me every day, it was possible to hope that Father would somehow be able to hold out.

The Strange Case of Chaim Rumkovsky, King of the Ghetto

Toward evening, when I was sneaking to Dudu's barrack, I heard a voice behind me: "Excuse me, please!"

I stopped in my place. What words were these? This was not the language of Auschwitz.

Before me stood a shaven figure like me, but when I looked closely at him I saw a young man who looked very confused, as though he did not grasp where he had landed. His blue eyes were filled with terror.

"Where are the bathrooms here?" the man asked me. I looked at him, not believing my ears, and almost broke out in laughter.

"How long have you been here?" I asked the man instead of answering.

"Since today." He stopped talking as though he were thinking to himself. "I don't know if we got here hours ago or ages ago, so many terrible things have happened since then. Even my watch was taken away from me, along with everything else."

"Now I understand," I replied. "There are no bathrooms here as you remember them. There," I pointed with my finger, "are toilets—that is, boards with holes in them, but you'd better not go there yourself. All of the residents of the barrack go together to them. And if some kapo sees you wandering outside your barrack he will hit you vigorously."

"And why are you wandering here by yourself?" asked the man.

"I don't wander around. I run. I already know the laws of Auschwitz well, and if I see some kapo coming close, I jump right into the nearest barrack. Depend on me!"

"My name is Yitzchak Epstein," the young man introduced himself and I once again almost broke out laughing. I looked at the man, doing my best to hold in my laughter, with a kind of pity: he still did not understand where he was. He needed help. "Sir," I replied to him in his own language, "here there are no names. In a very short while you will forget your name altogether. Here a man has no signs of identity. There are only numbers. Every man is a number. No, no, excuse me, I was mistaken," I corrected myself. "Here you aren't even a whole number, but rather a small fraction of a number. Here a whole barrack, numbering hundreds of people, go to the bathroom. Even if you have to take care of your needs immediately, at this very moment, you must hold it in, and wait until your time comes and the kapos order you to take care of your needs. And if you can't hold it in you have to do it in your pants. They will dry."

The man stood opposite me, his mouth gaping. I thought that he should learn the reality of Auschwitz as quickly as possible, and that all this was for his own good.

I soon realized that Yitzchak Epstein had already begun to understand the reality. He told me that he had arrived here from the Lodz ghetto. For a moment I felt a sort of tugging at my heart, a kind of jealousy for the few extra days the man had been lucky enough to stay in the ghetto, in conditions infinitely better than those of this death camp, Auschwitz. And especially, he'd been together with his family.

"Tell me," I asked him, "are there still people left in the ghetto? Are they sending everyone away?"

"A few are still left there," he answered me. "I think one more transport remains in the ghetto, among them the firemen and the *Zonder Kommando* (special police). I arrived here with our king, Chaim Rumkovsky, and his police. We were happy that we were sent with Rumkovsky, for we were certain that we would get preferential treatment. Who could have imagined that such a place as this existed." The man spoke more to himself than to me: "This is the most horrible day of my life. They separated me from my family, they took everything from me...."

Whoa! I interrupted Yitzchak Epstein's torrent of speech, "Rumkovsky also arrived here? That's the reward he received from the Germans for his cooperation with them? And what did they do with him, with our king?" As I spoke I was surveying the area to make sure that no kapo was approaching.

"And so, he did in fact earn a special reception," answered Yitzchak, "Rumkovsky arrived here in a separate, special car for himself, his young wife, and adopted son, a beautiful fifteen-year-old boy. Rumkovsky's brother and his wife also arrived in the same car. In addition, the Germans allowed our king to take whatever belongings he wished with him. In the cars next to Rumkovsky's were his policemen. When the train arrived here, high-ranking German officers awaited him on the platform. I saw Rumkovsky, despite his advanced age, jump from the car, as was always his habit. He walked with his head held high and his gray forelock sticking out of the crowd. His boots were shiny, and he walked directly to the group of officers. I stood not far from him," Epstein continued, "and I saw how he took out a letter and handed it to the officer of the highest rank. I even heard him explain that this was an 'iron letter' from the Gestapo. The officer took the letter from him and read it with interest. The other officers also turned their heads to the letter and read it. We were sure that they would treat Rumkovsky with honor. They asked who else was with him, and he informed them that in his car were his wife, his son, and his brother with his wife. The officers sent a few kapos there, who, with great courtesy, brought them and stood them all together. After a few moments a special car arrived. It was closed, and from its roof a chimney pushed through. I saw Rumkovsky enter the car followed by the rest of his family. Before the door of the car closed, the highest ranking officer assured Rumkovsky that his belongings would arrive later. The crowd on the platform made room for the car as it began to travel. The car increased its speed and when it was some distance from the platform we saw thick white smoke coming out of its chimney. One of the kapos who was there at the time suddenly raised his voice in laughter and called out: "Chaim Rumkovsky, the king of the Lodz ghetto, is now ascending to heaven."

Yitzchak Epstein's voice became silent. And I felt paralyzed. We thought of the death of Chaim Rumkovsky, who was all-powerful in the Lodz ghetto, who had ruled absolutely for five years over the lives of a quarter of a million Jews, and who operated a tremendous industry in the Lodz ghetto for the benefit of the German government.

"After the car with Rumkovsky's family had left," Yitzchak continued his story, "the kapos began to enforce order on the platform. Most of Rumkovsky's policemen had arrived in Auschwitz with their police hats and shiny uniforms. They were now arranged in fives, headed by the chief of police, Rosenblatt. But the moment Rosenblatt was placed at the head of the police, a fat kapo walked towards him. He was Moshe Chasid, a man from the underworld in Lodz, whom the chief of police Rosenblatt had exiled in one of the first transports. Moshe Chasid now grabbed Rosenblatt by the neck and landed a blow with his fist on his face. 'I have been waiting years for this moment!' he shouted. 'Now I will pay you back for having separated me from my family and sending me here!' He knocked the chief of police down on the ground and kicked him mercilessly. One of the German officers took out his pistol. But Moshe Chasid turned to the officer and said: 'No, please. Why waste your bullet? I'll finish him off.' And that is indeed what he did. Then they marched the policemen, and they marched beautifully, as they had practiced. They were not taken like the rest of the people to the barracks in Birkenau. They were marched directly to the building with the tall chimney. I later heard two kapos talking and one of them said to the other: 'Such stupid people, to arrive here in uniform'."

Excited and agitated, I left the man. Even though I was already used to the suffering and the horrifying sights, Yitzchak Epstein's words had an extremely severe impact on me. On my way to the kapo Dudu's barrack I thought a lot about the chief of police who was slaughtered by Moshe Chasid. I thought about how much history repeated itself. The German did not have to waste a bullet on Rosenblatt, for there was a Jew who would put an end to his brother with his own hands. Just like the story of Moses in Egypt.

The Fateful Promise

Father's plight grew steadily worse. He got weaker with every passing day; he barely stood on his own feet. During the runs to the apels, to drink water, or to the toilets, my friends and I used to make a sort of wall around him so that they would not sense his weakness. Melech Appelion would run in front of him, Aharon Gustinsky at his side, while I was behind him, pushing him and giving him support. Father tried with all his strength to make it easier for us by running, but he would stumble and fall, stumble and keep going.

Dudu kept his promise. Every day I would find on his plank a slice of bread for me. We also repeated our operation for getting soup. It succeeded every day. The people who carried the heavy vats changed every day, and this made it easier for us. When the kapos appeared in the barracks to choose the people who would bring the soup from the kitchen, nearly everyone would pounce on them. Even those who could barely drag their feet were anxious to carry the heavy load, hoping to receive a little extra soup in exchange for his work. The kapos would be "forced" to use their clubs in order to choose several "fortunate ones" for this work.

I protected the clog that Dudu gave me. He was right when he said that this shoe, a simple wooden clog, was a real treasure in Auschwitz, a treasure to which no golden jewelry or diamonds could compare in this place. But the slices of bread I received from Dudu and the additional sips of soup that we endangered our lives to obtain were not enough to bring my father back to health. I thought that he needed a larger portion, so I would drink last from the soup. I drank just a drop or two, something I could not ask of my starving friends. But this didn't help him either. Father was already very sick. He was broken physically and spiritually. One day I took advantage of the commotion aroused in the barracks when people shoved and shouted that the distribution of the soup should begin on their side, and the kapos wielded their cudgels to impose some sort of order. When all this was going on, I grabbed a small pot, which I hid under my broad coat. From then on we had a pot in addition to the clog, and that meant we had more soup. We changed our course of action. Melech Appelion would run by an unguarded pot, dip the vessel into the pot and flee with the precious liquid. I would chase after him and threaten him with my clog, and at the appropriate moment, I would put the clog inside it, take out soup, and quicken my pace. And then Aharon would appear and chase after me as he screamed and cursed. Our schemes worked, but each and every day we reexperienced the terrible fear that some kapo might catch us.

Unfortunately, even the thick and salty liquid was not enough to help my father. He began to cut himself off from the world. A dark depression overtook him. He spoke much of the past, of Mother and Talka. "If only I could meet them in the next world," he would say occasionally to himself.

Of this world he asked nothing, except to be left alone. Even so, when he heard the whistle, he would try to run as we supported him. I knew that he was doing this for me. I saw his battle but I felt that I was losing him, and despair ate away at me. Father also tried to strengthen me. One day he asked me to swear that I would always fight for my life, and that I would not let them overcome me.

"Your life is all that you have. Even though in the eyes of the Germans the life of a Jew is of no importance, it is very precious. Remember that we are born only once. And you are young, strong, and fast. You have a chance to get out of here. You have an obligation to get out of here."

I looked at my father. His face had a sort of radiance, as though the spirit of prophecy enveloped him. His eyes widened and a light smile appeared around his lips. "I feel, Luzer, not only feel but know for certain, that you will get out of here, out of this hell. And then, in a different world, you will tell what *Amalek* (the name for the ancient enemy of the Jews) has done to us because we were Jews. And perhaps," my father continued to daydream, "perhaps you will reach Israel and live out my unrealized dream. You will have a family and continue our line."

I felt Father's words anointing me with strength, despite the horrible conditions in Auschwitz.

"Father," I tried to strengthen his spirits a little as well, though I didn't really believe it. "Father, I will fight not only for myself but for the two of us. I am sure that both of us will get out of here."

But Father only sighed. "No, my son, it's better that you get used to the thought that the day will come when you will remain without me. I will not get out of here. I know this for certain. And, believe me, it's better that way for both of us. It will be much easier for you to manage without me. I only weigh you down and endanger you as well."

Of no help were my pleas or my explanations that my worry for him only strengthened me. Father tried to explain to me that his soul had died the moment they took Mother and Talka, and only his body suffered. For me alone was he trying ceaselessly to fight his weakness, without success. He explained that it was unimportant if he continued to suffer in this way another day and another day.

"If only the next world really existed..." said Father and did not continue. This was the only time I ever heard him doubt his religious faith.

To reassure him I promised my father that I would protect my life, that I would not give it up easily. At the time I did not know how difficult this promise would be to fulfill. I could not imagine that the time would come when I would wish to die, and that only this promise would prevent me from bringing about my end.

The "Days of Awe" in Auschwitz

My father's health got worse from day to day. His body was tortured in the frequent runs. As soon as we heard the first whistle for the apel we tried to get him up so that he would not be late, God forbid; we immediately surrounded him. Each time I left the barrack for bread or additional soup, I was terrified that I would not find him in his place when I returned. At a wild and breathless run I would fly across the distances separating the barracks, and only when I saw him lying in his place would I relax somewhat.

One day when I returned—by a twist of fate it was a day in which I returned happy since Dudu had left me two portions of bread—I did not find my father. My friends waited for me beside the barrack. They notified me, with downcast eyes, that just after I had left the barrack Father had asked them to help him get up. He parted from them and requested through them to deliver his parting words to me. He went to the revier.

I felt my head spinning, as though the walls were swaying. My friends supported me so I wouldn't fall. Only when a stream of tears burst forth from my eyes did I feel a little bit better.

What I had feared had happened. I knew that this time I had lost my father forever.

Even so, I still did not give up. I immediately ran to the revier. I could not knock on the barrack walls, for the revier was separated from the rest of the barracks with a barbed wire fence. Only its entrance was not surrounded by a fence, but the heavy door was closed.

I returned to my barrack and lay down in my place. On that day and the next I did not go to get additional food. Neither did my friends. Perhaps they did not dare try our operation without me. We all lay silently on our plank which was now more spacious.

I remained in shock for two days, but then I started running to the revier again. I was frightened. Who knew if Father was still there? Perhaps they already had taken him to the gas chambers?!

I lay in wait outside the barrack. I did not move from there. How could I know if Father was still inside?

When people came to the revier carrying a pot of soup on two poles, I hesitantly approached them and helped them. The heavy door was opened and we went inside. I quickly scanned the interior of the revier. The conditions here seemed inestimably better than in the ordinary barracks. Each man lay on his own plank and the sick people were covered with dark blankets. I quickly proceeded along the planks and on one of them I found my father. He also lay covered with a blanket. He was taken aback to see me, but at the same time, happy.

"Get out of here quickly, and don't you dare come here again. The main thing is that you can see with your own eyes that I am better off here. We don't go out to the rollcalls. Now, flee from here," Father said hastily.

I slipped out before anyone had noticed me. I radiated with happiness. I had seen my father. He was lying on his own plank and was even covered with a blanket.

Maybe what Dudu had said was not true, I thought to myself. Perhaps they did take care of the sick here.... I was calmer when I returned to the barrack. The sight of my starving friends lying on the plank touched my heart.

"Aharon, Melech, get up!" I turned to them in a thunderous whisper, "We're going hunting!" (That's what we called our soup operation). They raised their heads in disbelief.

"What happened? Have you seen your father?" the two of them asked at once.

"Yes," I replied, "Imagine, I was in the revier and I saw my father. He has his own plank and even a blanket."

"A blanket?" cried out Aharon Gustinsky in amazement.

"An entire plank?" added Melech Appelion.

As soon as I told my friends that we were going to get some soup, the two of them seemed to suddenly return to life—they were filled with newfound strength.

From that day on we had enough soup. We divided the soup from our hunt equally among the three of us. But with every swallow I took, I felt as though I were choking—for Father was no longer getting his share. I had enough to eat and he was certainly hungry.

I was unable to sneak inside the revier again, even though I stood there for hours each day. I was hoping to enter if only for a moment to give my father the bread or the soup which I kept for him. The heavy door was always closed, and when the soup was distributed only the kapos and their helpers went inside.

Each day, when I went there, I felt unsteady and frightened; who knew if the sick people were still there, or whether they had, God forbid, been taken from there already?! Each day I was relieved when I saw that they brought a pot of soup into the revier. That was a sign that the sick people were still there.

Meanwhile, the New Year arrived, Rosh Hashanah in Auschwitz, and with it the days of repentance. Why were these days called "the days of awe"? Were there days more awful than those in Auschwitz, when each man was torn from everything that was precious to him; in which the human form was erased hour by hour, turning each person into an unidentifiable figure, humiliated and starved?

We also used to call those days the ten days of repentance, during which Jews prayed to God for pardon and forgiveness for the transgressions they had committed knowingly and unwittingly. But here in Auschwitz, we Jews were already being punished for the sins of all the generations put together, and much more on top of that.

I found out about the arrival of Rosh Hashanah early one morning when I heard a quiet rumbling coming from outside the barrack. Afraid, I leaped off the plank and peeked outside. Beside the barrack adjacent to ours, many men stood and prayed. Amazingly, no kapo was anywhere to be seen. I asked someone what this prayer was about and was told that it was Rosh Hashanah.

I knew that the adjacent barrack, which had been emptied after the selection held the day before (in which the healthy men were chosen to be sent to a work camp while the weak were placed on the left side to be killed) had been filled by a new transport of men from Hungary. The Hungarian Jews, who had not yet experienced the terrible hunger which we had known already for years, looked better than the Jews from Poland. They even remembered the dates of the holidays. But there were among us also religious Jews who despite all that had happened to them had not lost their faith but somehow were able to cling to it. My father was one of them; even here he kept track of the days that passed and knew the dates of the holidays.

A few men from our barrack, who went out like me upon hearing the noise, joined the praying men. I did not join, but I thought of my father. I was sure that if he were here he too would join the service. I slipped once again to the revier block. Immediately my breath was taken away from me: on the far side of the barrack, behind the barbed wire fence, I saw figures wrapped in blankets, standing and praying. I moved closer. The darkness had begun to lift a little. I stood on the other side of the barbed wire fence and scanned each figure. One of them, wrapped in a black blanket as though it were a tallith, raised his head. It was my father. He recognized me and even smiled at me. I stood in my place and could come no closer, as we were separated by the barbed wire. Through his smile I could see the tears which covered Father's face. Tears covered my face as well.

The following morning, I too joined those who stood praying in the square of the adjacent barrack. All was still dark. From within the darkness I could distinguish a gray block of men swaying in the tempo of prayer. Voices ascended from within the block, the thin voices of young boys. Before darkness lifted I left this group and again ran to the revier. Father stood in the same place I had seen him the previous day. I saw satisfaction in his eyes when our eyes met. I had just turned to leave when I noticed another man leaving the revier, the assistant of a certain kapo. He was alone. I'll try my luck, I said to myself. I approached the man and stuffed in his hands a slice of bread that I had with me. Then I pointed to my father, told him that I was his son, and he should give this bread to my father. He looked around to make sure that no one was watching us and promised me he would fulfill my request. I saw this as nothing less than a miracle. I returned, happy, to the place I had stood in the beginning, from where I had first seen my father standing and praying.

"Father," I called to him in a whisper, "I gave bread for you to the assistant kapo." Father nodded his head and continued in his prayer.

That sight, the image of my father wrapped in a blanket as though it were a tallith, swaying here and there in prayer, will remain with me as long as I live. This was the last time I saw my father.

From then on, whenever I went to the revier, the door was locked. And on the following days guards were also placed there. It was impossible to be anywhere near the place. I was seized with fear. These were the most horrible days that I had known since my arrival in Auschwitz.

One day, when we stood in an apel, before the Germans had arrived to survey us, I saw the assistant kapo to whom I had given the bread for my father. The man held a note in his hand and as he walked he looked around him and whispered: "Luzer Zyskind, Luzer Zyskind." I trembled all over. "I'm here, I'm here," I whispered in his direction. He tarried beside me and pretended he was bending down to remove some obstacle from his path. At the same time he handed me a note.

"My son Eliezer," Father wrote to me.

My son Eliezer,

As you know, I am in block 24. Please see if Dudu Wiesel can come here today. We hope that with God's help you will be able to send me a little soup.

Your father

"It's been two days since the sick have received food," the assistant kapo whispered to me.

Inside my coat I held a pot of soup. I always carried some kind of food with me. I always thought that I might be able to give it to my father. I took out the pot and told the assistant kapo: "Give this to my father. God will repay you for this." He hid the pot under his coat and left.

I have no idea how Father found paper and a pencil in Auschwitz. But this note, the last sign from my father, has stayed with me as though it were the biggest treasure in the world.

I don't know if the soup ever reached my father, but I would be prepared to give up years of my life just to know if he did indeed eat it.

The day before Yom Kippur they brought trucks to the revier and took away the sick. The revier was left empty. One could now approach it freely.

On Yom Kippur eve we heard the *Kol Nidrei* prayer from the square of the adjacent barrack. I went outside and looked at the red heavens toward which sparks of fire and pillars of smoke ascended from the giant chimneys, and I knew that my father's soul had also ascended to the heavens.

The Selection

I was left alone. On Yom Kippur I fasted without feeling it. The soup that they gave out in the barrack I only brought to my mouth, but did not drink. I ran together with everyone to the faucets, but no water touched my lips. My mind was left emptied. Only two sentences repeated themselves relentlessly: "Father was asphyxiated to death in the gas chambers. And Mother and Talka ended in the same way."

For two days I lay on the plank like a machine which had stopped working. Nothing interested me. Both my friends, Aharon and Melech, were like brothers in their sincere concern and it was they who brought me out of it. On the following day, when they brought soup and I pushed away the pot without tasting any, I suddenly felt a strong slap on my face. Melech Appelion had hit me.

"Drink," he said forcefully, "or I'll slap you again. Now we are all equal. We also lost here all that was most precious to us, we also have been left alone. Thank God that we are together and can help one another. This way it will be easier and maybe we will even get out of here. We must continue living. Remember the promise you made your father."

"Tomorrow we will continue our soup hunt as usual," added Aharon Gustinsky.

But the following day we did not go soup hunting. Early in the morning we heard a sharp whistle. "What is that? An apel?" everyone asked himself. But this time it was not an apel. When we were in place out on the big square, a group of kapos appeared. They walked among us shouting: "Selection! Get undressed!" Every person in Auschwitz knew the meaning of a selection: who would live and who would die.

Suddenly, a new spirit awoke in me, and I wanted to live. My father was right, I said to myself. I must protect my life. They must not take it away from me easily. The three of us must live. We must get out of here, be sent to work. Indeed, we were thin, but we were young, and in contrast to the adults and the weak skeletons of men, we looked quite good. Also the supplementary food that we obtained by scavenging, when others were dying of starvation, gave us added strength and even a little confidence. Still, fear gripped us. Suddenly we felt how strong our bond was to one another, how precious we were to each other. "God," we prayed (at such moments we turned to God) "don't let them take any one of us, let us remain together."

There is nothing in the world comparable to the selection. While it is true that a flock of sheep also stands under similar scrutiny (which will live and which will be slaughtered), it does not go through such degradation, and the sheep remains until the end as it was created—with its coat of wool and fur. Only we, the Jews, stood there with the very form of man taken from us, naked and bent figures, skin and bones, with shaven heads. We knew what awaited us and there was nothing at all we could do. We had to pass before a group of armed German officers, tall, hardy, and impeccably dressed, who next to us looked like gods descended from Olympus. The differences between us and them were immeasurable. But even though we looked like an inferior race, inside I was full of rebellion. I tried to imagine what those same officers would look like if they were in our place, starved and beaten for years, with shaven heads, without their splendid clothes. Indeed, these officers looked like proud peacocks in their shining boots and coats with velvet collars embroidered with silver. Beneath their white gloves I saw in my mind's eye their bloodstained hands. Were it not for my humiliating position, I would have certainly broken out in laughter as I imagined the sight of a plucked peacock, without its beautiful feathers and glorious tail.

Suddenly I remembered Gereck. Perhaps he was among them? How great would be his shame if his friends knew that a subhuman figure like me had marked his forehead for the rest of his life. For a moment I was filled with a wave of pride; but I quickly sobered up when I thought of how long ago that was. How much my humiliation and suffering had lowered my stature since then. I was no longer like I was then, when I had looked straight in his eyes during the rollcall in Bzezin. I was now afraid to steal even a quick look in the direction of the officers. Whatever I did could lead to my downfall. And I wanted to live.

Even though my head was bent I could still see the disgust and contempt which the Germans' eyes projected towards the "stain upon the human race" that stood before them. One of them, who stood a few steps in front of the other officers and even seemed taller than the rest, decided people's fate by merely moving his finger. We all knew this man's name. He had somehow received the title of doctor which meant that he had taken an oath that he would help people. And, indeed, that's what he did, for with the motion of his finger he put an end to the suffering of the weak and sick by sending them to the gas chambers. Dr. Mengele's name was famous.

Now he stood opposite us. Through the monocle over his eye he hastily glanced at each naked figure and pointed his finger to the right or to the left, to life or to death. He decided very quickly. He did not speak. There was no need for words. The movement of a finger was enough. Everyone carried out his decision unquestioningly.

I saw people who had been directed to the left try to run to the right side. Woe to the man who tried to disobey the decision of Dr. Mengele. A group of kapos, waiting for any sign of refusal, ran after the rebel and with rubber clubs punished him for his defiance, for his will to live after Dr. Mengele had decided otherwise. They would drag the man, who was by then dripping with blood, to the side which Dr. Mengele had decided upon.

Before our turn arrived I tried to give some advice to my two friends, who stood trembling with fear. I told them that we had to walk by freely, not look at the Germans, breathe in a lot of air so as to fill ourselves up with it, inflate our cheeks a little, and to stick out our stomachs. I went first. In one hand I held my clothes. I inflated my stomach and cheeks so that I would seem stronger. From the side I saw Dr. Mengele's finger point to the right, to life. I breathed a sigh of relief and stood beside the group destined to live. I now anxiously watched my friends. Thank God, luck was on their side as well. Our joy knew no bounds. If we hadn't been afraid, we would have jumped on top of each other, crying and kissing. But it was forbidden to move or show any emotion whatsoever. We were still within sight of the Germans and the kapos. Our hands just felt their way to hold each others' hands, squeezing one another's hands until they hurt. We would get out of here, we would get out alive from Auschwitz, we would be sent to work.

The clog remained in my pocket. On the next day we renewed our soup operation. We now felt more confident, stronger. And indeed from that day on we performed our "soup hunt" with great ease.

I once again visited Dudu. He understood when I stopped coming to him, that they had taken my father. He was happy that we had survived the selection. He even told me that he was jealous of us, for now we would be sent to work. That day he gave me two portions of bread. I was happy when I returned to my friends, and I divided with them what I had received. Four more days passed by. On the morning of the fifth day the familiar whistle was once again heard. This time we were run in a different direction. We were certain that they were sending us to work. I was sorry that I hadn't had the chance to say good-bye to Dudu.

We were run to the square behind the revier. In the center of the large square between the revier and the barrack which served as a laundry for the kapos' clothes, a sort of gate had been installed, made of three poles. Two of them were stuck in the ground and the third was set upon them horizontally. Beside the gate stood a group of officers and with them was that despicable man, the devil incarnate, Dr. Mengele, with white gloves on his hands and a magnifying glass in front of his eye. What was this supposed to be, we all wondered.

Our bodies trembled. Another selection? We had thought we were already chosen. It was already decided that we were fit to live. It quickly became clear to us that the previous selection was not the end of the road. But we had no time to think.

"Undress! Quickly, everyone undress!" the kapos yelled.

Apparently the gas chambers were not full enough, I thought to myself as my whole body broke out in a sweat. And that indeed was the case. To the Germans, masters of order and economy, it was a shame to empty boxes of gas when the cell did not contain the maximum number of people that could be compressed inside. The Cyclon B gas was too expensive and it had to be used to maximum efficiency. They therefore had concluded that it was necessary to hold another selection. Those who passed through the gate, whose head did not touch the horizontal pole, would be sentenced to death.

The three of us watched in fear as the people passed through. We saw clearly that the horizontal bar was higher than we were. So all was in vain after all. This was our end. We saw men who had also believed that they were chosen for life, now running on the tips of their toes, trying to jump up in order to touch the bar. But all their attempts were useless. The kapos saw through their charade. It was impossible to fool Dr. Mengele. Like hungry wolves they chased after the victim and with brutal blows dragged him to the left side. The kapos were joined by two overgrown dogs that helped them. The dogs stood panting, their long tongues hanging out, prepared to pounce. These dogs were well-trained and they would quickly catch their victim, insert their teeth in him and drag him to the correct side.

Melech Appelion went first. Aharon and I stood breathless. Melech started at a run. Beside the poles he gave a jump upward, and even touched the bar. But Dr. Mengele saw through his trick and his finger pointed to the left. Two kapos took hold of Melech and dragged him to the side of those who were sentenced to death.

Aharon's turn arrived. He was white as a ghost. He did not run. He walked on the tips of his toes. Again the all-powerful master's finger moved to the side of death. Even before the kapo's blows landed on him, I saw Aharon turn himself to the left side.

I knew that my fate would be like theirs, that I also would not reach the height of the bar. My mind raced. At least we will die together. It will be easier that way. We'll hold one another's hand even in the gas chamber, where everything must happen very quickly. And actually it will be redemption. Father, forgive me, I tried everything. Then a thought occurred to me. I had to fight for my life. That's what I had promised my father. So what if a dog stuck his teeth in my flesh? I would die anyway.

I stretched my body and with rapid steps began to approach the gate on my tiptoes. In my head I already had put together the plan. I had to try to do something to stay alive. I had nothing to lose.

I didn't continue walking all the way to the poles. Some distance before I arrived at the poles I sprang out to the side. Before the officers and kapos understood what had happened, I broke into a wild run. Even in my childhood, in which I earned the title of running champion, I had never run so fast. Before the kapos began chasing me I was already beside one of the barracks. From a distance I heard screams, curses, and even shots. I heard the whistle of a bullet as it passed right by my ear. With a jump I reached the barrack and clung to it. I had apparently undermined the whole order of the selection. I heard orders and shouts that they would catch me, but I had already climbed up the wooden wall of a barrack and had reached its roof. The slanted roof was flat in the middle. I quickly crawled across its entire length. I knew that at the end of each barrack there was a pit covered with a round concrete lid. Before I jumped from the roof I heard the barking of dogs and the screams of the kapos who had apparently reached the barrack and could not figure out where I was. With a quick leap I jumped off the roof, and reached the pit. I pulled the concrete lid and jumped inside the pit, as I held the lid over my head. I was lucky that the pit was not deep and I could remain standing as I closed the lid over my head. Darkness enveloped me. It was a blessed darkness. The kapos had apparently left. They had to return and restore order. I did not envy them at that moment. A few days later I heard that such a thing had never happened in Auschwitz. Never had a prisoner escaped from a selection while armed officers and kapos with dogs were on hand.

I don't know how long I sat in that pit, crumpled up and afraid. My throbbing head felt heavy. A strange noise

hummed in my ears. I was not satisfied with my accomplish-
ment. I did not want to live. I wanted only to be with my
friends, to die together with them. This was the first time I felt
the weight of the promise I had given my father. I had been
orphaned again, this time from my two friends. Only now could
I appreciate how close and dear they were to me—like my
brothers, my flesh and blood. And now I was left alone.

The silence in the pit began to be oppressive. I slowly
lifted the concrete lid. Outside it was dark. I barely managed
to lift the lid. My strength had apparently left me. Finally I
crawled out. I covered the pit and slipped into the barrack.
There was now plenty of room on the plank. Only two other
figures lay upon it. With my coat I covered myself over my
head and cried silently.

I don't know how many days we remained in Auschwitz.
Nothing interested me any longer. Like an automaton I ran
with everyone, like an automaton I knelt on my knees during
the apels. I no longer went to steal soup as in the earlier days.
In any case I no longer had the clog. It must have fallen out
of my pocket when I ran. Nor did I go again to visit Dudu.

It turned out that the man who remained on our plank was
Dr. Warhaft, the doctor from Bzezin. The way we looked, our
heads shaven, dressed in rags and starving, it was hard to
recognize one another. But Dr. Warhaft recognized me and
spoke to me. Still in shock from all I had undergone, I did
not hear or understand what he wanted from me.

I think that despite the promise I had given my father, at
that time I could no longer have fought for my life even if I
had had to stand in another selection. Fortunately, I did not
have to go through that again. One day the people of our
barrack were run with people from other barracks in the
direction of the gate of Auschwitz, the gate upon which it was
written: "Work makes you free." The big gate opened up and
we went out to a freight train that stood beside the platform.

I left Auschwitz. I had gotten out alive. It did not manage to swallow me, but it had taken everything from me, everything that is dear to a man in this world. It took my mother and father and my little sister, as well as my two friends Melech Appelion and Aharon Gustinsky.

The Bronshveig Work Camp

I continued to be indifferent to everything that happened, letting it pass over me as though it did not concern me, as though it all belonged to someone else while I was only standing and looking in from outside. Everything in me and around me was empty. I suppose I was better off that way, for otherwise I would surely have gone mad. Even so, I would occasionally return to the moments of happiness with my two friends after the three of us passed the first selection, to those hopes that we would finally leave Auschwitz and be sent to a work camp and that maybe we would even live to see the end of the war.

But those moments were few and far between, and I was so depressed that even the stories of the men in the railroad car, stories of which I was the subject, could not pull me out of my depths. These men did not stop talking about their amazement at the escape of one of the prisoners from the very midst of a selection. I myself was feeling so faint that none of the stories seemed to touch me, as if they had nothing to do with me. They continued to talk of the escape, and it seemed to me that this event gave them added strength and aroused in them new hope. They spoke of what happened afterwards in the selection yard: of the order which was disrupted, of the rantings of the Germans and the punishment received by the kapos. One of the German officers took a rubber club from the hands of one of the kapos and beat him till he was senseless, while the officers slapped and kicked other kapos. Even Dr. Mengele, usually so miserly with words, only moving his finger to the right or to the left, now screamed and cursed. Everything I heard, which at another time would have moved me deeply, could do nothing to lessen my depression.

For a long time the train sped ahead covering great distances, when suddenly it stopped opposite a platform and a big sign upon which was written the name "Bronshveig." Here too I continued to be indifferent and marched along with the other men, arranged as we were in fives, in the middle of the street of the big city. I don't know how long we marched like that, thousands of barefoot men with shaven heads, dressed in rags, surrounded by armed soldiers, who ordered us to march in time to their command: one, two, three!

We arrived at the outskirts of the city. As though on a screen I saw a big camp stretching out in front of us, encompassed by barbed wire fences. We saw a giant barrack in front of the camp, and two giant barracks inside the camp. The barracks were much bigger than those in Auschwitz. With indifference I climbed onto one of the planks of which the second half of the hall was full. Here and there could be heard calls of admiration for the sacks filled with straw which were given us as bedding. At the apel to which we were called after a short while, we were given wooden clogs and portions of bread.

"I hope," I heard the voice of Dr. Warhaft, who lay on the plank next to mine, "that we will be able to get through the war here. I hope conditions will prove to be different from Auschwitz. I should think we'll receive more food."

I did not answer Dr. Warhaft. My heart only ached because my friends had not made it, especially since they had come so close.

Dr. Warhaft's hopes that conditions would be better were quickly deflated. Not much time passed before it became clear that here too conditions were unbearable, that we were programmed for gradual death. But before we died we were to give over whatever remained of our strength to the German machine. Eventually I thanked God that my father never had to be here and was thus spared the additional months of torture.

That night, our first in Bronshveig, at four o'clock in the morning, a whistle blew like in Auschwitz. Into the barracks burst a gang of kapos who spurred us on with their clubs to go out to an apel.

There was a large space between the two barracks, which served as an apel yard. The kapos, apparently very bitter over having been awakened in the middle of the night, turned their rage against us. Amidst brutal blows they arranged us in rows. We had to stand at attention for two full hours in the chill of the night, which penetrated to our bones. With the break of dawn the count and the attendance check began. Everyone was called by his new "name," which here too was nothing but a number.

As six o'clock approached, we sensed a special excitement, like an electric current passing through the air. At exactly six o'clock the gate opened and a group of German officers accompanied by soldiers entered the camp. They surveyed us contemptuously and gave out orders to the kapos who ran about submissively. Thus they prepared us for the arrival of the great ruler, the camp commander, the *obersturmfuehrer*. He entered in measured steps, accompanied by S.S. officers. The officers and soldiers saluted him. He passed through the whole length of the inspection and looked over his slaves. Every once in a while he landed a blow with his whip on someone's head, whoever he felt was not standing properly. Afterwards he stood before us and began a speech filled with hatred and venom, using words like filth and shit, which left his mouth in the staccato rhythm of machine gun fire. From this speech we understood that we should work quickly and devotedly. We would not receive any free bread here. He forbade us from speaking with anyone at the factory, especially with captives from other nations. Everyone who broke this law would be sentenced to flogging until he would be *kaput* (finished).

If one of the *heftlinge* (slaves) should see that a Jew committed an illegal act and did not report it, we would all suffer the penalty, and there would be no food on that day. But a reward would be given to anyone reporting such an act; he would earn an additional portion of bread.

Next the speaker explained to us that before the war ended, all the Jews would be destroyed. When the speech was over we could see that the obersturmfuehrer was pleased with himself. It was clear in the triumphant look he directed to the stooped figures standing before him.

"And now march! To work!" he shouted.

This speech, as we heard it then, would repeat itself every day, with minor changes in the abominations. These speeches were enough to take away any crumbs of hope which we still had left when we were taken out of Auschwitz to the work camp. I used to think to myself sometimes that if we were doomed to die anyway, why didn't they just finish us off in Auschwitz. Why make us continue to suffer? Why did we have to work for the Germans?

I later learned that such speeches were given at all of the work camps to which Jews were taken. Everything here was thought out in advance—not only the speeches, but even the distances between the camp and the factory were taken into account in advance, so that we would tire ourselves out going and coming. The Germans who directed the camps—there were many throughout Germany—underwent a special course in how to exploit every ounce of Jewish strength before it finally gave out.

I was not at all bothered by his speech. Because of the

deaths of my father and friends I preferred that my life be terribly difficult, for then I would not be so sorry that they had died. What would happen to me was unimportant. I saw my life as a role I was meant to play out.

Despite the speech, we nonetheless had to raise our heads, straighten our backs and walk like soldiers, nicely and quickly, seven kilometers back and forth. Whoever did not do so was taught his lesson with a club.

We walked in the middle of the street, through the big city, which for some reason seemed empty of inhabitants. We were surrounded by kapos and soldiers. That day, although walking on the end, I didn't look at the residential buildings on the two sides of the street. I looked about me in a dazed stare until we arrived at the factory. Before long we saw a giant building, or rather two big buildings connected by a sort of bridge, which was hoisted above them like a gate. In the middle of the bridge was placed the symbol of a lion, and above it the inscription: Bisingwerke. This was a factory for the production of heavy vehicles and diesel engines.

We entered a big courtyard and were lined up in rows. Germans in civilian dress stood on the side. I looked at their faces. Their expressions showed wonder and disgust at the same time. Yes, we certainly looked contemptible compared to them. We, shaven figures, terrifyingly skinny, dressed in rags—and they, dressed in clean, tailored clothes and neatly combed. These were the work supervisors, called the meisters. Each meister received a group of however many people he needed for work.

I joined a group who followed our meister. He refrained from looking at us. It was clear that he was still not used to human monsters like us. We entered a giant hall filled with machines. I was the first one in the group that the meister signaled to approach a big machine and wait for his return. I stood beside the machine and he continued ahead with the group. After he had scattered everyone in their various places he returned to me and asked me if I understood German. With the exception of the first days of the war when my Aunt Chandzia and I sold butter to the German soldiers, this was the first time that a real German, a member of the superior race, had spoken to me directly. I replied by nodding my head. He told me to watch. Then he took a block of metal and inserted it in a special, lowered area in the machine. He then turned on the machine and it began to chisel. After a while a sort of cone was formed; I had no idea what it was for. I had to pay close attention and measure it with a special device to make sure that the height and width of the cone were in accordance with the exact dimensions required. When the cone was ready, the meister put it in a basket which stood on the side and took a second block of metal. This time he gave me the block and I was to put it into the machine and chisel it until it took on the appropriate form and size.

At first this was not so simple. Each time I thought it was still a little too big I continued to chisel, until the cone was too small and had to be thrown into a different basket for defective parts. The meister got angry and shouted. The two soldiers posted at the door as guards looked at me with open anger. I saw that I had to try to do my work better, and I did so. In truth, I strongly desired to ruin many blocks of metal so as to sabotage the German product, but I knew that that would have to wait for some other time, when the meister was far away. Thus I continued doing my work. When the meister was sure that I understood my job and could complete a cone successfully, he left me for the other workers who waited beside their machines. Once he left me I could, in addition to the cones I had damaged in the beginning of my work, intentionally sabotage several blocks of metal. I was not afraid of the soldiers who stood at the entrance. I was sure that they didn't know how to determine the quality of my work. Unfortunately for me, it wasn't as I imagined. The meister returned to me, for some reason, before he completed his explanations to all the other members of the group. I didn't see him come and stand behind me.

"Donnervetter!" (Dammit!), he raised his voice at me, "Can't you see that you have already chiseled too much, that we'll have to throw all this into the furnace to melt back down. With determined steps he walked over to the basket containing the defective parts, turned it over, and poured its contents out on the floor. He bent over the floor and counted the number of defective pieces.

"Listen," he said with emphasis, "if you mess up so many pieces again, I'll have to notify my superiors about it, and you know what that means. This material is very expensive and must not be wasted." I didn't answer him, but I understood very well that it was dangerous for me to act in this way and that my behavior had been foolish.

Within a few hours I had learned the work, which became easy and even pleasant. But that was just the beginning. As the hours passed my legs felt heavier, my back began to hurt and the hunger got oppressive. The long day, which had begun at four o'clock in the morning, continued endlessly. When the clock on the wall showed that it was only ten o'clock, the meister sat down near me and took a sandwich wrapped in white paper from his case. The powerful aroma of smoked salami reached my nostrils and drove me out of my mind. I swallowed my saliva and turned my head so as not to see the meister as he devoured his food. At the same time the soldiers who sat beside the door leaning on their rifles dipped their hands into their packs and began to take out food. One of the soldiers held a hard-boiled egg and began to peel it. I looked at him as though I were in a trance. God, I had completely forgotten that such things existed in the world. How many years had it been since I had eaten an egg? But what am I thinking about, of delicacies such as eggs?, I thought to myself. Just my fill of dry bread would be enough.

Another two long hours passed. At exactly twelve o'clock we heard a bell. That meant we had to arrange ourselves by the exit. Two rifle-bearing soldiers led us to a big hall in which stood tables and benches. At the end of the hall were kapos beside big vats of soup. Even from far off the aroma of the soup was potent. The smell alone was enough to drive us mad because nothing had entered our mouths since the evening before. It's no wonder we each pushed toward the vats in an effort to receive our portion first. That sight delighted the German soldiers and they hurried to call the meisters so that they too could watch the show, Jews pushing and cursing one another in order to be first in line to receive the soup. I sensed that my indifference began to diminish, as my entire being rebelled at the sight of those coarse and sated faces, filled with contempt. If you were in our places, if you were hungry like us, how would you behave, I thought to myself.

With the aid of the kapos' clubs we arranged ourselves in lines, and my turn arrived. I, along with everyone else, received a metal bowl with a spoon, a real spoon. Here, in the factory, we ate with spoons, not like in Auschwitz, where we ate with our hands. The soup that I received was very hot, nearly boiling, but I didn't have the patience to let it cool. I devoured it in a moment, regardless of how hot it was. It did not satisfy me. In fact it only stimulated my appetite. So I remained hungry. Meanwhile the kapos were busy beating those who tried to sneak into the line to receive additional soup.

Soon the eating break ended and we had to return to work. We worked an additional eight long hours until eight o'clock in the evening. The meister and the soldiers would prepare meals for themselves at various intervals, the smell of which reminded me of the distant home I once had, and our stomachs refused to recognize the fact that we were now sub-humans who must make do with what we were given.

At eight o'clock in the evening we heard a whistle and were ordered to arrange ourselves in the courtyard to begin walking back to camp. After such a day, being so tired and hungry, the way back seemed several times longer than it had in the morning. But our guards made sure that the marching in the streets was proper and uniform. It was nearly ten o'clock at night when we arrived back at camp.

While we were marching I had only one thought—to reach my plank and rest my head on it. That plank now became my most precious object. Before I even had a chance to lie down, another whistle split the air. But this time it was a redeeming whistle. They gave us a little soup and bread, an eighth of a loaf of bread per person. We received the food in the front section of the barrack. Despite our exhaustion, once again confusion and chaos took over, and again the kapos began to restore order with their clubs.

I finished drinking my soup while I was still on my way back to my plank. I didn't touch the piece of bread. I shoved it into my coat pocket resolving to keep the bread until the next day and eat it at the factory.

I was unable to carry out my decision. The dry piece of bread gave me no rest. I lay on the plank and could not fall asleep. Finally, I decided to slice a tiny piece. Then one more crumb. Then another crumb, until all that was left was a small remnant which I angrily finished in a moment. I was upset with myself for not having been able to overcome my hunger, and I tried to convince myself that if I had not eaten my portion it would certainly have been stolen from me. Finally I fell asleep. It seemed that my eyes were closed for only a short moment when the hated whistle aroused us all again from the planks. Only now did I feel the full fatigue of the previous day, but there was no time to think. The kapos

already stood in the barrack and as usual they waved their
clubs and beat us, shouting at us to move faster. We had no
choice but to go out. Once again it was four o'clock in the
morning and a work day began.

Autumn was already well under way—which meant cold and
powerful winds. Again the apel lasted two hours although
that day it seemed much longer. The obersturmfuehrer's
speech seemed more poisonous, the workday at the factory
continued endlessly, and even the hunger was stronger.

Again the following day, the big whistle awakened us to go
out to work. That day, I remember my stomach hurt terribly.
I tried to get to the toilets which were in the front part of the
barrack. But I didn't make it; the kapo pushed me toward the
exit. "Quickly," he yelled, "the apel is beginning!"

All the while the apel continued as usual for two hours.
During the march, which lasted an hour and a half, I felt that
my stomach would explode, but even when we arrived at the
factory I was unable to relieve myself, for first I had to begin
working.

Going to the bathroom entailed an entire procedure. The
bathrooms for the Jews were in the factory courtyard, in a
small wooden cabin which appeared to have been recently
built. Here there was not a collective bathroom as in
Auschwitz; each seat with a hole was in a separate cell and a
door even closed in front of it. But in order to go there one
had to raise his hand and request permission.

Now we were dependent on the kindness of the two soldiers who guarded us. We were allowed to leave the machine
and stand at a distance from the soldiers. Only when one of
the soldiers nodded his head did you know that in a little
while you would be permitted to go out and relieve yourself.
In a little while and not immediately, for you had to stand
and wait until another five heftlinge also asked permission,
and only then would one of the soldiers, his rifle slung over

his shoulder, go out with the group going to the bathroom. The amount of time we could stay on the toilet was limited, and when the soldier who was waiting outside decided that enough time had passed, he would knock with his rifle on the outer door and shout that we had already wasted enough time or that perhaps someone had fallen asleep?

It was, therefore, clear to me that I would not be able to earn such luxuries immediately upon arriving at the factory, and only after it seemed to me that enough time had passed (for I could hold out no longer), did I raise my hand to attract the attention of the soldier. But the soldiers, who ordinarily never took their eyes off us, chose now to ignore me completely. When one of the soldiers finally deigned to notice my outstretched arm, he shook his head in an absolute no and with an angry look: how dare I make such a request just a short time after arriving at work. I suffered horribly until I finally was allowed, with five others, to go to the bathroom.

There were many other nights when I did not manage to overcome my hunger and keep the little piece of bread for the next day. After a while I stopped trying to fight with myself. I knew that I would not conquer the hunger, so as soon as I lay down on my plank I devoured the whole portion at once, and I did not regret it.

On the third day after our arrival in the camp a torrential rain poured down on us as we stood in the apel. The rain wet us down to our bone marrow. It stopped, as if by miracle, before six o'clock, when the Germans entered the camp. The sun came out from behind the clouds and began to shine in all its splendor. I now hated the sun; it seemed to me that it too was mocking us, the Jews.

That morning, as we marched through the streets of Bronshveig—our clothes soaked and sticking to our bodies, while our water-filled clogs clattered and made walking more difficult—I suddenly rid myself of my indifference, and said to myself: I am happy that my father did not arrive here. He avoided all this additional suffering. His body was so tortured. He would not have been able to take this suffering for even a single day. It was not surprising that they only chose the young and strong. Then I remembered my friends, who were young and strong and could have coped as well as the others, but luck had not been on their side. Was this indeed luck? Would we be able to hold out for long in these conditions? Would not the hunger and the hard work take its toll? Perhaps the obersturmfuehrer was right when he said that after the war not a single Jew would be left in the world.

That was the first time I raised my head during the march and looked around me. On both sides of the street I saw tall buildings, and in them were windows covered with curtains and plants. Flowers were on the windowsills. I saw human figures hiding behind the curtains, watching the long convoy of monstrous men marching in the middle of the road, guarded by armed soldiers.

Sundays

We knew that the factory would be closed every Sunday, since that was the Christian Sabbath. Desperately, we looked forward to that day in which we would not have to march fourteen kilometers to and from the factory, we would not have to work twelve hours, and perhaps there would be no roll call. For one blissful day we could lie on our planks and not move, just lie down and sleep.

The long-awaited day arrived. The familiar whistle awoke us and we all ran to the apel, but outside it was no longer dark, as in the apels during the rest of the week. The grayness in the air had already begun to scatter, and we were greeted by the first light of early morning.

So it's true! Today we will finally be able to rest and gather strength for the following week, I said to myself. They quickly made us realize our mistake. While they did not wake us at the usual hour of four in the morning, and we were not ordered to walk the great distance to the factory, this was not a day of rest for us. This was a day of backbreaking labor, immeasurably harder than on ordinary days.

During the morning apel after the obersturmfuehrer's habitual speech filled with slander, abominations and insults to the Jews, he informed us that a pile of bricks had been laid in the incorrect place, and we were ordered to move them from one end of the camp to the other. We had to perform the work as quickly as possible, and only then would we be permitted to rest.

I was horrified when I recalled the mountain of bricks laid at the edge of the camp. How would we manage to move them to the other side of the camp during a single day, a distance of about two kilometers? But the Germans had their own plan. German soldiers, as well as kapos with sticks and clubs in their hands, were placed along the length of the giant camp to watch over the workers and guarantee that the work would be done rapidly.

As soon as the apel ended we were run to the pile. Kapos, who made sure that we did not take too few bricks, stood here. I loaded three bricks on myself, one on top of the other, and turned to go, but the kapo stopped me.

"Slob!" he yelled and piled on another two bricks. I began to run; the load was heavy but I comforted myself with a secret plan. I decided, on the way when no one was looking, I would throw two bricks aside. Also, I wouldn't walk too fast. This is work for many hours and I must protect my strength. But I was not able to do that, for there was not a single part of the way that was not guarded, and the distance from kapo to kapo was too short. Even when we ran by them, and were doing everything perfectly, they sometimes hit us on our heads with their clubs. In fact, it was usually those who had dropped a brick by mistake who were beaten, and not those who had done it on purpose. I was barely able to complete the two kilometers, burdened as I was with the five bricks. On the way back I pretended to be running, but I didn't run fast. Each time I reached a place where there was a kapo I slipped quickly by so that he would not have a chance to beat me over the head. On one of the rounds I loaded four bricks. I was out of the kapo's field of vision, so I succeeded in fooling him. I lifted the bricks high and rested my chin upon them, so that it looked from the outside as if there was no room for an additional brick, and they couldn't tell that I had taken only four bricks instead of five. Even four bricks were very heavy. My legs and back hurt. We ran back and forth while time crawled by slowly. The day, like the pile of bricks, was endless.

That sight—of Jews running piled with bricks, while task-masters with clubs in their hands beat them—reminded me of something from the distant past. My sister Talka, who was then a little girl and still didn't know how to read, received an illustrated Haggada on Passover night. On the first page there was a picture of slaves and slavedrivers, and under the picture were the words: "We were slaves unto the Pharaoh of Egypt." Father explained to Talka the meaning of the words, and we all pitied the miserable Jews of yesteryear, even though we knew they were no longer alive. We pitied them year after year.

But now I envied them. We would have been better off if they had enslaved us with hard labor and even beat us, but had not separated our families, and not starved us. The Jewish families in Egypt stayed together. And I never read that they were hungry for bread or that they were murdered in gas chambers. In those days, God had mercy on His people, heard their cries and helped them to freedom. Because of such thoughts I sometimes slowed down, and the lash of a whip on my back would remind me where I was. Why didn't God hear us now?

Day was turning to evening when we finished moving the bricks to the other end of the camp. Tired and broken, much more so than on a regular day, we dragged ourselves to our barrack. We were so tired that we forgot about eating. The kapos arranged us in line for soup and bread. This time we all stood quietly. We were just too tired to push.

After a while we understood that they hadn't mistakenly placed the bricks on the edge of the camp, for on the next Sunday we had to take them back to their previous location, and so on and so on.

I eventually found out that each Sunday that same hard labor was the lot of the Jews in all of the work camps, even those containing women.

Two Kapos

During our first week in the camp, I got to know the *lageralteste* (elder, or head, of the camp) and our kapos, who were many and varied. Two of them are unforgettable because of their cruelty. One of them was a strong, burly man, with a dark face, and black forelock and black moustache. We called him "the Gypsy." We were told that he actually was a gypsy, who because of his great strength had been chosen to be a kapo. After his entire family had died he had become completely unemotional and very cruel.

The second kapo, whose name was Herman, was also strongly built. He had a pugilistic face with a flat nose and looked like a bulldog. We called him "Boxer." He was pure German; that was his pride. He was also proud that he had been a professional boxer. He would sometimes roll up his sleeves to show us his muscles. He, like the lageralteste, had been locked up in prison for many years, and had been let out in order to serve as a kapo in the concentration camps, a role which he filled faithfully. He demonstrated his hatred for the Jews at every opportunity, much more than was required.

One Sunday, Herman strutted into our barrack, and, even before they began distributing food, jumped up on the table, rolled up his sleeves and announced loudly that he wished to box with one of the heftlinge. He promised that anyone who volunteered to box would receive an extra portion of bread, and whoever defeated him would receive a full loaf.

A tense silence filled the barrack. We looked at one another in fear. None of us moved an inch. But the kapo Herman, fresh and well fed, had an urge to use his muscles against us. His fists were itching. After no one responded to his call he pointed to someone who stood close to the table.

"You!" shouted Herman at the man, "Come here and give me a box. I give the first shot even to a stinking Jew."

The man lowered his head. His whole body trembled and he didn't move from his place. But Herman was used to having his way. He jumped from the table like a cat, grabbed the man by the collar of his coat, and dragged him to the middle of the hall.

Terrified and breathless I watched the scene. Right beside me, one of the residents of the barrack sobbed. I didn't know if this was a relative of the man or not, because I also felt like crying. Herman still tried to provoke his victim to hit him first, but in vain. The man stood paralyzed and motionless.

"So that's it!" screamed Herman, "Miserable Jewish coward! It's not enough that I let you go first, you don't even listen to me. Take that!" And the kapo let his fist fly at the man's belly. The man doubled over from the blow, almost to the floor, and then Herman, in a well-practiced move, grabbed him under the chin and straightened him up. Now he struck him a second time, on his head, and the man fell unconscious on the floor.

"Take this trash away from here!" Herman shouted and appointed two men to carry out his order. Before the two had a chance to leave with the unconscious victim the kapo had already turned to us again.

"So, who's in line now?" Everyone tried to make himself smaller, we all wanted to be invisible and the Earth to open up its mouth and swallow us up. Meanwhile, Herman measured us with his small, narrow eyes and then he pointed to his next victim, and again he hit him from all sides, until he too fell unconscious to the ground. Herman eased up on the third man when a stream of blood burst from his nose, and after him came the fourth, the fifth and the sixth, weakened and dangling figures who fell down one after the other. When they were taken out, Herman found others.

Filled with hatred, I clenched my fists and watched what was going on. If only a miracle that would make me a strong man would happen, I could teach him a lesson. Of course I did not know how to box and I did not have muscles like Herman, but the will to kill him made me fantasize. I would not stand there silently and wait to be kicked like a straw-filled sack. If called on, I would prove how fast I was. I would kick with my wooden shoe perfectly, right in his groin, and then watch this putrid Herman crumble, unconscious, to the floor. Thus, I would reap revenge for everyone. Even if I had to pay for it with my life, it would be easy to die knowing that I had wounded this cursed devil. As my mind raced with these imaginary thoughts I was about to move forward into his line of vision, and then my entire body began to tremble. The miracle did not happen. Instead I remembered the promise I had given my father to protect my life and fight for it. I shrank. Now for the first time in a long while, since Rosh Hashana, I turned to God in prayer, asking him to protect me and not let the man named Herman point to me and take me out. Miracles don't happen in our day, I said to God in my prayer. I know myself and I know that I am not a hero and there's no way I'll be able to stand before that well-fed mountain of muscles...before that Jew hater.

Luckily God heard my prayer that time and I didn't have to stand the test.

More victims fell at Herman's hands before he decided that the day's game was over. He jumped lightly onto the table and with a victorious smile praised himself:

"That's it! You have all seen what it means to be a real unbeatable German boxer. Now, you stinking sissies, line up for your food!"

I was so tired that I barely made it to my plank. On my way there I finished my soup. The bread remained in my pocket. I was too tired to touch it. Before I fell asleep I figured out that it was no later than eight o'clock in the evening, and I would have lots of time to sleep until the four o'clock apel.

I slept so soundly that my neighbor, who slept on the plank above me, shook me vigorously. "Get up quickly!" he yelled at me. "You didn't hear the whistle for the apel. Everyone's already outside."

This was not the usual night apel. It was eight thirty in the evening, only half an hour after I had lay down to sleep. The kapos divided us into two groups. We were told that now we would work in the factory in two shifts: a day shift and a night shift. That week I was chosen to work in the night shift. We were also told that the night shift would begin at eight in the evening, but this time we had been lucky and would begin work at ten.

We marched into the night against a strong wind, which made it more difficult to walk. After we had covered only half the distance, an annoying rain began to fall. Within a few minutes it had turned to heavy hail. The balls of ice hit my face, slid over my shaven head, fell on my neck, and down my back. I felt them melting on my body. But in a sense that was good. I kept hoping the cold would take the cobwebs out of my head, the sleepiness from my body.

But I was not that lucky. I think that was one of the longest nights of my life. The whole night I fought off sleep and was barely able to stand. I looked yearningly at the floor—if only I could lie on it for a few minutes and close my eyes! But I could not even lean on the machine. The two soldiers who sat opposite me guarded well. And the meister, who certainly must have rested throughout most of the day in preparation for the night shift, would pass by me occasionally and give me a push, to make me work faster. He had not spoken to me since that first day when he explained my work to me. He would pass by me, look in the basket at the finished cones, and then turn to the second basket to count and list the number of defects. This time he stopped right beside me and said something I didn't understand. My eyes wanted to close even with him next to me.

Fortunately, I recalled the slice of bread that I had not eaten before falling asleep. Every once in a while I picked off a crumb and chewed it. This helped me stay awake until the crumbs were finished—which happened very soon. At midnight we heard the redeeming whistle. We received hot liquid, but my battle against sleep continued. I found a trick: I raised my hand to ask permission to go to the bathroom. The wind that blew on my face when we went out to the courtyard woke me up a little and gave me some strength. In the bathroom I sat for a moment with my eyes closed. In fact, I actually fell asleep as I sat in the bathroom, and was awakened by a soldier banging his rifle on the door. Later, when I noticed that another group was organizing to go out to the bathroom, I raised my hand again and was allowed to join that group. In this way I managed to go out four times that night, but when I raised my head a fifth time, one of the soldiers shook his head. He must have noticed that I had already gone out a number of times.

I thought the night would never end. When we finally arrived at the camp and had been given our portions of bread and soup it was nearly eleven 11:00 a.m. I was too overtired to sleep immediately. The night shift was the hardest. The nights were endless, and days miserable, since we never got any rest. We usually had five hours for sleep, from 11:00 a.m. till the apel at 4:00 p.m. We always stood in the apel until 6:00, when the lageralteste appeared to deliver his familiar speech. Apparently even five hours sleep was too much in the opinion of our captors. They therefore disturbed us in the middle of our sleep. At about 2:00 or 3:00 p.m. we heard the familiar whistle—this time it was an intermediate whistle. A truck had arrived in the camp with a load of potatoes, or a truck with a load of vegetables, or coal, and these had to be unloaded and taken to the kitchen. At such times the kapos did not need to make us work faster, we ourselves hurried to finish the work so that we would be able to sleep a little more before the long night began.

Hunger and the accumulating exhaustion took their toll. I got so thin that I could count my ribs. I continued to be withdrawn and spoke with no one—including Dr. Warhaft who lay on the plank next to mine, who was from my home town, who used to come to our home, and who had known me since I was born. He was a distinguished gentleman. Even the Poles showed him respect, for he had served in the Polish army as a high-ranking officer. I could remember his magnificent uniform.

Now he was a shadow of a man, alone, tired, weak, and hungry, with shaven head, in rags like everyone else. On the plank above me lay another doctor, also famous—Dr. Ser from Lodz. My parents had always preached to me that I must study. They would explain to me that coins were round and could be lost, but one didn't lose that knowledge. It remained in one's head and could be used anywhere in the world. Here were two learned people, who carried with them the knowledge that could be used anywhere in the world... They were lucky, these two respected doctors—at least the kapo Herman did not choose them as boxing partners.

That week finally ended. On Sunday, when we returned to camp, we were immediately put to work transferring bricks from one side of the camp to the other. The people who worked the day shift had been toiling with the bricks all day. But I envied them. They, at least, had managed to snatch a few hours of sleep.

After we finished moving the bricks, I dragged myself with everyone else to the barrack to line up for food. My feet were so heavy that it seemed to me that instead of feet I was dragging two tree stumps that did not belong to me. Only now could I understand how my father felt when he said that his feet didn't carry him—he carried them. I looked hopefully at the soup they put in my bowl. Perhaps it would give me some encouragement and a little life. I was so tired that I didn't notice that the kapo we called "the Gypsy" had climbed onto the table and was swinging his club. Only when I passed by him did I hear his shout: "Move already!"

But that was too late because before I had a chance to realize that he was shouting at me, his club landed on my head. I lost consciousness and heard nothing more. When I opened my eyes everything was dark and quiet. I was lying on the floor and didn't know where I was. A strange noise buzzed in my head and my left ear hurt terribly.

As my eyes began to adjust to the darkness, I could see that I was in the bathroom in the front part of the barrack. Suddenly my entire body trembled: My soup! What had happened to my soup? The bowl was still in my hand but it was empty, it had all spilled when I had fallen. In vain did I try to scratch the sides of the bowl with my fingernails. Nothing was left. Panic stricken, I put my hand in my pocket and found a piece of bread that was still there. Thank God, I could breathe a sigh of relief.

I slowly got up on my feet. My head was heavy. With failing steps I sank down on my plank. Everyone else was already sleeping.

I realized that I had to be more careful if I wanted to live. Another blow like that could easily finish me off. I must not let the hunger and exhaustion overtake me. I must be more careful, I thought as I swallowed my dry bread mixed with tears. I didn't cry because of the blow I had received. I cried for my lost soup.

The Motor Repair Division

The winds and the rains got stronger. Each day it became colder. Winter had begun and we stood in the apels shivering from the cold, soaked with the rain, hungry and tired. All those who until now had held out began to collapse. The revier, which was in a small barrack near the entrance to the camp, filled up with sick people. The first ones were victims of Herman, the kapo. One of them died after a few days. He was the the first casualty in our camp. Herman, the boxer, had broken his ribs. They took him out of the camp in a wheelbarrow and buried him without a sign. I was filled with despair when I saw what was happening. That day I believed that perhaps the threats of the obersturmfuehrer and the lageralteste — that no Jew would remain alive after this war — would indeed be fulfilled.

On that gloomy day in which we buried our first dead, the lageralteste was in a particularly fine mood. He was apparently a great lover of music and poetry. After his speech he informed us that he had written a poem and had even composed a melody for it. The latter-day hero claimed it was a march and that on Sunday we would learn it.

When Sunday came, after the roll call, the lageralteste began teaching us the song. It was very cold. The first snow began to fall on our shaven heads, which had begun to grow a little hair. It was a horrifying sight. Thousands of men, dressed in rags, standing in the snow, shivering from the cold, looked in desperation at the pile of bricks that shortly would be theirs to drag. People, so hungry that they didn't even have the strength to speak, had to sing loudly, to rehearse the first line of the song, to repeat it again and again, to sing it even louder. I thought I would faint. There was a time when I had loved to sing. People said I had a beautiful and clear voice. I sang in the choirs in school and in the synagogue. I had always thought that one sang from happiness and for pleasure. I had never thought that singing could be so unbearable. But the lageralteste enjoyed his composition. He wanted us to learn all three verses of the song right away so that everyone would recognize his talents.

"From now on," he told us, "as you leave the camp and as you return to it, I want you to sing in a loud voice! Sing and march in time!"

From that day on, after twelve hours of work, we had to march while we sang the lageralteste's song. If the marching had been difficult before, now it was seven times harder. I pretended to move my lips, but only when a kapo or a German soldier was near did I really sing. The others did the same thing so of course the singing was ruined and all we got for our efforts was a beating on the head. Thus we marched, totally worn out, singing the song we all hated:

"Beside Hamburg stands a camp
Surrounded by barbed wire,
Three times a thousand young men
Live in this concentration camp."

The song went on to give a precise description of how we marched in the streets of Bronshveig, arrived at the factory, and in the third stanza—how the factory received us with black smoke spewing from its tall chimneys.

Even before the week of the day shift was over I was afraid of the coming week when I would have to work the night shift. While working and marching I would think of the endless nights of work, the endless workweek, and the hardships which accompanied them. One day I got lucky. A certain fat meister turned to my meister, pointed to me and asked him something. My meister nodded and then with a movement of his hand showed me that I was to follow the fat man. I did as he said.

We crossed the courtyard to a big garage filled with completed and dismantled motors. Besides the meister there was only one other worker, a German youth about my age. He was dressed in a *Hitler Jugend* (Hitler Youth) uniform, a blue-visored hat and a yellow shirt decorated with swastika buttons. The boy ignored me, as though I wasn't there at all. The meister explained briefly what I was to do. He gave me two big screwdrivers and ordered me to tighten screws. Afterwards I had to spray water from a rubber pipe on different machine parts, then load other machine parts onto a wheelbarrow and take them to another place. The parts were very heavy, but I was pleased. This work was not monotonous and each time I had something different to do. The day passed much more quickly than it had when I worked at the lathe. What's more: here the soldiers were not sitting opposite me. The Germans did not have enough soldiers to guard one lone heftlinge. Actually they didn't need a guard for me, since the two workers, the meister and the Hitler youth, were always with me and watched me carefully. I could go out to the bathroom only when I saw a group of workers passing by in the courtyard accompanied by a soldier. But the most important thing was that in the garage they did not work at night. That change brought me real happiness.

Once in a while the meister and his assistant spoke to each other, mostly concerning work. When he spoke to me the meister would call out, "Hey, you!" and would show me with his hands what I was to do. But that was only in the beginning. After a while, as he became used to me and my strange appearance, he would talk more. The boy, however, never turned to me at all. Occasionally, when he thought I wasn't noticing, I would see him stand on the side and look at me. This manner of staring used to get me angry: it was as though I were a rare animal in a zoo. I wanted to stick out my tongue at him, so that he'd really have something to look at. But I immediately remembered where I was and who I was, and what my punishment could be for such an insult.

From now on the days passed more easily. I found the work interesting, even though it was very difficult. All of the loads which had to be moved from place to place were given to me. Here too, as in the big hall, I worked standing up. The meister and his assistant, the German youth, had two chairs, on which they rested whenever they felt like it. Here, too, hunger continued to eat away at my insides, especially when my two employers took a break to have their meals. About three times during the shift they would sit down by the table, right next to me, to eat. The smell of fresh bread, salami, eggs, and strong coffee that they poured into their cups from thermoses, the apple or other fruit for dessert, would drive me crazy. I often had an overwhelming desire to pounce on that food and devour it, even if they punished me by beating me to death—just not to suffer so much from the hunger and for once to eat my fill.

Luzer!—I would catch myself, their blows could kill you, and you must live. You promised!

In the hall too, where I had worked before, I had seen my

meister and the soldiers that guarded us, eat to their heart's content. But there they were at least some distance from me, while here the two ate right next to me.

Pigs! You should choke on your delicacies!—I used to curse them silently. Can't you give me a little something, you have so much. If I were in your place I would share with you. Why must a Jew be hungry? In order to rid myself of the maddening irritation, I would leave the hardest work for the times when they were eating. Those were the times when I would load the heavy parts on the wheelbarrows and take them where they were supposed to go—anything to get away from them while they were eating and from the temptation which I feared I could not withstand.

With time, despite their shaven heads, skinniness, and raggedy clothes, I learned to recognize the other heftlinge. Some I remembered from before Auschwitz. There were two guys always together, whom I was sure I had met somewhere. The skin on their faces had dried up and wrinkled so their blue eyes stood out and looked tremendous. I stretched my memory to discover from where I knew them. Then I remembered that they were Yitzchak and Moshe Urbach, whom I had known in the Lodz ghetto.

I was happy that I was able to identify people and distinguish between them, but I never spoke to them. In this camp I lacked the strength to speak to anyone. Besides, there was no time. We were always busy, whether with work or with the apels, walking to work or sleeping.

One day I ran into a young man whom I recognized immediately and whose appearance here made my blood freeze. He was the assistant kapo from the revier in Auschwitz, to whom I had given a piece of bread for my father. He was the one who had handed me the note from my father, the last sign of his life.

When I saw him there I wanted to run after him, ask if he

had given that pot of soup to my father, if Father had indeed eaten the soup. Suddenly I stopped. No, I said to myself, I cannot go to him. I just can't ask him. What if he said that the soup didn't get to my father? I felt that if that were so, something terrible would happen to me, and I would not be able to fight for my life. Until that moment I had not realized how important it was for me to believe that Father had eaten the soup, and how carefully I had repressed any thought that the soup never got to him. I would give years of my life if someone could verify that he did eat that soup, and did not leave this world hungry.

I lowered my head so that the kapo from the revier would not recognize me, but his presence in my barrack was always disturbing. I fully understood the importance of fulfilling the last request of a dying man, particularly if he was your father.

The Lauzenstrasse Haircut

This year, winter began earlier than usual. It got colder day by day. The winds and snow blew fiercely during the apels and they had no mercy on the three thousand men standing nearly naked in the middle of the night under the open sky. Our outer garments hung on us for they were too big for our bodies. We lacked undergarments. Our clothes were not enough to protect us from the cold that went right through them. Our fingers and toes felt as if thousands of pins and needles were sticking into them. To march in such weather was terrible; we had to battle winds which blew against us and slice our way through them. Sometimes I thought they would blow us away, skeletons who weighed no more than a feather. Even so, all our torments during a march were preferable to standing in place, for the movement helped us warm ourselves a little. At least the factory was heated, and that gave us a little added strength.

Although the hours in the factory crawled by and hunger drove us crazy, we still wished the week would not end, that Sunday would never arrive. That day scared us to death. Among all the other troubles that were purposely designed for Sundays, in addition to carrying the bricks, at the end of the day we also got the kapo Herman's boxing practice, plus searches of our bodies and our planks. We all knew this was to postpone as long as possible the hour when we were fed and permitted to go to our plank and lay our tortured body on it.

I used to wonder during the searches: what could they possibly find? In Auschwitz they had already taken everything from us, had left us naked. Our ragged clothes had been searched thoroughly. And still the kapos always found something when they searched. There were among us those who succeeded in hiding a piece of bread for the night shift by shoving a slice into the mattress, and that treasure the kapos would uncover and appropriate during their inspection. Those who returned to their plank and did not find the bread which they had managed, with such tremendous effort, to save, would sometimes break out in tears. At such moments I was happy that I had not succeeded in saving anything and had finished the entire portion at once.

All too soon Sunday came with its back-breaking work. During the first part of the day the sun shone upon us, but in the afternoon our luck ran out and a snow storm began to rage. Only towards evening did we enter the barrack, tired and wet to our bone marrow, to receive bread and soup. Then, just before the distribution began there was another deafening whistle, calling us to an apel. What was it this time?

We didn't have to wait long for an answer. Into the camp walked the lageralteste. By his stride it was clear that he was very drunk. He could barely stand on his feet. With a wicked smile he informed us that today we would get new haircuts:

they would divide us into groups and the kapos would shave the hair on our heads. About six weeks had passed since we had arrived shaven from Auschwitz. Now our hair had begun to grow back, once again giving us a somewhat human appearance and even protecting our heads a little from the cold of the apels. But we didn't think now about the loss of our hair, but rather the loss of our sleep. We could only dream about reaching the plank and giving our bodies some rest.

Soon we realized that this was not a simple shave, that the lageralteste had not laughed due to his drunkenness, but rather at his malicious intrigue. The kapos, equipped with shavers, went to work immediately. The shave was quick and the first "customers" soon appeared. Our breath stopped; monsters from another world stood before us. Up the middle of their skulls was a bald line the width of a shaver, from the forehead to the back of the neck, while on both sides the hair remained. The haircut weirdly divided the head into three parts. We called this haircut lauzenstrasse, which meant: lice street. We looked at one another and burst out laughing, which soon turned to tears. Everyone whose shave was completed was ordered to go to another kapo. He took a broad paint brush from a pail full of red paint and smeared a broad red stripe on our clothes, from the collar over our back to our pants.

I thought then how our appearance would amuse the inhabitants of Bronshveig when we walked through the streets of the city. This time they would really have something to look at, and also in the factory our meisters would have a good laugh.

"All this is so that you won't be able to escape," said the kapo whom we called "the Gypsy," as he enjoyed the new invention.

As if we had a chance, I thought to myself, to slip by the barbed wire fences, the watch towers, the eyes of the kapos and the soldiers, who accompanied us even to the bathroom with their weapons ready. As if we had a chance to escape from here after they counted us three times a day, once in the camp and twice in the factory, when we arrived and at the end of the work. And if they were off on the count even by one, they counted again and again, searched through the planks, beat and kicked us as though it were our fault. In such a case we remained standing for a long time in the apel. Even if this took away work time in the factory they persisted, until they remembered that the missing person was the one who had died and who was buried outside the camp, or the one who had been transferred to the revier.

Our new appearance was quite an attraction when we arrived at the factory the next day. Even before that, when we stood for the apel, the meisters ran to see us. I felt my blood rise to my head. Hah, how the sight of us amused them. For some reason I recalled that moment in the biblical story about Samson, when the Philistines ripped out his eyes and ordered him to dance before them. I remembered his prayer that God give him strength to take revenge on his captors and his words, "My soul will die with the Philistines."

God!—I thought in my heart—do something! Perform one of those miracles.

I noticed that not all the Germans laughed when they saw us. A few of them lowered their heads. Or maybe it only seemed that way. In any case, my meister was among them. That entire day he did not look in my direction. It was one of those in which the Hitler youth did not come to work. I eventually learned that those were days in which the Hitler Youth went to training camp.

Despite my appearance and the depression it gave me, I worked as usual. I already knew what I had to do. Only occasionally would I steal a look at my meister, to see if he might require anything else of me. I watched him from a distance when he sat to eat his meal, but this time it seemed that he was beckoning me to come to him. However, I couldn't be certain since he quickly turned around and continued to eat. Afterwards I saw him open a package wrapped in white paper, take out two slices of bread, look cautiously at the door and then at me, and then put the package aside. I was afraid to delude myself and continued working. After a moment the meister got up, took the package in his hand, and put it on the motor near him. He saw that I was following his movements and again made a sign to me, as though he were inviting me to something. My breath stopped. I didn't know what to do. Maybe he wanted to test me so that he could later inform against me that I had taken bread from him? No, no,—I said to myself—I must be strong and resist temptation. I therefore continued to work and to ignore the package which was placed on the side. I was relieved when I heard the whistle concluding the work day. But that entire night I could not sleep. The bread had stayed on the motor, and the meister had hinted to me that I should take it. I could not forgive myself for my stupid behavior. I decided that if the bread was still on the engine the next day I would take it no matter what. I could no longer withstand temptation.

As soon as I arrived at the garage where I worked, I turned my head to the engine and saw that the package was still in its place. On that day too the boy did not come to work, but today the meister also behaved differently. He peeked outside and then closed the entrance door, and now called me to come to where the package was and clean the motor. When I was near him he whispered: "Take this and eat it quickly." I couldn't believe my ears; I thought I was dreaming. When he was some distance away I grabbed the bread and fled with it to the end of the garage, where I hid behind a big engine and rapidly devoured it.

Back at camp that night as I lay upon my plank, I couldn't

stop thinking of my meister and his behavior. Could it be that my meister did not hate Jews? Maybe he just had pity for me like one pities a hungry dog? But it didn't matter, I said to myself. The main thing is that I received additional bread and was less hungry. One thing was clear: my meister had been afraid when he put the two slices of bread on the engine.

On the following day the boy returned to work and I received nothing from him. But what amazed me was that, even the Hitler youth, who all the time refrained from coming close to me, did not laugh at my appearance, and in him too it seemed that I could detect a flash of participation in my sorrow. Nevertheless, my meister was wary of the boy.

From that day on I would occasionally find a dry slice of bread, but only on the days when the Hitler youth did not come to work.

After a while it became clear to me that the boy had also changed his attitude towards me. He began to talk to me, even if this meant throwing a few lone words at me, primarily concerning work matters.

One day, when the meister left the garage, the boy sat as usual beside the table to set out his meal. I distanced myself from him, but he knew that I was watching. I saw him take a sandwich wrapped in paper from his bag. He opened the paper and put the salami that was in it onto one slice. The second slice he rewrapped in the paper, got up from his place, and demonstratively threw the bread into the garbage can. Then he turned around and walked away. I didn't know what to do: did that mean that the bread was intended for me, or did he just happen to put it in the garbage can. It was unimaginable that a boy who was a member of the *Hitler Jugend* would do such a thing. But the slice of bread in the garbage gave me no rest. I couldn't live with a slice of bread that would be thrown away together with the rest of the garbage at a time when I was so hungry. When I was sure that the boy was not watching me, I stole to the can before the meister returned. I took the bread out of the paper. I threw the paper back into the garbage can so it would look just like it did when the boy had first put it there.

It was fresh bread soaked with the smell of salami, something out of this world, something divine. In a split second I already finished the bread and then was sorry that it was finished so quickly.

It seemed amazing to me, but every few days I found a piece of bread in the garbage can. Even so, I wasn't sure whether he did this in order to help me, or just happened to do so. In any case, it was a fact that each time he put the bread in the garbage the meister was not in the garage.

Naturally, the pieces of bread that I received every few days were not enough to satisfy my hunger. But still it was something. Each day that I had an extra piece of bread I was filled with new strength. If that happened because of the lauzenstrasse, I thought to myself, then even that was for the best.

Every three weeks, we received a new "lice street" shave. The name lauzenstrasse was apt for we were plagued with lice: a new enemy, a dangerous enemy which we were powerless to fight, that nearly defeated us.

The one and only shower we had was when we had first arrived at Auschwitz. Since then many months had passed in which we hadn't showered and hadn't changed our clothes. The miserable rags we received in Auschwitz became an inseparable part of our bodies. We didn't take them off for a moment. We slept, walked and worked in them. It's true that there was a concrete area in the front of the barrack where faucets were installed. But we didn't have time to wash ourselves. Every hour of the day was filled with other things— the hasty running to the apel, standing in it, walking to the factory and work. After a day of oppressive labor we had a long march to the camp, where we barely had the strength to stand in line for soup and bread. All we wanted to do was crawl to our plank and lie down. In addition, it was already well into winter, a very hard winter. The water in the faucets was frozen. How could one even think of washing? The lice multiplied until they were countless. They sucked our blood so that in a short while our thin bodies were covered with bruises and wounds. We suffered terribly, indescribably. Their bites drove us mad and prevented us from falling asleep. We tore our flesh scratching so much.

In the evenings, after finishing our diluted soup and dry piece of bread, some of the inhabitants of the barrack would sit on their plank naked, or wrapped in the worn out blankets we had received before winter, and begin to pick the lice out of their clothes. We sat that way for hours. There was no end to the lice. No sooner had we finished this work, shaken the clothes and the blanket and finally gone to sleep, than we heard the hated whistle for the apel.

The air in the barrack was filled with vapor, that came out of the many mouths and gathered on the ceiling as drops of water. These drops would drip onto the upper planks and the floor, making puddles in which you could see the lice as they stirred and moved about. We didn't know which plague was worse: the hunger, the lice, the standing in the apels in cold temperatures that reached many degrees below zero, or the marching to the factory on roads covered with a thick layer of snow into which we sank and from which we were barely able to pull out the wooden shoes on our feet. The snow would stick in hard chunks to the soles of our shoes, and this would occasionally cause one of us to fall. When the road was covered with a layer of ice we would also slip and fall. Every time, our sentence was the same—beatings from our guards.

"Lord of the universe, why must we continue being tormented so?" I would argue with the Creator. "I'm sure we won't get out of here alive." I had no doubt that the obersturmfuehrer's words would come true.

Those were days in which despair ate away at me. If only something would happen that would free me from the promise I gave my father. There were hours in which I was angry at the father who had bound me with this difficult promise. What did he know of the unbearable tortures that awaited me? Even in the conditions of Auschwitz could he have possibly imagined that such terrible things existed? No, I must not be angry at my father, I argued with myself, he could not have imagined that such things existed. I must look at the good in all these horrors. What was good for me at the time was that Father's life had ended in Auschwitz so that he was prevented from having to undergo all this.

In order to find some contentment in life I would try in my own way to take revenge on the Germans. I already had learned to put together the parts of the engines in the factory, and now I also knew how to ruin them. I could not, God forbid, do something which might arouse even the least bit of suspicion towards me, so I didn't do it often. At the same time I knew that there wasn't any practical value to my acts, since sabotaging one engine would not change the disposition of the German forces in this cursed war. I was doing it for my own good—it was my private revenge.

Meanwhile, the mortality rate in the camp was on the rise. Every day someone died. During the apel one of the tortured figures would collapse suddenly and not respond to the blows of the kapo. It would remain lying on the ground, and only after all the slaves went on their way, marching and singing, did they take the body in a wheelbarrow and bury it in the distant sands outside the camp.

When the plague of lice worsened, I used to stay away from the meister and the boy at the factory. I didn't want them to see the lice crawling on me. I didn't want them to receive additional confirmation of the degrading name they called us—filthy stinking Jews.

One night I awoke before the apel whistle. The lice woke me up. This curse will finish me, I thought as I scratched my body till it bled. Suddenly the thought came to me again: I have to fight for my life, I must not die without a fight. Had I really tried everything to fight these lice? It was impossible to fight them, I tried to convince myself. But I realized that I hadn't convinced myself. I knew I could do something. I quickly jumped from my plank and ran to the front part of the barrack where the faucets were. By the dim light of the bulb that was inserted in the middle of the ceiling, I saw that I was not the only person there; naked men, covered with sores, stood under the streams of cold water washing their bodies. Until a place opened up beside one of the taps I shook out my clothes and blanket. Eventually I too stood under the open tap. My breath was taken away by the contact of the ice water on my body. I thought I would freeze then and there. But this burning cold was many times better than the irritation and stings caused by the lice. I had nothing with which to dry my body so I wrapped it in the blanket. I had tried to make sure the blanket would not get wet, but was unsuccessful and stood wrapped in the wet blanket shivering from the cold of the night. I didn't even manage to dry off before the deafening whistle for the apel.

That day I actually felt something of relief. In the evening the blanket was still wet, but all this was better than the suffering caused by the lice. From that day on I would get up before the apel and wash my body with the icewater. One more change occurred in our tortured bodies. During the days of terrible cold we no longer felt the needles in our fingers and toes because they were so frozen. Our feet, two blocks of wood that didn't belong to us, were covered with congealed blood. We particularly suffered at night, when we warmed up a bit. Only then would we feel that we had feet, that they were ours, and the pains we knew then kept us from falling asleep.

The plank, which until now had been our place of respite, was turned into a place of suffering because the terrible cold, the lice and the pains in our feet and legs kept us from falling asleep. The thin blanket we had was not enough. From then on we slept in pairs, hugging one another, in order to warm up and be covered with two blankets instead of one. I sometimes slept with Dr. Warhaft and sometimes with a boy my age, Avraham Zelig from the Lodz ghetto.

In the factory I found a remedy for frozen feet. When the meister and the boy were away I would take paper out of the waste basket and wrap the soles of my feet in it. Many of our people did this to get relief from the cold.

My Knife

I continued to work hard for twelve hours a day, standing, without rest. I would carry heavy engine parts while I was mad with hunger. But the work in the factory was still the lesser evil. The work hours were the best hours of the day. The meister and the boy had by now gotten used to my presence in the garage. Every once in a while they threw me a few words about work matters, every once in a while I would find a piece of dry bread on the motor, an act of mercy from the meister, and sometimes a slice of bread from a sandwich, which the boy would throw in the garbage. Sometimes they would even go out for a few minutes and leave me alone. They knew that I would not run away, that I had nowhere to run. They knew that the appearance the Germans had given us would give me away immediately if I tried to escape. I even used to get some pleasure from the fact that they trusted me. During such moments, when they left the garage and I remained alone, I had a chance to rest, to lean or sit on some machine. While I rested I was always alert, and as soon as I saw someone approach I immediately began to work. But even those few moments of rest were something of a relief.

One day an idea flashed through my head. It happened while I was looking at the various pieces of metal that rolled around the garage. One piece that particularly caught my eye was some steel in the shape of a ruler. I could make this steel into a knife. A knife would protect me. At the same time, I was aware of the danger if a knife were found on me, and I tried to push the idea away. "I don't really need a knife at all, in my situation a knife can't help me," I would tell myself. I wasn't about to attack the lageralteste or a soldier or a kapo. If I did they would kill me on the spot. And I had to live. If they so much as found the knife on me I would die. That was a wise thought, but the will was stronger than the thought. I tried to convince myself that one never knew what situations one might get into and I could use a knife to defend myself. When I picked up the piece of steel I was filled with uncertainty. Nonetheless, I took it and hid it. I knew that the idea of the knife would give me no rest, and I was right. It used to accompany me during the march to the camp, as I lay on the plank and while I picked out the lice. I even found a place to hide the knife. During the apel, when the obersturmfuehrer gave his diabolical and slanderous speech, calling us all kinds of degrading names, I realized that I had to have a knife.

Later that same day I waited impatiently for the meister and his assistant to leave the garage. Even before that I kept all my work as close as possible to the sharpening machine. Every moment that I remained alone I took out my precious piece of steel and began to sharpen and file it. I knew that I had to be very careful, that I could pay with my life if I was caught doing this. But that didn't stop me. At the sound of even the slightest noise I stopped the machine and stuffed the steel up my sleeve.

At the end of my workday I hid the unfinished treasure inside an idle machine in the garage, and on the following day I would take it out again. Although I worked feverishly this took many days. Finally the knife was ready. It was shiny and sharp. I now made an incision in the inside of my coat near the buttons where it was a little stiff and shoved in the knife. I suddenly felt a new kind of strength; if someone wanted to kill me, and I knew that I had no chance otherwise, I could unsheathe the knife and kill him. I would not give my life up easily, I thought, as I felt the place where my knife was hidden.

After that I felt stronger, my body stood taller, I raised my head higher. Even the way I looked at the meister and the Hitler youth was different.

A few days later I began to be bothered by the thought that they might search our bodies. Because of this I took the knife out of its hiding place in my coat and hid it in my plank. I made an incision in the straw-filled mattress and inserted the knife. When I thought it was safe, I felt better.

About two weeks passed. Each night, before going out to the apel, I would touch the blade as if parting from it for the day. In the evening, back in camp, when I finally climbed up onto the plank, I searched feverishly to touch the knife. Only when my fingers felt it would I be able to relax and sleep securely. Even while I worked in the factory I would think of the knife that awaited me, so to speak, in my bed. It was now my closest friend, my only friend.

Thus things continued until that Sunday, when we stood in line for another lauzenstrasse shave. At the same time we heard that they were searching the planks.

"Funny," I heard one heftlinge say to another, "what do they think they're looking for. Don't they know such searches are superfluous? What do they hope to find—money, diamonds?"

This information was a terrible shock to me, and at the end of the shave I dragged myself in a daze to the plank. I tried to make myself believe that they couldn't possibly find something like a knife inside the straw. I climbed up to my bed. I straightened it out and put my hand inside the straw, hoping to find the knife, but I didn't find it. I feverishly tore the whole mattress and scattered the straw over the plank, but there was no sign of a knife. I plunged down on the plank, my face covered with the scattered straw, and cried like a little boy.

I was in a state of shock for two days. Even in the garage I didn't pay attention to what the meister said, and only his shout, "What's wrong with you!" brought me back to reality.

What really was happening with me, I admonished myself. What was I mourning about? A knife? How could I be sorry about such a thing after they took everything from me, my parents, my sister? How could I act this way and not remember that the meister could complain about me and then they'd return me to the big hall, where two soldiers who sat opposite me all day would guard me continuously, where I would have to go back to working the night shift as well, to go through all the torments I had experienced then? I must not get the meister angry. I must recover. As for the knife—I would make another. And if they took the second knife from me I'd make another. I must be prepared for that. I should be glad that they did not investigate whose knife it was and that I wasn't punished. Probably one of the kapos took the knife for himself. Consequently the incident passed quietly, without a special investigation.

Within two weeks I had a new knife. But now I knew better than to put it in the straw of my mattress. I went back to hiding it in my coat next to the row of buttons, in the same place I kept the note I had received from my father. It was a tremendous risk to hide the knife on my person, but I did it anyway.

A Spark of Hope

Half a year passed since my arrival at Bronshveig. Sometimes it seemed that I had been there forever. Time crept by so slowly, each day identical to the next in all its suffering. The only change was the happiness upon finding a slice of bread on the engine or in the garbage can. Then one day my meister disappeared, and with him went my happiness. He was replaced by another meister, older and more nervous. He didn't speak to me but would shout commands in a grating, annoying voice.

The Hitler youth also stopped coming. Avraham Zelig told me that many of the meisters were drafted into the army and sent to the front. From this he concluded that the Germans' situation in the war had clearly degenerated, but this information had no influence on me. On that day in particular, during the apel, I thought not of the situation at the front, but of our situation here in camp. I would look around me at the skinny figures who barely stood on their own feet, and think of the snowstorm which raged and the bone-freezing chill. These were my brothers, the Jews, members of the cursed people, the bonded slaves of the twentieth century. I knew many of them were already on the edge of death, many were spitting blood, afflicted with tuberculosis, and all were eaten by lice. Each day a few more died.

How long could we hold out? I looked just like them. How long could I hold out? I too would probably be touched by the hand of disease. We won't even last till the end of the war, and if we do, they'll just kill us then. The commander of the camp had promised us this. Such thoughts plagued me especially now, when it seemed to us that the tide had turned against the Germans.

Then, again I was put back to work on the night shift. The pace of the work in the factory was quickened even more. The nights were terrible and endless. My eyelids closed on their own—I really had to battle them. The new meister would stand beside me and shout. The hunger sucked my insides. All this was enough to drive a person crazy—but I was not a person. I was a stinking Jewish slave who had to keep living in this hell.

Avraham Zelig told me that not only my meister but all the meisters were nervous. In fact, all the Germans were nervous. Something was happening. But in the garage I felt no change until that night.

It was a night like any other, a night in which I battled my need to sleep. I was hungry and tired. Like the other nights I saw my meister sitting by the table, beginning to eat. I wanted to lean on one of the machines for a brief moment to rest, but I knew this was forbidden. I knew that the moment I leaned I might fall asleep and the blows I would receive for this could kill me.

Meanwhile, the meister opened his bag of food and poured pungent coffee from his thermos, and I, as usual, breathed the smell of the coffee and nearly went out of my mind. If only that pig would give me one drop of that liquid to warm my insides and dissolve my tiredness. If he would only throw some remnant into the waste basket, to quiet my hunger and help me overcome my sleep. But all these were mere fantasies. The old pig had a healthy appetite, and he finished everything down to the last crumb.

Before the old man finished his coffee a loud siren shook the air. The meister leaped from the chair and ran to the door. When he reached the door he turned around and shouted to me to hurry after him. I saw that he was pale as a ghost, trembling from head to toe. The siren continued blasting. I didn't know what was going on and ran after him.

When we reached the courtyard we heard the droning sound of many planes flying ever closer.

The giant courtyard was full of people cursing and running in every direction. The noise and commotion mixed all of us together: soldiers, meisters, prisoners of war, and us, the Jewish slaves. Only the Germans were in a panic, running like wildmen. We, the Jews, did not hurry. We were delighted that we had lived to see this sight and filled our eyes with it: a squadron of Allied planes was bombing Germany. It had been worth surviving to see this: the "superior race," the arrogant masters, well-fed, confident, scrambling like terrified mice. This was an indescribable happiness.

I was invigorated by that sight. My tiredness and despair evaporated into thin air. How great to see the sky filled with planes whose bombs shook the air. Before I had a chance to see the skies redden with anti-aircraft fire, I felt the strong impact of a rifle butt on the back of my neck.

"Stinking Jew, you want to be killed?" I heard the voice of a soldier who was running to the shelter.

Yes, I said in my heart, I want to be killed, but together with you. You cannot understand how happy I am to see you, you big hero, so terrified.

Of course I didn't say anything out loud.

The shelter was terribly crowded. Here everyone was equal in the face of death: superior and inferior, beaters and beaten. The one difference was that the beaters were afraid of death while the beaten waited for death as a redemption.

I hoped the Germans would catch our lice when I saw everyone crowding together. Maybe it's your time to be filthy.

I looked around me. The faces of the Jews which until now had been so expressionless, acquired life. The blank eyes sparkled. Like me, I am sure that everyone was prepared to die, but so would our enemies. I hoped for a bomb that would kill us all. Again I thought of Samson's pledge: "My soul will die with the Philistines...."

"The Germans must not see that we are happy," I heard a friend whisper. "They will take revenge on us afterwards." I turned my head to the speaker. Beside me stood a blue-eyed boy—Moshe Urbach.

Indeed his words came true. They took it out on us, as though we were guilty of dropping bombs. The kapos treated us even more cruelly. We entered the shelter as equals, but as soon as the all-clear siren sounded they beat us on our backs and heads. After that the kapos and the soldiers persecuted us even more vigorously. They hit us whenever they saw us: when we ran to the apel, while straightening the rows, when we stood in line for soup, and when we dragged bricks.

Even the obersturmfuehrer, in his daily speech, mentioned that we had no reason to be happy and hope for the end of the war. He reminded us that as soon as the war ended so would our lives.

But we were happy anyway. Despite his diabolical speeches and those of the lageralteste, despite the increasing cruelty of the kapos, we were full of hope that the end of the war was coming. Our persecutors couldn't understand that in our eyes death meant an end to our suffering. With all our might we wanted to see those invincible heroes lose the war. We were ready to die with them in order to see their defeat.

That day, after we returned from the factory, when we finally lay down on our planks to sleep before the night shift, I suddenly began to sing. I sang a sad song filled with yearnings for the Land of Israel. I sang quietly, as tears streamed from my eyes:

"On a starless night, starless night.
We'll go up to our homeland, our homeland
You are a mother to me, you are a brother to me,
You are my outstretched hand, outstretched hand."

I hadn't noticed that the youth Avraham Zelig from the second plank was listening to my song. He liked the song and asked me to teach it to him. We sang it together over and over. It must have been a strange sight, two starving and lice-ridden boys lying on the planks singing, and all this before the apel which awaited them, before the seven kilometer march and twelve hours of work through the night.

The bombers came back each night. From that night on, I was reborn. The work at night became almost pleasant. I no longer felt tired and didn't have to wrestle with sleep. From the moment I arrived at the factory I eagerly looked forward to the sounds of the siren, the airplanes, and the shells. Each time the meister sat down to eat, I wished that the siren would suddenly sound. With each siren the meister would grind his teeth and curse, while I was happy. Sometimes the bombing continued for hours, and I could rest. In those hours I would sit in a corner, lean against the wall and sleep like a baby. I slept as the sweet music of bombs over Germany hummed in my ears, and in my heart I thought that the Germans must be in very bad shape if the Allied planes had reached here.

I would wake up from my nap when the all-clear siren announced that the shelling had ended, hurry to get up and slip past any contact with the kapos, and return to the garage, equipped with renewed strength.

The bombings of Bronshveig's giant factory became more and more frequent. There were nights when the raids were one after the next so that another siren blew before we had even returned from the shelter. Work in the factory nearly halted. There were attacks during the day, too. One day, while we were in the shelter, a plane actually struck one of the factory buildings. We heard the noise of explosions and thought the whole factory had crumbled. But when we left the shelter we saw that only a relatively unimportant building had been hit and destroyed.

That day we didn't return to work beside the machines. All the Jews were used in clearing away the rubble. The building was empty of people during the shelling, with the exception of one kapo. We found him dead among the ruins.

The Death March

The war continued and we now felt its full impact. Nothing happened on schedule except nature. The snowstorms had stopped, for spring was approaching. The cold was not as oppressive. Now the skies opened up and released torrential rains which tormented us during the apels. Work in the factory stopped entirely. We remained in the camp and no longer went to work. Only the apels in the middle of the night continued as always. Now the Germans had spare time to arrive at the apels later, so we would stand for a long time before they came. As always, the camp commander and the lageralteste delivered their loathsome speeches. They tried to keep us busy with all kinds of work: we carried bricks from place to place; we sawed trees, unloaded coal and vegetables from trucks that arrived at the kitchen. But chaos was felt everywhere, and we knew that the war would soon end. The only question was whether we would live to see it.

One day all the sick were evacuated from the revier. One group of men was also sent from the camp. We didn't know where they were taken until we heard, during an apel, from the lageralteste that immediately after the apel we would go on our way. We weren't told where we were going or how long we would walk. The lageralteste only warned us that we must march in uniform time and not slow down. He emphasized that if someone delayed or lagged behind he would be killed on the spot with a bullet in the head. He also ordered us to leave the camp singing our "anthem."

We didn't know how to react to this information. With all our might we wished to leave this camp, which we hated.

On the other hand, we had no idea where we were going. We had learned that things could always be worse no matter how bad they already were. We felt that the Germans were taking us away from the approaching front. The bombing of Bronshveig continued without pause.

We went on our way and as we left, I touched my knife. We left the Bronshveig camp marching and singing, as the lageralteste had commanded. The date was March 21, 1945. We knew this because we had heard the Germans mention it. We left behind our filthy planks with the puddles from the water which dripped from the ceiling, filled with millions of lice squirming around. We left behind sand dunes in which many of us were buried, Jews, brothers in suffering who had died in this camp, nameless, unidentified, as numbers only.

The song quickly faded from our lips. It made the marching more difficult. Towards the beginning the soldiers and kapos still beat us for this, demanding that we continue to sing, but they eased off when we approached the streets of Bronshveig.

The march went on and on. Soon we left behind the city of Bronshveig and went out to a wide road. The kapos and soldiers continued to push us to go faster, that we shouldn't slow the pace. They didn't let us rest for a moment. We had to continue quickly, to the rhythm of their repeated commands: one, two, three, four; one, two, three, four—on and on.

The sun, which in the beginning had shone upon us, now hid behind the clouds. For a moment it peeked again, until it disappeared totally behind a heavy cloud. Big drops of rain began to fall. Within minutes the drops turned into a flood which soaked us to our bones. The walking became more difficult. The soldiers and kapos, despite their tall boots and clothes which protected them from the rain, were angry, and they, of course, took their anger out on us.

After about an hour the rain stopped and the sun came out again. It seemed that the sun too was mocking us. We had already walked for hours, passing villages and forests. The scenery around us was spectacular, but we weren't in the mood to pay attention to the beauty of nature. The contrast between the beauty around us and our ugly appearance was too sharp and embarrassing.

We went out to the main road. From the opposite direction people came towards us traveling in wagons, on bicycles, in cars. They passed by us as though they didn't see us, as though we were ghosts. It occurred to me that I also had once had my own bicycle and could ride it wherever I wished. But that seemed like many centuries ago.

We continued to march. The sun was setting but still we walked and walked without a moment's rest. How long would this march continue? Where are they taking us? Every one in the convoy asked himself these questions.

Our feet got so heavy they didn't want to obey us; they even refused to obey the soldiers and the kapos. Our feet didn't care that our heads and backs were punished because of them. Our feet also became our enemies, became a body separate from us. Instead of them carrying us, we had to drag them.

After our march had lasted at least twelve hours, I felt I couldn't go on. All I wanted was to sit down and not get up, no matter what happened. The main thing was to sit down. But the Germans pushed us on—and I would not let myself give up. I had to keep going. Perhaps the Germans intended to kill us in this manner, by walking. If that was their intention, then I had to be the last. I had promised my father.

The first shot was heard. Someone had remained behind. He couldn't go on any longer. They finished him, those dogs, I said in my heart. After all the effort and all the suffering to get this far. Here, of all places, to be murdered by them!

But be comforted, my Jewish brother, that your suffering has finally ended. Then I thought, it's too bad you didn't try, my brother, to rest earlier. Why did you need to continue until your strength gave out? I myself, were I not tied by this terrible obligation to my father, would have sat long ago. I would have stopped walking so they could finish me off. But even that is not quite true, for people, as long as they are still alive, want to live. They want to try more and more. Surely no one knew better than I, who had faced death so many times, that as long as his body breathes a man believes a miracle might occur. But here there were no miracles. For the Jews the miracles ended after the exodus from Egypt.

The convoy continued on its endless journey. Although it began to get dark we continued to march. The fear of death pushed the walkers, now far beyond exhaustion, to take one more step and then still another step until the final collapse. The shots became more and more frequent. The Germans kept their word and shot anyone who lagged behind, after which the kapos kicked the dead bodies to the side of the road, so that they wouldn't get in the way of the traffic.

The march lasted throughout the night when it rained again. Our clothes stayed wet and clung to our bodies, adding weight to our march. But the rain was a blessing in a way, for it provided us with water to drink. The shots continued to echo and the ranks thinned out more and more. Each time one of the marchers dropped, someone from the rank behind him had to come forward to fill his empty place. The Germans loved order, and kept us marching in ranks of five.

Darkness began to fade. Before long the first rays of sun began to shine upon the marching convoy, whose members dragged themselves with their last ounce of strength to some unknown place. The next afternoon we saw in the distance a giant camp, surrounded by barbed wire and watch towers. The man who dragged himself next to me whispered, "I can't go on any more, I can't," and stumbled. I supported him with the little strength I had left. "Look, we've already arrived at our destination. Soon we'll be able to rest," I whispered back to him. But he didn't hear me. Right then and there the man collapsed and was shot, and the others passed over him. He wasn't the only one shot before the entrance to the camp. Just when we had finally arrived at our destination, a few of the walkers collapsed.

We had walked for thirty hours without a moment's rest. A few minutes before the camp had come into view, I had been ready to give up: "Father, forgive me, Father," I murmured to myself, "I wanted to keep the promise I gave you, but I can't. I have to sit down. I too am allowed to end my suffering." I wanted to sit down and let them shoot me. Then I saw the camp. Miraculously I was filled with the strength to continue.

We entered a camp called Vatenstaat. We were now no more than half the number we had been when we left the Bronshveig camp. The other half had fallen and remained by the side of the road.

The Vatenstaat Camp and Hermann Goering Werke

As soon as we passed through the gate of the camp we all collapsed on the ground of the big square. To lie down forever—that was all we wanted. As far as we were concerned, they didn't have to give us anything, not even food. We were so tired we didn't even remember that, except for the few drops of rainwater we drank on the way, we hadn't eaten for nearly two days. Now we felt pain in every part of our bodies. I closed my eyes. I wanted to sleep a little, but I was unable to fall asleep because of the pain.

Fortunately for us, they let us lie that way for many hours, until an order came to move to the barracks. We could barely lift our heads. They gave us soup and bread. Then each of us received a dark and worn out blanket. We were ordered to hand over our clothes for disinfection and wrap ourselves in blankets until we got our clothes back. We rested some more. A second before handing over my clothes, I remembered the note my father had written me that day in Auschwitz, and my knife. I was mad at myself for having almost forgotten them. Quickly I removed them from my coat and wrapped them in the blanket's edging.

The next day we received disinfected clothes, but they came back all mixed together. Again I received clothes much bigger than my size. In fact, everyone received clothes much bigger than his size since we had all become thinner. I think that the weight of the heaviest person among us was no more than 85 pounds. The first thing I did after receiving the clothes was to make a slit in my coat for the knife and the note.

New kapos were assigned to us. We were divided into groups for the apel. My group was called the Leichen Kommando. I didn't understand what this name meant until I started working. Then I discovered it meant Commando of the Dead. As soon as the apel was over we went out to work. We had to drag and push big flat carts over a distance of several kilometers outside the camp. When we arrived at some big buildings we went in and descended into dark cellars. Here we were hit by the terrible stench of corpses—piles of human corpses.

I leaped back involuntarily. I felt my throat convulse; I wanted to vomit. So this is Hell, I said to myself, and I am standing in the middle of it. Maybe those corpses are better off than I am. They are already dead and don't feel anything, while I must touch them and move them. My punishment was worse than theirs, for I had to continue living in this hell. But why had I been punished so? I asked myself. What sins had I committed when I was a child that I should deserve such a hell? I continued to complain to God that he chose the Germans, of all people, the followers of Hitler, to be his guards in Hell.

At times I couldn't decide if this whole scene was real or just a nightmare. I stood inside the cellar and could not move. I was unable to touch any of the dead and naked bodies. The blow that landed upon my head quickly taught me that I was indeed able. We were ordered to work fast and arrange the bodies inside crates, four bodies per crate. Then, with three others, I had to carry the crate up the stairs and out of the building. We put it in the cart, which we dragged about three kilometers to an open field with big open pits. Here we unloaded the bodies. Inside the pits we arranged the bodies one on top of the other. Then we returned with the empty crates to the cellars, came back with a new "load," and on and on.

When I stood inside the pit in broad daylight, straightening bodies, I knew this was no nightmare; it was a horrible reality. I began to tremble. I looked into one corpse's eyes, blue eyes looked back at me—familiar blue eyes. Then I remembered that this boy had been in Bronshveig with me. There was no doubt about it, this was Moshe Urbach. When they buried my grandfather, someone told me it was forbidden to leave a dead person's eyes open. With my fingers I closed Moshe Urbach's eyes and straightened his body.

"Hey, what are you doing down there so long!" one of the kapos shouted. "Hurry up and bring the second crate, you stinking lazy bum!" I did as he said. Now I didn't curse him, as I had once cursed the meister in the factory. This time I only cursed myself, for if I had to be a slave I would be better off if my senses were blocked and I didn't understand what I was doing.

The next day in the apel as the darkness of the night began to lift, I turned my head and saw those same blue eyes. They belonged to Yitzchak, Moshe Urbach's brother. Yitzchak whispered to me:

"I lost my brother. He was sent from Bronshveig in the group before us. Who knows where he was sent or if I'll ever see him again. All the time we tried not to separate, to be together."

I know where your brother is, I thought to myself, I closed his eyes and buried him, but I won't tell you about it. Who knows how long we have left to live, why should I cause you such sorrow? I just shrugged my shoulders and I said something inane, just to say something. Yitzchak continued whispering: "They took our group to work in the factory. Imagine, they have giant factories."

"Factories?" I asked Yitzchak. "I work in the field." I didn't tell him what I did, only that during the day I walked many kilometers and never saw any factories.

"Yes, that's a German trick. From the outside you can't see anything, but just the same there are factories there. We work underground, inside salt mines that the Germans have transformed into workshops to make weapons. We descend deep into the earth, to rooms where walls sparkle like crystals. The machinery there is very sophisticated. These are the factories of Hermann Goering. Conditions there are better than they were in the factory in Bronshveig. I wish my brother were with me."

The conditions in Bronshveig? The factory, the garage—I could visualize all that now as though it were a lost paradise. I touched my knife. It was in its place. It looked as if I would have no use for it. Probably not much time would pass before I, too, would be in the same place as Moshe, Yitzchak's brother.

The work was unbearably hard. Dragging the carriage and the bodies wore me out so much that I was barely able to climb onto my plank at night. Every day was an eternity. I tried not to look into the faces of the corpses, and only when I saw eyes open did I close them. That was the least I could do for my Jewish brothers.

Three or four days after we arrived in Vatenstaat it, too, was bombed by Allied planes. Here there were no shelters; the Germans had hidden trenches and they would run to them in a terrible panic. We wandered about outside and looked in desperation at the heavens. We knew that luck would not be on our side, that no bomb would fall directly upon the camp and kill us all together.

If the front comes close again, they will transfer us to yet another place and we will once again have to march like we marched here. If that happens then none of us will remain alive, I told my heart.

The Death Trains

On the tenth day of our stay in Vatenstaat, after a shelling which lasted an entire night, we were ordered to take our only property, our blanket, and get organized for an apel.

"Apel"—I said to myself, "now begins death march number two." More than half of the people died in the first march. Now those who remained would die.

Fortunately it wasn't a long march this time. After only one hour we reached a station where a train of freight cars stood. On the roofs of the first and last cars sat S.S. soldiers with machine guns. The other cars were roofless.

Before boarding the train each of us received a quarter of a loaf of bread, in which the kapos made a hole with their fingers and filled with honey. Each of us also received an additional blanket.

This time won't be too bad, I thought. We won't have to waste our energy marching again. This time the train will take us. The bread they gave us was also somewhat encouraging. But the main thing for me was that I would not have to continue burying the dead. In the train I would be able to rest a bit.

The German soldiers began to pack us into the cars.

"Dammit, hurry!" their shouts echoed.

Russian prisoners of war, who had arrived at the platform, were loaded with us into the cars. Because we were mixed together I had confidence that no harm would come our way.

The hope that I would be able to rest in the train was shattered very quickly. The S.S. soldiers compressed so many people into each car that it was impossible to move. We lay literally one on top of the other. After they filled the car in this way, two S.S. soldiers came on board, and with their rifle butts pushed the people right and left. In the middle of the car remained an empty space in which the soldiers sat opposite one another, as they leaned on the heavy iron doors on both sides of the car.

Ah, if only they would let us come a little closer to the space between the two sides so that we could straighten out our bodies, I said to myself. Those two pigs needed a third of the car, while we had to lie one on top of the other.

These were vain thoughts. We were lucky the cars had no roofs. Otherwise we surely would have suffocated from lack of air. As it was we didn't have air to breathe, and only when the train began to move, after an extended delay, did we feel a breeze that alleviated our suffering somewhat. If it weren't so crowded, things would actually be good, it occurred to me. To ride in a train, to hear the clatter of the wheels without being pushed and beaten. . . . Were it not so crowded!

I remembered my last journey with my parents and Talka. Then we were all together, and we still believed everything would be okay. That was only a few months ago, a little more than half a year, but in truth that, too, was an eternity away.

I pushed the memory of my dear ones from my thoughts. I had gotten this far, and I hadn't gone crazy during the days that I worked in Leichen Kommando. I had to protect my sanity, especially now, when a faint hope stole into my heart that they would not kill us.

I began to think of the positive aspects of this journey: the distribution of the bread and the blankets, and the Russian captives in our car.

I divided my quarter loaf of bread into two halves and ate one. The train sped up and I watched the little clouds float above my head, fleeing in the direction behind us.

We traveled for hours and hours. I wanted to sleep, but I couldn't because of the pressure on my feet, my hands, my limbs, and the rest of my body. The second half of my loaf of bread "burned a hole in my pocket." With all my strength I put off eating it. I wanted to save it for the next day. I tried to convince myself that we were likely to travel for a long time without their giving out any more bread, but I was so hungry. I searched for justification in the claim that if I were to fall asleep my bread might be stolen. Still, I hadn't yet touched it and I struggled with myself. With all my strength I tried to fall asleep without touching my bread, but I just couldn't. The hunger was stronger than I was, and in the end, after a real battle, it won. By the time I ate my last piece of bread night had already fallen and the train was galloping into the darkness.

I fell asleep despite the crowded conditions, and when I awoke the gray that precedes morning was in the air. The moon and stars became increasingly pale until they disappeared altogether. My entire body was pressed upon, I could barely straighten out my legs. But what awoke me now was a torturous thirst. I wanted to drink. To drink. Water.

The dry bread, dipped in honey, that I had eaten, scorched my insides. My whole body screamed for a little water, but there was none to be found. The men who lay beside me also groaned: "Water! Water!"

I recalled the thirst in Auschwitz, I remembered the rain

that we drank during the march. If only rain would fall now and save us. I looked at the sky, but the little fleeing clouds showed no signs of rain.

Those damned Germans! Even now they abuse us. They put honey on the bread on purpose. Even now all they thought about was how to add to our suffering. If only the train would stop somewhere so we could drink.

I swallowed my saliva. It seemed to me that my saliva was also dry. The others also writhed in thirst. The Russian captives cursed, but after a few hours they became silent. They seemed to understand that speaking dried out the throat even more, and it was necessary to protect one's strength. Only the two S.S. soldiers sat comfortably and even conversed with one another. They looked with disgust upon the compressed rabble who couldn't find a place for themselves, groaned, cursed, and bothered their friendly chat. The train continued to swallow up distances, while time crawled by at a snail's pace, lasting an eternity. And the thirst got worse and worse.

The sun sent out its first rays, notifying one and all of the dawn of a new day, and then it came out in all its splendor. And its rays, which at first were pleasant, grew stronger till they began to beat down cruelly upon our heads. There was no shade to protect us. The heat of the sun heightened our thirst, which had already been so strong. God almighty! How long must we travel like this? When will we finally get somewhere?

The train began to slow down. It must be approaching the station. When it stood still, everyone got up on their feet and tried to push to the door. But the orders from the S.S. soldiers and the shots in the air returned us to our places.

"Stay in place! No one gets off!" shouted the soldiers.

The car door opened and two soldiers entered. They came to replace the previous ones.

A short rest for the engine, a sharp whistle, the screeching of metal on metal and the train jerked forward, first at a crawl, and then increasing its speed until it returned to its earlier gallop. The train sped on and on, while our time crawled and crawled. Our insides shrank and cried out for water. It seemed to me that this day would never end. The day faded into evening, the sun set and made way for the moon and stars. This was our second night on the train. I tried to fall asleep, but thirst kept me awake.

Then we heard a heavy and vague noise, a distant sound that got louder and louder. The train slowed and the noise grew stronger. Suddenly, the heavens lit up as though an infinite number of flares were in the air. At precisely that moment the bombing began. Explosions could be heard everywhere. The S.S. soldiers opened the doors of the car and jumped out, but as they jumped they did not forget to close us in from the outside. We also heard shots from around us on the ground. We didn't see the planes, they must have flown at a high altitude. The flares also prevented us from seeing what was going on above. The noise was deafening.

"God," I prayed, "perform a miracle. Make a bomb fall directly on our car and free us from this terrible suffering, and free me from my promise." But God did not heed my prayer.

The shelling continued for a while, until the planes dropped their bombs and disappeared. The S.S. soldiers returned to their places in the car, and the train continued on its way. For some reason it seemed to me that we were now traveling in the direction we had come from. Maybe they were taking us back to the Vatenstaat camp. If only that were true. At least Vatenstaat had water. There we could drink to our heart's content. But we had already traveled for two days from Vatenstaat—would we hold out until we returned there? Could we keep from dying of thirst before arriving?

During the shelling the thirst had bothered us a bit less, but now it returned in full force. The two S.S. soldiers, who had been very afraid at the beginning of the bombing, calmed down and continued their interrupted conversation. The flock of sheep on their two sides, desperate for water, did not bother them. I looked at them and thought: these are people like me. The same human form, the same figure, sitting in the same car and even prone to the same danger from a falling bomb, yet how great was the gap between us. The gap between us and the Russians had already been blurred. They too lay like us Jews while their parched lips pleaded for water. Not one of us thought now about food.

I recalled the story I had been told by the kapo Dudu, how the Germans had broken him with thirst. I was no longer surprised that because of the burning thirst he had agreed to be a kapo.

I must have fallen asleep for a moment, for I was startled by a strong rattle. It was the death rattle of the Russian next to me. He was already unconscious, but nonetheless he clearly pronounced the word "water." It was terrible to see a man dying, and to know that a few drops of water could save his life. The rattle continued a while longer. Then the man lay motionless, dead. After a while we heard the same rattle from the other side of the car. The S.S. soldiers looked on at the victims of thirst with total indifference, while I looked at the two soldiers and thought: here are two people totally bereft of human feeling. If they had given the dying people a little water from their canteens or thermoses, they could have saved them. They had plenty of water, as did the soldiers who came to replace them.

Toward evening, before dark, the train stopped. The heavy metal door was pulled aside and into the car walked a number of men with stretchers. The soldiers in the car pointed out the dead, a total of four, and their corpses were taken from the car. In another day or two they would take my corpse too, I thought.

The place of the dead man who had lain next to me was vacated, and I moved right up to the wall. I now saw a thin crack between the boards of the car wall. I was too exhausted to be interested in anything, so I didn't look through it, but suddenly it seemed to me that I heard the sound of flowing water. My whole body trembled. Outside there was definitely water. I tried to put my eye up to the crack, but it was too small for me to see anything. I lowered my head and remembered that thirsty people walking in a desert were victims of mirages. It seemed that I was now in the middle of a hallucination. Could there be water here, in a place where only train tracks passed? The noise would not go away and it continued to bother me. I knew that nothing would stand in the way of my finding out if there was water outside the car, even if they killed me. This time I was exempt from my father's promise. Quite the opposite. I was going to keep that promise for if I did not get water, I would die soon anyway.

I pushed to the open door. The two soldiers stood below outside the car, talking with their comrades from the next car. They were now taking the dead bodies out of all the cars. With newfound strength I slipped out of the car.

A miracle happened. My senses had not misguided me. This was no hallucination. At the edge of the road was a narrow canal, and in it was a slow flow of shallow water. Without thinking I jumped over the short distance from the train to the edge of the road and I went right up to the water canal. I was not the only one beside the canal. Many people lay on the road and, like dogs, licked up the water. It was dirty, muddy water, but it was the most delicious, best water I have ever tasted. It was the water of life—and it returned me to life.

We could not pull ourselves away from the water, even when we heard the whistles and shouts of the soldiers who began to hurry us back to the train. It turned out that the S.S. soldiers had seen us leaving the cars and drinking. Why hadn't they told everyone to come drink? I had no answer. Anyway, they didn't prevent those of us who had dared leave the train from drinking. Perhaps they acted in this way because they felt their end approaching?

Before I pulled myself away from my source of life, from the water canal, I happened to see the S.S. soldiers taking pictures. It wasn't every day that one saw such a rare sight, men crawling on all fours in order to lick water like dogs.

With renewed strength I returned to the place where my blankets lay. Once again I had been reborn. Once again I was given the opportunity to extend my life. Until when?

The train continued its journey. It traveled forward, changed tracks, and continued in the opposite direction. There were hours when it crawled, hours when it galloped, and hours when it took a special break in order to remove the dead bodies. At night, when heavy shelling rained down upon it, it stood still.

Now that a little of my strength had returned after drinking the water from the canal, I pressed my eyes up to the crack in the wall, through which I saw other trains, sometimes filled with wounded German soldiers. Through the big windows of these trains I saw stretchers positioned in two layers, similar to the planks in the work camp, with bandaged soldiers lying on them. There were also trains loaded with heavy weaponry: tanks and artillery. My own eyes were witnessing the disintegration of Germany. I said to myself that even if I were to die now, it was good that I had been given the opportunity to see this stirring sight.

Two days had passed since I drank the canal water, and this still kept me alive. I looked now at the dying people around me and felt both pity and guilt, that I wasn't so thirsty and was able to hold out.

I had already lost track of how long it had been since we left the Vatenstaat camp. A week had probably passed but I wasn't sure. Even though I tried to convince myself that I wasn't as thirsty as I had been before, I once again began to feel that my strength was draining hour by hour.

That night we were hit by a heavier shelling than usual. It seemed that the planes had noticed our train and decided to destroy it. A mighty explosion suddenly shook our car. Fire and smoke raged all around us, but nothing happened to us. The two last cars were destroyed by a bomb that had fallen directly on them. In one of those they had put the dead bodies, and in the second car were captives. From the screams and curses of the S.S. soldiers we understood that Germans had also been killed in the same shelling.

A Miracle

Once again the shelling had left us alive but had not freed us. At the end of the shelling the two ruined cars were separated and the train continued on its way. This time it traveled only a very short distance before it stopped. The doors opened and we were ordered out. Some distance away was a camp surrounded by barbed wire and watch towers: the Oranienburg concentration camp. The mere sight of it gave us a little added strength. We prayed for a piece of bread, and, especially, that we would be able to drink plenty of water. To our surprise, only the S.S. soldiers were allowed to enter. We, the heftlinge and the Russian captives, remained outside. After a while the soldiers returned, their faces red with rage, and they explained to the other Germans that the lageralteste of this camp was unwilling to receive additional people. We were ordered to return to the train and look for a different camp.

I shivered all over at the thought that I had to reboard the train. At least they could have given us something to revive our souls—a piece of bread, a little water. How much longer could we continue like this?

The stooped figures dragged themselves back to the train. And here occurred a true miracle. Trucks arrived with the symbol of the red cross. Polite and smiling people greeted us and distributed packages, one per person. We didn't understand what was going on. Feverishly, with trembling hands, we opened the packages.

It could not be! This could not be for real. This time I was certainly hallucinating, I thought.

The packages contained food, real food! We hadn't seen such food for nearly six years, since before the outbreak of the war. We had long ago forgotten that such food existed in the world. There were packages of biscuits and cheeses, cans of preserves and chocolate, real chocolate, and packs of cigarettes. We even found a can opener in each package.

I became confused and thought I had gone mad. Or perhaps I was dreaming, or maybe I had already left this world and had arrived at the next world, paradise, and there, in exchange for and in reward for all the suffering I had known, I had received these delicacies?!

Whatever was going on, I said to myself, I must take advantage of the situation, even if they were delicacies that one saw in a dream, and eat quickly so as not to lose any time. I must taste each thing before I wake up and they take the package away from me, before it disappears.

I began to eat. All the tastes mixed together—cheese and chocolate and mashed potatoes, meat together with biscuits. I lit a cigarette and inhaled the fragrant smoke.

The other people did the same. We all looked like madmen. People shouted, cried, and ran wild. The German soldiers with their rifle butts, and the kapos with their clubs, were unable to restore order. We didn't even feel the blows that landed on us. Our eyes saw only the food.

Time passed until the soldiers and kapos succeeded in getting us back on the train. We were different people when we boarded the cars. We had newfound strength and new hope that things would soon be better.

I no longer cared how long we continued to travel. I was busy chewing, each time something different, guarding my food so that it would not be stolen, God forbid. I didn't shut my eyes as long as I still had something left to eat. Cases of theft began to multiply in the car, causing quarrels and fights. Those who had already finished their food stole from those who still had some left. Even the nightly shelling disturbed no one. We were totally absorbed in the morsels of food, and the shelling seemed insignificant.

On the following morning we arrived at a giant camp, Ravensbrueck. Once again we were lucky that we didn't have to tax our strength walking great distances; the train pulled right up to the gate. They pushed us in and we joined those who were already imprisoned there.

A camp is still infinitely better than the cars, I said to myself. Even though we are in absolute confinement, at least we are free here in comparison to the confinement we knew in the cars. Here there are faucets with water and there is no danger of dying from thirst. Here there are also planks to sleep on, and we would certainly receive a piece of bread.

This is what I thought when I entered the camp. Before long I could sense that chaos reigned here. There was no way to keep so many people busy, and since it was absolutely forbidden for slaves to wander idly, they kept us occupied with endless apels. We would barely return from one apel when we would hear a whistle announcing the next. Day and night, in winds and rain, apel after apel.

Meanwhile the front had advanced this far and the shellings became more frequent. Food in the camp was exhausted and no new supplies arrived. A number of days passed in the camp, and nothing but water had come to our lips. The packages that we had received from the Red Cross were long forgotten. (The incident of the packages was engraved in my memory as a wonderful dream, not from this world.) And now, while lying on the plank after hours of standing in the apels, as I was thinking of this dream and all its implications, I put my hand into my coat pocket in order to feel Father's note, which I continued to keep—and my hands felt two cigarettes from those that had been in the package. I must have put them in my pocket without thinking. I took out one cigarette and brought it to my nose to smell. Then I took a bite from it, chewed it and even swallowed it. It tasted strange, but even so I ate the two cigarettes with appetite, in order to have something to fill my empty stomach. Again we heard the whistle for an apel, but even before everyone got organized in lines, I managed to run to a faucet and drink water. That evening, then, I had a meal which extended my life.

One Last Try

The day and night bombings on the Ravensbrueck area became more frequent. Once again they decided to transfer all of us to a different place. Once again we were taken to a train and squeezed in far beyond the capacity of the cars, crowded one on top of the next. But this time everyone knew that there was nothing to worry about, since the train would become less crowded very quickly. This time I was seized with fear—I was overcome by a feeling that this was my end, that there was no way I could go through this hell again, without food and water.

Again we traveled day after day, forward and backward. During the bombings the train would stand still. It also stood still when the dead were removed. Then the car would become less crowded. Once again I lost track of time but I was certain that we were on the train for many days—perhaps two weeks or more. It seemed to me that we had already passed through the whole world. All the while, hunger sucked away at our insides and drove us out of our minds.

"How long can a man live without any food at all," I asked myself. "Essentially I know that one person dies sooner and the other later—a sign that the first is less strong then the second. I certainly belong to the stronger ones if I am still living."

Now I began to feel that the hour of my death was approaching. I began having hallucinations from days long past. I saw myself as a little boy. Mother, Father, and Talka were with me in our home. That was paradise, in all its splendor. In this paradise also belonged the synagogue in our town, in which I sang in the choir and my glances met those of my grandfather, who was filled with pride over my clear singing. I sometimes saw my mother lighting and blessing Sabbath candles, and Father returning with me from the synagogue, our house lit up in an extraordinary fashion. The holiness of the Sabbath peeked from every corner, the wonderful fragrance of fresh *challot* (Sabbath bread), and Talka walking around with a pink ribbon in her light hair. Then Father would burst into song, "Shalom Aleichem," and I would join him. Still another picture. Father and I were building a *sukkah* (temporary shelter used during the autumn festival of Sukkot), and Talka was preparing decorations.

Next, the Passover holiday, the festival of freedom, and again Talka was with me. We were stealing the *afikoman* (special piece of matzo) and demanding ransom for its return. I shook myself out of the mist and looked around. I was not in paradise, but in a death car, surrounded by death rattles.

And still I thank You, Lord, that You granted me these visions, that You returned me to my lost paradise, even for such a short while. It was wonderful. If death was accompanied by such visions, then it wasn't at all hard to die. Perhaps I would have more such visions. I so wanted to return to the pictures of paradise I had had in my misty dream. But now the train stopped. People bearing stretchers again entered the car in order to take out the dead bodies. A German soldier entered and gave the two S.S. soldiers two loaves of bread. Long brown loaves of bread. I stood some distance from the soldiers, but the smell of the bread reached my nostrils and made my head spin.

The German soldier left, and our two guards put the loaves of bread into their knapsacks. One of them held his knapsack on his knees, while the other one laid it in front of him, on the floor. I noticed that during the shelling he left the car without taking his knapsack with him. He must have been sure that no one would dare touch the property of an S.S. soldier.

The thought passed through my mind that if I could take the bread that was in the knapsack I would be saved from death. It was possible, perhaps, during the shelling. But I immediately gave up the idea. Even if I succeeded in stealing the bread, all the others in the car would pounce on me and kill me. Anyway how did I dare think about stealing bread when even the Russian captives were dying of hunger and didn't dare do that. Some of the Russian captives most certainly had knives.

But the thought of the bread in the S.S. man's knapsack would not leave me alone. I couldn't stop thinking of the bread.

Day turned into evening, the world became gray and the train continued endlessly. People in the train died. The man beside me ceased stirring and no longer moved. And then I saw something that made me tremble all over and nearly faint: a Russian took out his knife, cut through a dead man's clothes, sliced a piece of thigh from the dead man's flesh and ate it.

This was already the deepest Hell. Now I was sure that nothing could be worse. I wanted to call out God's name, but I could not bring His name to my lips.

Absolute darkness descended upon the car. I was still thinking about what I had seen when I heard a blood-curdling scream:

"Nyet" (No), was the scream, "Don't cut me! I'm still alive!"

In the darkness someone had made the mistake of cutting into a live man.

My hair stood on edge. My decision was made: I no longer had anything to lose. In a little while I would die and they would cut my flesh too. Nothing mattered anymore. I had to try to take the bread from the S.S. man's knapsack. This would be my last try. With this decision new blood began to flow through my veins. I hatched a plan. I was sure that that night there would also be shelling. When the two soldiers left the train in order to hide under the car, I would get to work.

I removed my knife from its place inside my coat. I wrapped myself in my two blankets and began to move in the direction of the S.S. soldier, slowly, so no one would notice my movements. A slight move, and then a rest. Slight move, then rest. And indeed no one noticed. Perhaps they thought that someone was just straightening his limbs in the crowd.

Soon I was near the area between the soldier and us, the people of the camps. I was completely covered and I waited with excitement for the shelling. I trembled with excitement, and didn't think of any consequences. At the same time, I was happy about the new strength I seemed to have. My only fear was that they wouldn't bomb that evening. Time crawled by. There seemed to be no shelling in sight.

I had despaired when I finally heard the heavy sound of planes. The train stopped as usual. So did my breathing. What would I do if the soldier took his knapsack with him?! The sliding door opened, the soldiers jumped out, but the knapsack remained in the car. I breathed freely. The shelling began. Planes dropped their bombs and fire was shot from the ground, while I, covered by my blankets, continued to crawl towards the knapsack. At last I was next to it. Without thinking I covered the knapsack with my blanket. I continued to lie there. No one noticed. I was just another person covered with blankets, a human package, maybe a dying one.

Under the blanket I groped in the knapsack with my trembling hands. I reached the bread. I felt it. Now I had to act quickly. The shelling could end soon. I slit the knapsack with the point of my knife and continued to cut until I felt the bread in my hands.

"Father, I did it." I whispered silently. Now I had to get back to my place. I moved slowly, so no one would notice. Before leaving I turned the knapsack over, putting the rip underneath, so that the German would not notice that his knapsack had been slit.

It seemed to me that the crawl back was endless. I was afraid to hurry, worried that I might arouse someone's attention. I had to eat the bread quickly, I said to myself, in case they made a search. I prayed silently for the shelling to last. It did continue until I reached my place. Now, covered with two blankets, lying on my stomach, I began to tear off big pieces of the bread and stuff them into my mouth. I didn't chew them, I only swallowed whole pieces, like a snake swallowing a mouse. My stomach hurt from the sudden load of the big unchewed pieces. I finished in a matter of seconds. A wonderful feeling filled my heart.

I was full, I had new strength. And you, you stuffed German, may you burst when you notice that someone stole your bread! Thus I cursed him in my thoughts.

The shelling ended. The planes disappeared. The S.S. soldiers returned to the car and sat down in their places. It was still dark and I couldn't see anything, but still I didn't take my eyes off the soldier. After it became light, I saw him bringing the knapsack closer to him. Everything that was in the knapsack poured out. The soldier lifted the knapsack to see what happened. Suddenly his face became red as a beet. He got to his feet, trembling from head to toe, drew his pistol from its holster, and began to shout.

"Who did this? Who took my bread? Who slit my knapsack? I'll kill that dog!" He looked at the people who lay close to where he sat.

"You!" he shouted at an overgrown Russian who barely breathed, "get up quickly!!" He dragged the man by his neck. The confused Russian didn't know what he wanted from him, and only shook his head no. The German slapped him in the face, then picked up a second man, and a third.

"You!" he shouted "You!" as he waved his pistol and put it to their heads.

I felt I was choking. All kinds of thoughts raced through my head. I must not let an innocent man die because of me. Suddenly, it seemed a shame to die. Now, when I was no longer hungry and had the strength to continue coping. But there was no choice. I had to pay for the loaf of bread.

I quickly got on my feet, before I would change my mind, before it would be too late and someone else would be killed.

"I, I stole the bread," I called out. No one paid attention to me. No one heard me. The clatter of the train and the shouts of the soldier overwhelmed my voice. I decided to shout in a louder voice so that he'd hear me. "I!" I called out, "I stole it!"

The German soldier didn't even look in my direction. It didn't occur to him that someone from the end of the car had taken his bread. Meanwhile he decided that the overgrown Russian must be the thief. I began to clear a path for myself between the people lying on the floor, and I continued to call out in a loud voice. But my voice went unheard. The noise from a squadron of heavy planes drowned it out. A new shelling began. The Germans quickly left the car. I didn't believe my eyes. Once again I had been saved. Maybe I was destined to live after all.

After the shelling subsided and the soldiers returned to the car, the bread wasn't mentioned again.

Light in the Valley of Tears

Thanks to the bread I continued to live for two more days. There were many who breathed their last during those two days—among them the overgrown Russian whom the German soldier had picked on. At the end of those two days, toward evening, the train stopped and we were ordered out. A few hundred meters from the train sprawled the Ludwigslust camp. As usual we were run by the kapos and the S.S. soldiers, but before we entered the camp I took a look at our group. I was certain that there were now fewer than half as many people as had left Ravensbrueck.

The Ludwigslust camp was smaller than most of the camps we had been through. It was a new camp that was not quite completed. It didn't even have planks in the barracks so we had to lie on the floor. Here, too, there was disorder, and we could feel some type of expectation or nervousness among the Germans about what was going to happen. The nervousness of the Germans expressed itself, as usual, in apel after apel, and in the blows that they dealt us. But we were used to it, and one more blow on the head or back was insignificant to us.

I had long ago stopped making comparisons between a train and a camp—where was it better and where was it worse. Did it matter where one died? There, on the trains, we were desperate for a little bit of food and water, and here, in the camp, all we wanted was to be given the chance to lie down and rest, so that we would not collapse in the apel which lasted for hours.

During our first days in the Ludwigslust camp each of us received an eighth of a loaf of bread. There was also water. Nonetheless, people continued to die. We were already in such a state that the little piece of bread that was given us once a day, and the few ounces of water, were not enough to save us. After four or five days even this distribution was stopped. New supplies of bread didn't arrive, and during each apel there was always some figure that collapsed. The starving people would drop and the kapos would get them up with blows. Only when a man did not respond to the beating would they leave him where he fell.

Despair descended upon me. I recalled the two cigarettes that I ate. Again I began to search in my pockets, but I found nothing. Even the thought of the bread of the S.S. soldier was only a distant memory. I was often attacked by weakness and dizzy spells.

One day we suddenly heard the vague sounds of shooting, similar to the distant thunder preceding rain. No one paid attention to these sounds. Nothing had any impact on us anymore.

That same day, towards evening, we were ordered to march to the gates of the camp. A few hundred meters farther we saw a freight train standing on the tracks. This time cars awaited us with closed roofs. It seemed to me that there were fewer cars on this train than on the train we had arrived in. They compressed us into these cars in such a way that it was impossible even to sit. We stood up, one against the other. The Germans pushed in more and more people. I held up my elbows to protect my chest, so that I wouldn't be squashed.

If only the train would get going already, so that some vent would give us air, I prayed. But hours passed and the train did not move. There was always a situation that was worse than what you could imagine. I remembered the open, roof-less cars, in which it was at least possible to breathe, while here I felt that I would soon suffocate. Here I didn't think about food or water—only about a little air. Air to breathe.

We stood like that through the night and the train did not move. Death rattles mixed with the sounds of shooting and planes. The smell of burning and smoke that reached us added even more to the suffocating lack of air.

Morning had broken when I felt that I was unable to go on. I don't know if I fell asleep standing up or if I fainted. A sudden burst of air, shouts, and the barking of dogs awakened me. I felt the pressure upon me decrease, and I fell forward. I don't know how, but I managed to grab hold of someone. The door to the car was open and beside it stood S.S. soldiers with rubber clubs and giant dogs. They took us out of the train and ran us back to the camp. Only the dead, who now had a chance to fall on the wooden floor, remained in the cars.

We were ordered to stay in the barracks. Whoever left would receive a bullet in his head. After such a night of terror all we wanted to do was to rest in the barracks. It seemed to me that if they held an apel I would not get up and go out, even if they beat me to death.

We lay like this for about two hours before S.S. soldiers appeared and informed us that they would soon blow up the entire camp. Whoever wanted to be saved could join them and leave. Not one of us moved from his place, with the exception of a few kapos who got up and went after the Germans. We heard the news that the camp would go up in flames with complete indifference. It was better for us to be blown up with the rest of the camp than to take one more step.

Hours passed. All around us was silence, a threatening silence. With an effort I left the barrack and lay on the sandy ground. Despite the prohibition against leaving the barracks, I could see masses of people lying on the ground outside.

It was an amazingly beautiful day, May 2, 1945. The contrast between the clear, splendid day and the horrifying sight of thousands of dying, gray figures strewn about on the ground was incredibly sharp. The threatening silence continued and continued.

I lay motionless. I no longer even felt hunger.

I prayed to God to be kind to me and bring on my end. I was still involved in my silent prayer when there was a loud noise, as though we were hit by an earthquake. I lifted my head to see a giant tank approaching the camp.

That's it, this is our end. They're coming to finish us off. My prayer was heard. Thank you, Lord!

Father, I tried everything to stay alive, but I did not succeed. I don't believe a single Jew will remain alive to tell this tale. Even those who went with the Germans will not stay alive. They will murder them all, so that there will be no witnesses left.

I moved forward. I wanted to die quickly, I whispered to myself. One more look around, at the valley of tears and death. The entire field was sown with corpses, human skeletons, one next to and one on top of another. Even those who still breathed did not lift their heads upon hearing the noise of the tank. Everyone knew what awaited him. Everyone waited for his end.

The noise grew louder. Following the first tank was a second and a third. I closed my eyes, so as not to see how they fired at us. I'll die with my eyes closed.

The noise grew louder and then was silent. Now there will be the order to fire, the tanks are already opposite us, opposite the barbed wire. What are they waiting for? Why aren't they shooting?

Slowly I opened my eyes. Right opposite me, on the other side of the barbed wire, stood a strange tank, without the emblem of the swastika. I saw only a white star on the tank.

The cover of the tank turret was raised. In the other tanks they were also lifted. I saw heads wearing unfamiliar helmets. The heads of those sitting in the tanks came up and stopped in their places. I saw their frightened eyes, looking anxiously at their surroundings.

From behind me someone shouted:

"American soldiers! The American army! We've been saved!"

I leaped up. I looked at the camp, at the skeletons and corpses all around. Countless corpses, which I had thought were dead, stood up suddenly revived, as I had stood up. An indescribable excitement and shock passed over those who were already on the edge of death.

"The American army! We've been saved!" the excited cries continued to be heard from around the camp.

I find it hard to understand how it happened, but it's a fact, witnessed by all those who were in that camp and remained alive—suddenly as though from a single throat, a song burst out with our anthem, "Hatikvah" (The Hope).

Many many people stood up at attention, as they sang and cried. I was among those many. My voice also sang out, and every word of the song was soaked with tears.

I turned my head in the direction of the soldiers who had meanwhile jumped out of their tanks and stood opposite us, opposite the barbed wire fence. They stood in reverence in the face of this horrifying picture, at attention with their helmets placed over their hearts. I saw their faces, I saw the crying eyes of the men—the American soldiers, who stood weeping like children. I felt intoxicated, like someone who was not from this world.

As I stood and sang, I recalled a different picture: Sabbath morning. Father and I sat by the Sabbath table covered with a white tablecloth, and Father read the verses from the Book of Ezekiel about the valley filled with bones, how the bones were covered with skin and ligaments and came back to life. I, too, was in the valley of bones, the valley of death. I too had come back to life. I was saved.

Freedom

After that everything happened quickly. With three young men from our camp I moved into an abandoned apartment. The Americans supplied us with plenty of food and clothes. They really spoiled us, as though trying to make up to us for all that we had been through. They also transferred the sick to hospitals, and brought in the best doctors and nurses to take care of them.

Epilogue

I wandered about freely in the very heart of bombed out Germany. Here I heard about the end of Hitler, the greatest enemy of the Jews in all generations. I saw the change that took place in the Germans: they were no longer fanatic anti-Semites who were more concerned for the life of a fly than the life of a Jew. Now it was the turn of the Germans, formerly members of the "superior race," to wallow in the dust and beg for a slice of bread.

And I, who so wished to stay alive to avenge the sufferings and deaths of my grandmother, my aunts and uncles, little Abonik, little Chana'le, Mother and Father, and my sister Talka—how strange it was, but I gave them bread, because I couldn't bear to see a person hungry.

I wandered about freely in defeated Germany, eating until I was nauseated. I was stunned and confused by conflicting feelings—joy and sadness, hope and despair. I was senseless from grief in those days of victory, sick from sorrow. There were hours in which I could not bring myself to touch the fresh bread that was within reach of my hand.

I didn't know what to do with my life now. I wanted to return to my birthplace, Poland, and at the same time, I didn't want to set foot on that blood-drenched ground, on the graveyard of my entire family and of so many other Jews. I dreamt of the Land of Israel.

Many of the horrors I had been through returned to me in my dreams. In one of them I saw us in our hideout in the Lodz ghetto, as the S.S. soldier knocked down the wall with his axe and captured us. In another dream I saw Father in Auschwitz, depressed and exhausted, me supporting him. I saw the death train, where they wanted to cut my flesh. I cried endlessly in my dreams.

Some days I would travel from place to place with the American soldiers, then I would return to my new friends, the other three youths in our apartment. I felt an increasing urge to return to Poland. I felt I had to go there no matter what, if only once. I could not explain this attraction, for I knew that there was nothing left there for me to find. So I kept putting off the journey. Weeks passed.

One day I met an acquaintance from the Lodz ghetto, from the Bnei Akiva youth movement. He told me that he had already visited Poland and met a few of those who remained from the movement and were organizing a kibbutz in preparation for the journey to Israel. The organizer and leader of the kibbutz was Sara Stern. Now I knew that the time had come for me to travel to Poland.

Nothing could stand in my way, not even the lack of transportation. I was not put off by the few trains, filled way beyond capacity with captives returning home. I pushed with the others and climbed up to the roof of the train. Many others who found no place inside the train did the same thing, and paid with their lives for it. But I arrived at my destination.

I was choked with tears when I set foot on the ground of

Lodz, which showed no signs that it had just withstood a six-year war. From the outside it looked as whole as it had before the war. I put off visiting the area of the ghetto for a while. First I went to find the kibbutz.

My heart raced as I entered. Zehava Urbach received me with open arms.

"Luzer! You're alive?!"

Her brother Yitzchak, the boy with the blue eyes who was with me in the camp, entered the room. He and his sister had met in the community council. They were so happy to find one another. I didn't tell them about their brother Moshe whom I had buried when I worked in the Leichen Kommando. They still waited and hoped that since he had been so young he too would return.

Sarah Stern received me with cries of joy. I felt that I had found family, that from now on this would be my home.

My glance fell upon the figure of a girl who stood by the window. It was Surtzia, Talka's teacher and my friend Lazer's sister.

"Surtzia," I called out happily, "Are your brothers also here?"

"None of my brothers remains," said Surtzia.

Someone walked into the room. I couldn't quite tell if she was a little girl or a young woman. This was Salusia. I felt my breath taken away.

"I know that girl. I know her from long ago. I remembered my parents, Talka, and me in the Lodz ghetto. A Jewish policeman was taking us to the apartment that had been allotted us. We were burdened with knapsacks and bundles. On the way we passed by the coalyard. There I saw a girl, with long, light braids, piling a bag of coal on her narrow back. I was still pitying the pale, thin little girl who had to carry all that coal when her bag tore and all the coal scattered over the street. The girl stood at a loss, tears poured down her face. I yearned to help the girl, but the policeman hurried us along, for he was on duty and had no time to spare. When we arrived at our apartment I told my parents that I had to go out quickly to the street to stand in line to receive bread with the new coupons we had received. Instead, I ran to the coalyard to help the girl. She was gone by then. Only the black stain with the little pieces of coal lying on the street testified to what had happened.

"I have to know," I turned to her. "Were you in the Lodz ghetto? And once did your sack tear and all the coal inside it scatter on the street?"

The girl stopped beside me. It looked like she was recalling some distant memory.

"Yes," she said, "It was so long ago."

Her bright eyes covered over with mist, and she quickly left the room so that I wouldn't see her tears.

From that moment my soul was linked to that girl's. She was now for me the most precious and beloved soul, like a remnant of my family. I knew that I had to protect her so as not to lose her in the trying days which lay ahead of us.

After years surrounded by torture and hatred, I now also felt Salusia's (Sara's) love. We were the first couple in the kibbutz. We were destined to face many more days of trouble and hardship, but from then on the hardships were tempered with the light of a great hope.

For two long years we wandered all over Europe, until we finally reached Israel. During those years of wandering I had to separate from the members of the kibbutz and from Sara. With an ex-partisan, Chaim Basok of Vilna, I was sent to distant places to organize people for illegal immigration to Palestine. It wasn't until 1947 that we finally set foot on the ground of our holy land.

Indeed, we endured quite a few hardships before we reached our little piece of land whose name Gereck and his friends already knew—they would call out after the Jewish children, that our place was not in Bzezin of Poland, but in Palestine.

I so wished to find rest here, after all the blood-drenched years. And indeed we were privileged to witness the rebirth of Israel, and to hear the noble and moving words of the Declaration of Independence on the day of the state's declaration. But we were not yet destined to find tranquility. The War of Independence broke out.

Sara and I both enlisted in the Israel Defense Forces, the Israeli army. This time, in contrast to the Second World War, when God turned away from us, He now came to our aid. This time we fought with weapons in our hands.

During the first lull in the fighting, Sara and I married. Peace did not come despite our victory. I had to go out and fight three more times. I did not go out to kill; I went to protect the house of Israel and the home that I had established, to protect my wife and children. We were privileged to raise three children, whom we called by the names of our dear ones lost in the Holocaust. With the passage of time our children grew and our son also participated in the wars of Israel, which to this day have not ceased.

We set up a new house, but the house of Poland, cut down by our enemies, continues to live within me whether awake or dreaming. An old Jew passing by on the street, a Jewish woman, or a Jewish child will sometimes bring my thoughts back to the old people there, the women and children as I saw them in the valley of slaughter. And I will never be indifferent to the sight of a slice of bread lying in the street.

Even the tree that grew near my house in Israel brought me images. It was tall and splendid, with deep roots, in whose broad crown I saw the glory of the Judaism that was, and in whose roots I saw the heritage of Israel. I loved to look at that tree and sit in its shade. When it was cut down, my soul found no rest. Each time I passed by the stump, I felt a pain slicing through my heart. Now I found an even stronger resemblance between the fallen tree, my family, and the Jews from the old country, who were also cut off from the land of the living.

Then one spring day, as I passed by the trunk, I saw that inside its bark, which I had imagined to be lifeless, thin green buds began to sprout. I was moved to the depths of my soul by the sight, for I once again found the similarity between what happened to us and this tree trunk. I asked myself: were we not like this murdered tree which has returned to life? Have not its deep roots fought desperately in order to sprout new life?

I once again remembered my father's will and testament—that I fight with all my strength to remain alive. The murdered trunk sprouting forth its leaves now symbolized for me our renewed life in the Land of Israel. In our children, grandchildren and future generations I see the delicate branches sprouted by our deep roots.

Thus when I am awake I relive our past. When I sleep I relive the past even more vividly in my nightmares. My nightmares will continue to haunt me as long as I live for it is then that I see everyone as I knew them in their pure and noble lives, and as I saw them oppressed till they were like dust. But above all I remember my promise to Father, which kept me alive...

About the Author

Sara Plager Zyskind was born in Lodz, Poland. Her experiences there and in Auschwitz during the Holocaust have been related in her first book, *Stolen Years*. After World War II, she and her husband, Eliezer, (who is Luzer in *Struggle*) emigrated to Israel, where they now reside. In the summer of 1988, Sara, Eliezer, and their three children made a trip back to Poland where they visited Lodz and Auschwitz—the places of her two books.